Small Vampires · Volume II
· MOÜSCH THE CROOKED ·

"*Although I am now well over sixteen hundred years old, I am unlikely ever to forget the smallest detail of the night that Corbeau came to our house, looking for* **the Chalice.** "

Moüsch and his best friend Chassignol are ordered by the Eltern to find the greatest of all the Small Vampire treasures – the Chalice. Hampered by visions that he cannot make sense of and physical disability he embarks on a quest, following Picus' steps from centuries before to England and beyond.

(Small Vampires) is that seemingly impossible take on the genre – funny, intelligent, imaginative story-telling that mixes Arthurian legend with faeries and vampires and comes up with a unique mix of all three. SSF Chronicles

… the world building is incredible and it's almost impossible not to become immersed in this fantastically realised world of charm and grandeur. SF Books Reviews

SMALL
VAMPIRES

knowe us by poppies in golden fields
of wheat splashd red lyke blood
〜⊷

The *Small Vampires* series:

〜

Mouïsch the Crooked

TRANSLATED BY ROBIN BENNETT

SMALL VAMPIRES

VOLUME II

MONSTER
BOOKS

Small Vampires. Moüsch the Crooked
(Aktuel Translations Ltd. 7043141. Monster Books)
Originally published in Great Britain by Monster Books, 2013
The Old Smithy, Henley-on-Thames, OXON. RG9 2AR

ISBN 97809568684-66 hard cover
ISBN 97809568684-73 e-book
A catalogue record of this book is available from the British Library

Printed in China by CTPS.
Set in *fiorenza* and Brioso
Typesetting & design by Medievalbookshop
(www.medievalbookshop.co.uk)
Cover illustration: the talented Rob Rayevsky©
Small Vampires device: the inspired Adam Curtis

As ever, I am bound to miss people out and feel guilty about it afterwards, but here goes: Thanks, once again, to Serena Jones for her invaluable editing and good advice, Barbara Newman for all her time spent writing complimentary letters to people about me, and to Patrick Walsh for his help and encouragement all the way back in 2008.

This book is dedicated to Father Anthony Sutch for encouraging me to write when I would rather have been playing cricket or watching TV.

'The Chalice defines Vampires
as the most powerful species
on the planet: it is our mother,
our father, our protector and
our avenger. It is the greatest
weapon we have.'

Kaier Slavdomi Krillinc ('Corbeau').
The Book of Truth.

Chapter 1

Corbeau

Although I am now well over sixteen hundred years old, I am unlikely ever to forget the smallest detail of the night that Corbeau came to our house, looking for the Chalice.

The Cracked Bell in the Keep had just struck midnight as I stared out of our attic window at the fires raging below. Terrified Vampires ran in short, panicked bursts between the houses, seeking safety in the shadows as the renegade Vampire knights, led by Corbeau himself, swept through the town, hacking to pieces or burning everything in their path.

To get a clear view of the street below, I had to stand on a pile of old boxes. I was nine. Alouette, my sister, dark-haired and quiet, was seven and Moineau, the baby of the family, plump and loved, was only two.

'Get down, Moüsch, you'll fall.' Alouette stretched up and took hold of my wrist. I still remember the feel of her hand – it was small and soft.

'Shh, Aly, I'm trying to see.' I was squinting with my weak eyes, craning out even further over the window-ledge. Cold seeped through my pyjamas from the stone and made me shiver, and my breath billowed white, then crimson, as the thatch on a house opposite collapsed into a whirlwind of sparks and flames.

Suddenly my father was at the attic door. 'Moüsch,' he said furiously as he strode in. 'I thought I told you all to hide.' We turned around. I saw a second emotion playing on his face, sheltering behind the irritation. It was fear. I had seen him angry before, but never frightened.

I jumped down as best I could and took hold of Moineau's hand. Then I turned to Alouette, who opened her mouth as if about to say something. Her back was to the window I had been looking out of moments before, and her white nightdress fanned out, as she raised her arms, blocking the flickering light from the burning street below. Somewhere further up the hill, towards the Keep itself, someone screamed and yet strangely my sister, her mouth open to reveal her small milk fangs, made no sound. Then she coughed and I saw blood well up from her throat.

And she fell.

Revealed behind her on the window ledge, framed against the infernal backdrop of his own making, was Corbeau himself; his wings beat slowly, and in his left hand he lightly held a tapered sword.

A solitary drop of my sister's blood ran to the tip of the blade and dropped like a tear to the floor as I stood, rigid with terror, my hand grasping Moineau's. I watched the tremoring orb of blood fall at Corbeau's feet. When it hit the ground, I was close enough to register how it exploded into dozens of smaller droplets, sending up tiny puffs of dust from the wooden boards.

I still recall how my whole attention was taken with staring in horror at the blood, so that I was hardly aware of my father, who flew past me, his sword unsheathed, slicing through the air in a single, fluid movement.

The speed and the ferocity of the attack almost worked.

Corbeau, with a look of mild surprise, only just managed to bring his own rapier up in time to meet my father's sword; a burst of sparks from the blades brought me back to my senses, and I pulled Moineau behind four large sacks of grain that stood in the attic corner.

Corbeau fought for his life as my father, his face deathly pale and savage, pressed home the advantage, bringing his sword down on Corbeau's in a brutal series of blows. Corbeau had flown down to meet him in the room but now had no choice but to retreat, forced back by the raw power of my father's anger. As with all great swordsmen, my father switched tactics abruptly: he stopped slicing and lunged once, then twice in quick succession. Corbeau managed to parry the first attack with a look of alarm on his face, but the second got through his guard and speared his free hand, pinning it firmly to the wooden rafter behind him.

I often think how different all our lives would have been had it not been at that moment, when he seemed on the brink of defeat, that one of Corbeau's renegade knights kicked the door open and dragged my mother into the room.

She had a deep gash across her forehead and the fingers of her left hand looked bruised and broken. As she looked at the small, bloodstained corpse of Alouette, a thin stream of blood escaped her broken lip in a silent wail. Moineau cried out, 'Mummy!' as my mother's soft brown eyes looked up and met ours.

All of my mother's gentleness, her fierce love for us and her regret were poured into that one brief glance that still haunts me down the centuries of my long life.

The knight pulled out a thin, curved dagger as my father turned away from Corbeau. From the corner of my eye, I saw Corbeau's sword arm move.

'No!' was all my father had time to shout before the knight sliced the razor-sharp steel across my mother's exposed throat in a terrible carving motion. At that same moment, Corbeau's sword pierced my father through the shoulder blade and found his heart.

I was too young, or perhaps simply too terrified, to be fully aware of what I was about to do: but at that moment I burst from my hiding place, grabbing my father's sword from the floor and brought it up between the legs of the Vampire who had killed my mother. He let out an unnaturally high-pitched cry and fell where he stood, dark red blood pumping onto the floor from his exposed inside leg. Even at that age, I knew enough about blood to recognise it was arterial. He would be dead within minutes. Then I turned, remembering Moineau. His pyjamas had always been too big for him, and so they slipped as he ran towards my mother, his eyes wide with the horror and his hands outstretched. Up until that evening all he had known was kindness.

'Get back, Moineau!' I shouted but my misshapen legs could not react fast enough.

Corbeau wrenched his speared hand free and strode forward; blood ran freely from the wound, yet his face was calm. Barely pausing as he passed, he swiped sideways and my brother's body flew into the air. As his head hit the wall, I heard an appalling crack.

Seconds later, with his sword raised at my own throat, he hesitated and something like puzzlement crossed his face. At that moment a commanding voice came from the street below.

'That's it, Corbeau, your murderous friends have surrendered ... it's over!' Still expecting a deathblow, I had closed my eyes.

When I opened them again Corbeau had gone.

'The Chalice is not a mere weapon!
Its true power may lie in peace. If used for
violence, it will surely become unstoppable.
The Chalice, wrongly used, has the power
to destroy everything we know.'

Qi LiFang. *Dragon Clan Chronicles.*

Chapter 2

the Mere Wars

Why Corbeau did not kill me when he had the chance remains a mystery. With my bent, distorted legs and stunted wings it may have been pity, though it seems doubtful. More likely was that he saw in me what no one until much later knew.

You see, I often get visions.

Most of the time they seem to be nonsense, but once in a while they tell me something important, which makes up for not being able to see anything further than about three inches from the end of my nose. It is as if these things that will happen lie very close by — through a dirty window. If I move my brain in certain ways I can peer through the glass to make out what is beyond, despite the grime.

These days, as I look around me in the Keep, I still fancy I can see the details that we all appreciate. The green leaves in spring, moonbeams etcetera … I feel the sun but I no longer see it, just as I feel the warmth of friendship that is now gone with the passing of the last of my fellow adventurers and friends. Only Grue still lives, cantankerous and snotty as ever. We are very old.

My name, by the way, is Prince Tærgu Mar, The Eight Hundred and Fourth of Vlad. Most people just call me Moüsch, or, if they are being unkind, Moüsch the Crooked.

And I'll be your narrator.

On that frozen night in winter when Corbeau disappeared, you Humans were embarking on your own hundred years of war a mere 1300 years after the death of your great prophet, that sanctifier of blood even we identify with, and likewise *cupholder*: Christ. Curiously, events in your history have often mirrored ours. As we were beginning to turn our backs on the magic that had been our birthright from the beginning, where we came instead to rely on our natural speed and strength for our survival, Weres began to gather at our walls. Thus our war began.

Some said Corbeau himself, exiled since that terrible night, now led them. For the past generation, the Weres had seemed to become more viscous, less *tame*, and more animalistic than ever. Once a shape-shifting race, brutal but intelligent, many of them now chose to shun all others of the Hidden Kingdom and hide in the great forests where they rarely, if ever, took on any form other than the wolverine. As a small child, with no mother to comfort me, the Weres' raging in the night kept me awake.

So now the hunter had become the hunted. No one is quite sure whether they wanted to destroy the Keep or whether they too were looking for the last source of our diminishing power, the Chalice: *our* sacred cup.

Peregrine, a Vampire Knight and one of those who had refused to follow Corbeau when he tried to take over the Keep, told the story better than most – probably because he was in the thick of it. When not actually fighting, he was given to telling bloodthirsty tales about different members of the Hidden Kingdom making mincemeat of each other. By this stage in the evening, he had usually drunk too much ox blood, fortified with cognac, so I'll have to give you his version, made suitable for family listening.

⁂

'It was a bitter, brutal time ours boys 'ad of it …

'The Weres attacked us, at first in small numbers around the outskirts of the Keep, but then gradually with more front and cunning until our general, the old Duke, had no choice but to raise an army of elite Vampire knights to fight the 'orrible cures.

'And so began the wars what were known as the Were Wars … s'cuse me …

'They raged to and fro for decades. Thousands were lost on both sides, the very young and the very old died too and many of us left

the Keep, to start new lives elsewhere, far from the bloodshed.

'Then, after generations of keeping them at bay in the woods of Transylvania, our Duke finally found their stronghold, the Lair, at the top of the Carpathian mountain range – ancient caves hidden amongst the black rocks and passes. For days he burnt 'ooge fires at the mouth of the Lair, to smoke those wicked Weres out and sent search parties in, what were never 'eard of again. It was only when he diverted the course of a nearby river, to flood the Lair with freezing water, that anyfing 'appened. Cornered, with nowhere else to go, they finally turned and attacked us in the open.

'At first they went for the Duke's vanguard in the dead of night, ripping and eatin' the flesh of our fallen as they swept in their thousands through the dark forests towards the Duke's main encampment. But the Duke was a wily old fighter, he was – over a thousand years old, and the victor of scores of campaigns. By putting his main force above the treeline, he'd lured the Weres into the open plain at the very top of the mountain. Wolves' Bane, it was ever after called by those who still have the stomach to dwell thereabouts.

'Dawn was a smudge on the 'orizon and the attacking Weres were no match for the fully-armed Vampire lancers on open ground. Our lads did us proud. Again and again the curs attacked the speared ranks of Vampires and each time their dead were left in piles of blood-matted fur and broken limbs scattered across the plain. As the new day turned the sky from grey to chill blue in the mountain air, the Duke ordered the Vampires to 'olster their lances and draw their swords. The pride of the Were packs was broken on the first charge, some say it never recovered to this day and even now they want their bloody revenge. The Duke wheeled his Vampire Knights around for a second charge and swept the howling Weres back into the dark forests and echoing caverns. An' good riddance, I say.

'But this wasn't the end of it, not by no means. The Weres had one last terrible card to play. As the Duke and his knights returned to the field of battle to care for their wounded and to bury their dead brothers in the forests, some of the stronger and cleverer Weres attacked the Keep, our 'ome. With no one left to guard the walls, they stormed the main gates easily, murdering indiscriminately, and it is said that they stole the Chalice from the Fast Tower and then kidnapped the Duke's great-grandchild, who was just a Milk Imp.

'The Duke's anger when he found out was terrible and even his closest friends and brother warriors said they no longer recognised him: that he became, at that moment, a monster, awful to look upon. He discovered the Weres had taken to sea, on ships bought by Corbeau from the Faies, so he sent half his great army to punish the Faies for their treachery and then raised a fleet, despite our distrust of water, and tracked the Weres down to a volcanic outcrop off of Africa, known as Truant Island.

'The battle that raged on its shores was bewildering and bloody. Vampires and Weres fought on the sea, the sands and in the dark jungles for days an' through nights and the smell of smoke and blood 'ung in the air for months afterwards. The Duke saved his great-grandchild but died of his wounds, badly mauled in the rescue. As 'e died, 'e 'eld the tiny child in his arms and his face became peaceful and kind once more.'

Peregrine usually fell over at this point – but you get the picture.

So this was the decisive battle that, in the way of nearly all so-called decisive battles, decided practically nothing but in which everyone lost so many soldiers that no one could see the point in fighting anymore and the survivors on both sides sailed away, both, no doubt, declaring great victories back home safely.

What was most intriguing and mysterious, though, was the next bit of the saga that is still told around campfires and bed-sides: that most of the casualties on that terrible day were not caused by the swords of the Vampires or the Weres' razor-sharp teeth but by a terrifying Hag who lived in the caves under the mountain at the centre of Truant Island. The story tells how she used her dark magic to turn both sides mad with fear and how they had thrown themselves into the water and sunk to the bottom, never to be seen again.

True or not, what is certain is that the surviving Weres and

Vampires all sailed away without the Chalice and that it hasn't been seen since; and nor has Corbeau for that matter.

'The harder we have tried to keep
a hold over the Seven Treasures, the
more elusive their power has become.
None more so than the Chalice,
whose true purpose remains a mystery,
even now. Parading It in a gilded cage,
It becomes a dead thing. Keeping the
Chalice hidden, will only make It try
the harder to break free or cause
mischief. The Chalice can never
truly be possessed.'

Eltern, *Edicts*.

Chapter 3

Search for the Chalice

It all kicked off again, as these things so often do, when we were least expecting it. The Were Wars had been over for fifty years and lately things felt like they were getting back to normal.

On top of this, it was a beautiful day and life in the Keep seemed idyllic. Not for long, though. Chassignol had been called before the three Vampire Eltern: Prince Vladimir van Pinsk, Duke Mazyr and Duke Limitri van Lud himself.

'The Chalice has been lost to us for too long and something's just cropped up, so we need it back urgently.'

And that was basically that.

As usual, the Eltern's attitude to anything important was vague at best: likewise their attitude towards anything trivial was equally hard to fathom – they had been known in the past to start wars over a game of checkers. However, the key to them staying in power was this: first up, they had a admirable habit of winning most fights they got us into and secondly, when the dust had settled and the full picture was known, the rest of us would realise that they had been right all along.

Prince Vladimir van Pinsk stared hard at Chassignol for a long time, then went on. 'You are the strongest and the bravest of all the young Vampires, Chassignol, so we command you to assemble a small band of the noblest amongst us, to lead a quest to search the four corners of the Human Kingdom and bring it back to us. Here, we've made a list of people you can take along with you if they're not doing anything else.'

'But how am I going to find it?' asked Chassignol, respectfully but at a loss where to start.

'Well, *we* don't know,' replied the Prince, a little crossly, taking off his spectacles and then almost immediately putting them back on again. 'That's your problem.'

'Oh good,' said Chassignol, bowing deeply. When he looked up the three Nosferatu had already gone off to play "snap" on the balcony. He stared pensively at the letter with his name on it he had just been handed.

Chassignol sighed. Like all relatively young Vampires he really didn't know much that could be counted as specific about the Chalice – except that firstly it was probably very important, secondly that it might have something to do with being some sort of weapon and thirdly, that it had a lot to do with blood. Unfortunately nobody knew where it now was – except that Corbeau didn't seem to have it, which was supposed to be something at least, or he would have used it by now and we'd all be dead in a dungeon somewhere.

He read the letter on the way over to see me.

After he'd explained what had gone on with the Eltern, we looked at list of people whom he was going to ask to come with us. If this was really to be a quest, it should have required some careful thought. However, Vampires are one of the least patient lifeforms on the planet, and, judging by the writing, the Eltern had simply scrawled down the first names they thought of. It seemed up to us then to make up reasons to invite them along.

 Looking back, it is just possible that the Eltern ordered me to go for reasons which only became apparent to the rest of us much later in our journey. For now it was enough that Chassignol counted on me to keep him out of trouble by using my brains, and I counted on him to do the same for me by using his natural charm or, failing that, his sword, or anything good and heavy to hand.

I read the names out as Chassignol stood by the window biting his nails.

'Count Chassignol: leader, proud to be chosen by the Eltern, yet so modest … hoping he won't let them down, steadfast of purpose … bla bla bla. Me: brains and beauty … '

' … Irritating know-all, more like,' commented Chassignol, spitting a bit of nail past my head out of the window. I ignored him. I had a policy, at the time, to discourage any of Chassignol's attempts at humour.

The next person was frankly a little hard to justify. 'Princess Chisnu-Cris, or *San-son-net*', I read out.

Chassignol's ears went bright pink. 'Err, after all', he coughed, 'we need to keep a balance'.

I kept my expression disdainful at the patheticness of that last comment and continued.

'Peregrine: a bit rough around the edges but he's the best swordsman we've got, except for you. He'll have to come. And then there's Grue down here. He's almost as good with a sword as Peregrine, and he's scary. That might be helpful'.

Chassignol's normally pleasant features clouded. Grue was just about the only person in the Keep whom he couldn't stand, plus Grue had been hanging around Sansonnet rather too much recently. As for his opinion about Grue, I agreed with him wholeheartedly. Grue was about as much fun as flu. Chassignol and I used to make fun of him when we were younger and I don't think Grue would ever forgive us for some of the pranks we played on him. Chassignol weighed his personal feelings against the importance of the Quest and, as usual, took the honourable course.

'I suppose so ... '

'Milan and Faucon are next on the list'. They were cousins who were more like siblings and everybody liked them. Also they were unusually square and muscular for our kind, full of unexpected sharp bony bits, which put people off picking fights with them. They rarely, if ever, took anything too seriously, but this wouldn't have stopped me trusting them with my life, if need be. Milan had a stutter, which didn't seem to bother him in the least. Faucon was marginally the more sensible of the two.

'Finally, Bud: very loyal, but isn't he what you might call *timid*, to be fair, and probably very unfit, given the amount of junk he eats?' I asked.

Chassignol shook his head. 'He'll be fine'.

To this day though, I honestly don't know why the Eltern included him. Bud was not what you'd call quest material – not that any of us really were – but everyone liked him and I guessed that it somehow seemed right to ask him along, almost as a tubby mascot. Also, Bud wasn't a Vampire. He was what some called a *Blutschpend*, or a *Sanguine*.

Originally they had been wild, flightless creatures, rather like chubby Vampires without wings, but the terrible truth is that over hundreds of generations we Vampires had bred them as a living food source. Sanguines had carried blood for Vampires when the Earth was mainly inhabited by fish. Cold blood tastes about as bad as it sounds, and insects' blood doesn't bear thinking about. As the mammals took over and blood became plentiful, the Sanguines' use changed from provider – much like Humans use cows for milk – to servant and now faithful companion. Each was attached to a particular Vampire family, sometimes for hundreds of years.

These days Bud was essentially a free agent, but his family had served Grue's since the beginning virtually. In fact Bud, with his mournful eyes and hesitant smile, seemed to be about the only living creature that Grue was truly fond of.

When the list was finished, we both looked at it in silence. Even for a notoriously impulsive species as Vampires, it all seemed sudden and surreal. 'OK,' Chassignol said, at last. 'You go and ask them; I have to arrange supplies and come up with a plan.'

I couldn't take it any longer, so I asked. 'Remind me why we're doing this?'

By way of an answer Chassignol gave me one of his looks. Then he sighed as he brought the palm of his hand across his mouth in a sort of wiping motion.

Now, I'd known Chassignol for years – his parents adopted me after my family was killed and so we grew up together – me, the cripple who had funny dreams, him, the handsome, over-achiever whom everyone liked.

In many ways, being sent to live with Chassignol's family was an odd choice. As one of the higher clan members, I could have been packed off to live with any one of a dozen or so distant clan cousins either in the Keep itself or off the map in some chilly castle miles away. However, the Eltern, who are in charge of these things, took note of my physical weakness but also my unexpected bravery in killing a fully-armed Vampire knight and decided to give me an alternative upbringing with a less wealthy family but one whose son showed great promise.

In many ways, it was an inspired choice and just goes to show that the Eltern aren't as stupid as they sometimes look. We made a good team; I helped Chassignol with his schoolwork, and he stopped me from getting the remaining sense I had being beaten out of me by the likes of Grue. Anyway, my point is this – the funny look was because he was not used to me questioning anything he did.

Many years before, when we were still kids really, deep within the Ice Caves in the north of our craggy little country, he'd saved my life, and so doing lost something no one should at his age. From then I vowed *fealty* to Chassignol, which basically, in Vampire terms, meant I had to do his bidding without question until I somehow repaid the life debt. Not being your swash-buckling type, I doubted I would ever repay him – and anyway, I was with the majority who liked and admired the guy, so usually I was just happy to go along with whatever Chassignol thought right.

Secondly, that hand gesture across the mouth told me that what he was about to tell me wasn't exactly going to be the whole truth, and Chassignol never could lie well. He cleared his throat awkwardly.

'Well, um, it's like this … Corbeau is back and there are even one or two rumours he has managed to summon the Thin Man himself.'

Time stopped.

When I eventually did look up, Chassignol had gone. I honestly hadn't noticed him leave. Outside the sun shone, birds did birdy things in the trees and a gentle wind blew ripples across the pond outside my window. Corbeau was back. Why hadn't the sky gone black, the trees wilted and the late spring grass dried to dust?

It was true that lately I'd been dreaming about Corbeau the traitor, which is never a good sign with someone like me. But the greater threat by far was the Thin Man. Older, it is said, than the Vampires themselves. If Corbeau stalks the dreams of Vampire children in their beds, it is the Thin Man who our adults fear. You Humans have a name for him too. You'd call him the *Devil*.

Nothing had been seen or heard of the Thin Man for thousands of years and some of the younger Vampires even claimed he didn't exist. On hearing this, older Vampires in the Keep would shake their heads and point out that if that were really the case, then why would no Vampire go alone into the deepest caves of the Craggy Vastness, and why would even our bravest warriors sometimes cry out at night, if it were not for some ageless fear of evil that dwelt in the quiet places and haunted our dreams?

The Thin Man might not always have a physical form, but he still trod the silent roads of our imaginations. It was said that he would offer sanctuary to our outcasts and our criminals for whom there was no redemption, which made me think of Corbeau and his disappearance up until now.

Anything to do with the Thin Man always brings on a mention of the Chalice. As said, without anyone knowing quite what it was or what it did, we had all been brought up to see it as our one effective weapon against the Thin Man, and therefore our last hope when things were at their worst.

So, as I hobbled up the road to the *Stagger Inn* where Milan and Faucon usually spent their days, I decided that it was what Chassignol had been holding back in that letter that concerned me most.

⤳

'If at first you don't succeed,
destroy all the evidence that
you have even tried.'

Faucon.

truant island

And so that was how, only three weeks later, we found ourselves bobbing about at sea, half-drowned and all wishing we were back in the safety of the Keep.

It was a blustery day and I was sitting on the prow of our boat, the *Sprite*, keeping a blurry lookout and shouting directions that no one was really listening to. Each time a patch of blue appeared, clouds raced eagerly across the sky to cover it up. The rest of our lot, and the rag-tag crew of Ship Wights we had hired, rowed toward a small island, as it appeared then disappeared with the waves that went up then down like medium-sized blue and white hills.

Sitting there in our brand new gear that we had bought for the trip we were all undeniably very cross and very damp Vampires. Vampires are really not meant to go to sea. There is a saying that a Vampire can get seasick just walking across wet grass, and everyone, with the exception of Chassignol and Grue, had been very seasick indeed. There had been a terrible storm the night before. The crew had insisted that it was nothing but a bit of *choppiness*, which I imagine was their idea of a joke. However, no one had got much sleep, and on top of that the last of the chocolate biscuits had vanished.

'Oo's pinched our lovely bikkies?' Peregrine had asked Bud the Sanguine, who almost certainly had something to do with their disappearance. 'Woz it you?'

'No,' said Bud, doing a very good job of looking completely virtuous. 'Actually I'm on a diet.'

Twenty minutes later Bud had been sick on Peregrine's shoes. Most of it was half-eaten chocolate-chip cookies.

Confronted by the evidence, Peregrine had taken matters into his own hands and thrown a bucket of seawater over Bud. It must have been freezing, and Bud was still sulking like mad. On top of this the boat, which our leader Chassignol had bought for too much gold dust from some North African Pirate Vampires, had started to suck up water like a giant spongecake a few hours after we left port. This wasn't surprising: most Pirate Vampires are in the business solely because they like the boots, the big shirts and the jewellery. The vast majority of them spend their days drinking fermented blood cognac and gambling, instead of actually putting out to sea. Nearly all Vampire boats are rubbish.

Now it looked as if we were all going to drown in the middle of the ocean before the Great Quest had even begun. I had tried to work out what the future held in store, but was feeling far too queasy for that.

The island was much clearer now, and we could see that most of it was dominated by a large mountain, rising up from the shore. The rock was pitch black and the wind and waves had eaten away at it over the years so that, rising up from the tangle of jungle below, the mountain looked exactly like a huge black claw clutching at the soft underbellies of the white clouds as they passed above its jagged nails. I shivered, and then turned to see that Chassignol was standing next to me, looking a little pale but on the whole a good deal healthier than the rest of us.

'Is this the place then, old chap?' he asked.

I stared at him. 'Old *chap?*'

Chassignol looked embarrassed. I shook my head, flattened out an ancient map I'd found below as best I could in the wind and pointed. 'I was worried that we were blown off course last night in the storm but this is the only land for a hundred miles in any direction.' We both looked at the tiny dot in the middle of the Atlantic where all those Vampires had died: '*Truant Island, no inhabitants, none welcome,*' said the map. Except for the witch, of course.

A tremendous screeching and grating noise, which didn't sound too welcome when all you had between you and drowning was an inch or two of soggy wood, put a temporary stop to my grisly thoughts of battles and bloated corpses lying on the sea bed. It was obvious that the noises came from under the boat, but it took us a few moments to realise that we weren't moving forward anymore. There was still a fair amount of open sea in front of us and behind. 'We've stopped,' confirmed Chassignol, peering over the side.

'What a relief,' I commented.

'What's goin' on 'ere, then?' Peregrine, the born psychopath, was already spoiling for a fight.

'We're not entirely sure.' Chassignol turned to the cousins, who were still running about pulling on ropes, as if we were moving. 'Milan, Faucon, jump over the side would you and see whether we've hit a rock or something.'

Milan unstrapped his breastplate, took off his shirt and tied a rope around his waist, so we could pull him back out of the water if anything happened, then jumped deftly over the gunwale. Instead of a splash, though, we heard a crash, followed by a tinkling sound. We all peered over the side. There was a rope, no sign of Milan and a jagged hole in the sea. We pulled the rope and then out he popped, soaked to the skin – his unruly hair, which normally grew like thick tufts of gorse on his head, was flattened against his scalp. He was looking puzzled, but OK. He coughed and spluttered and finally looked up at everyone waiting patiently for an explanation. 'The sea's made of ger-glass,' he said in due course, clambering out, 'and I've lost wer-one of my shoes.'

Ten minutes later Milan and Faucon were sliding about on the polished surface, jabbing bony knees and elbows into each other's ribs. Bud rolled his large, doleful eyes in mock despair at Chassignol, who just shrugged. We were standing on what seemed like a kind of lid someone had put over the water, starting about a hundred yards from beyond the island. The glass itself was perfectly clear and you could see fish and crabs on the bottom beneath us, weaving their way through the warm blue water, minding their own collective business. Strangely, the glass surface didn't move an inch; but as Milan had shown when he jumped in, it was no thicker than a finger, and it broke pretty easily.

'Magic,' said Grue matter-of-factly, as if he was the expert. 'Stops anyone getting too close to the island in a boat. I'd say that it's the work of this Hag everybody tells us about. And now she knows we're here,' he added ominously. There's nothing like Grue to cheer everyone up.

'Probably,' Chassignol was forced to agree. 'Well I suppose it saves us having to find a bay to moor the ship; we might as well bring some provisions and head towards the mountain.'

And so that's what we did. Being back on dry land (so to speak), with a warm wind in our faces, and in spite of Grue, we all felt our spirits lift for the first time in days. I even started to feel a little excited at the prospect of an adventure.

Moving along with curious little half-skating, half-walking motions we were soon stood on the beach, gazing up at the huge black claw of rock that seemed much larger and therefore more disturbing than ever. Looking at the coast, it was clear to me that there was no way we could have landed the ship anywhere near the island anyway, as the bay was littered with razor sharp-looking rocks lurking below the surface of the water, just waiting to gouge a hole out of the spongy bottom of the *Sprite*.

However, what little good humour we had faded quickly as we looked up the sand towards the dark and impenetrable jungle that blocked the path up the mountain. 'Nothing for it,' said Chassignol as cheerfully as possible, drawing his sword and swishing it a few times in the air. 'Let's start to cut a path here. It's the quickest way up the mountain and I think I spotted some a track at its base as we approached. Milan and Faucon, you make a start with me, and once we get tired, Bud, Grue and Peregrine can take over.'

'What about me?' said Sansonnet and I swear she almost pouted.

Chassignol looked sheepish – the fact is, Chassignol is pretty old-fashioned, and I think he was already beginning to regret bringing Sansonnet along. 'Er, OK, you look after Moüsch.'

'Oh cheers,' I said.

I might have had more to say on that subject but I had other things on my mind. The fact was that ever since we had reached the shoreline, I had felt uneasy. I was certain a pair of eyes watched us from high up on the mountain. I could feel them pass over our group like a searchlight, to and fro, a penetrating, baleful glare. For the time being I said nothing. First of all, because it's usually pointless to try to put the willies up a Vampire – they just hiss, 'Ahhh, blaahd and danger!' with a daft look in their eye and then go charging off into the bushes, which is a good way to get everyone killed. Secondly, I sensed that there were other things lurking much closer to us, from lower down in the forest itself. Whatever they were also watched us as carefully but with perhaps less malice – but, whatever their intention, we had to deal with *them* first.

❧

Anyway, Milan and Faucon drew their swords and started to hack their way deeper into the thick jungle, their arms knotted with muscle, looks of fierce concentration on their broad faces. Even now there was evidence of the battle from all those years before. Every so often we had to step over the sun-bleached bones of a Were or Vampire, often still locked together in combat, as if engaged in some macabre dance for all time. The cousins were getting into the spirit of the thing as the air became oppressively humid and the light went from gold to an ominous green, under the thick canopy of leaves.

Abruptly we came to a wall of rock. Towering above us, like giants, were a dozen or so worn rock sculptures. The figures were Human, though oddly stunted – their arms and legs looked too short for their stocky bodies. Bud, who before this journey hadn't got out much, seemed interested.

'What are they? They're *huge!*'

'As a matter of fact, they're relatively small,' Grue said, coming to stand next to him. 'For Humans. They are the forest dwellers they call pygmies.'

'They look nothing like pigs.'

'No,' said Grue patiently, 'it's Greek for *stumpy* – like I said, they're much smaller than normal humans.'

Bud looked thunderstruck at the idea that Humans could be larger than this. 'I suppose the rest of them must called *bigmies*, then,' he said, running after us to catch up.

A few moments later, Sansonnet fell into step with me with an apologetic smile.

'Is it me, or are you also beginning to wish you were back on the boat?' I asked.

'Chassignol knows what he's doing,' she said a little primly.

It was about this point that we all realised we were in a place full of insects. Whilst insects may be annoying to you Humans they are positively hazardous to Vampires. We've learnt to get around the danger of accidentally walking into a nest of thousands of ants, or being stung to death by hornets, by using a clever little discovery that was unearthed by one of our lot, long ago in a far-away place. The Memory Exception Crystal is something that every Vampire learns to carry with them from an early age.

As usual, no one can agree on one version. My favourite, though, is that the crystals were first discovered by Boris Gorky. History relates that old Boris was, to be blunt, cuckoo and that's how I like all my inventors to be. At the time, he was leading an expedition deep into the salt mines of Siberia to rescue a long-lost ancestor who had been bricked up in a salt castle there by a particularly cruel gang of ice Faies. Digging down into the salt castle, which lay hundreds of feet below the surface of the frozen tundra, some of his Vampire miners noticed some attractive crystals lining the walls of the cavern that turned from blue to green and sometimes red as you turned them in your hands. They were certainly very pretty and all Vampires like a bit of bling, so the rescuers made space in their packs for them. No one noticed anything odd about the effects they had on insects until much later, when on their journey home they ran into a swarm of swamp mosquitoes.

The story goes that the lookouts noticed them too late, which normally would have meant every Vampire for himself, and quite a few casualties; so everyone hit the deck, shut their eyes and thought of their mums. Imagine their surprise then, when the swarm simply passed over their heads as if they were invisible.

On their way home they tried out the crystals on many other types of animal and insect and in the end came to the conclusion that they worked in the following way: if you held the crystals in your hand or around your neck, the insect could see you but within seconds of doing so promptly forgot you were there. Each time it did remember that there was a delicious and juicy Vampire to eat in the vicinity, it promptly forgot and remembered something like one of its million or so aunties' birthdays, or the fact that it better make the most of the day as it was going to be very old or dead in half an hour.

Which is why, in the summer, when the Vampires are out, there are always loads of confused insects frantically rushing off to do things they didn't know they had to do.

As I say, very useful things, M.E.C.s, which is why it is all the more amazing that before setting out for a journey through an insect-ridden jungle nobody had remembered to bring one. We realized this when, without any warning, we heard a buzz, then a surprised cry as Sansonnet was almost lifted off her feet by a huge mosquito with beady eyes. It had this long spear they all have for a nose that it was presently trying to stab through the top of Sansonnet's head, if she would only stop wriggling for a moment.

In a single movement that was too fast for me to see, Peregrine had drawn his sword and skewered the mosquito neatly through the eyes, a look of grim satisfaction on his leathery features. Grue, who was never one to avoid a fight, I'll give him that, drew his sword and raced into the air with a graceful flick of his wings. There was a rapid parry and thrust, as the two remaining mosquitoes tried to spear Grue, missed and pretty soon three insect corpses lay on the jungle floor twitching erratically. By now we'd all drawn our swords and formed a defensive circle but nothing more came at us out of the jungle. The air was stifling. 'Everyone alright?' asked Chassignol eventually, putting away his slim rapier. We all nodded. 'OK, before we go much further, I suggest that Milan and Faucon go back to the ship and get the M.E.C.s.'

And so this just goes to show that every journey, large or small, always, *always* starts with someone having to go back and fetch something they've forgotten.

Now, normally, I would have had something to say about this and would have probably cracked a few jokes at Chassignol's expense, but I still had this nagging feeling that was growing by the minute. Sansonnet also seemed to be off-colour. Sansonnet wasn't exactly a Vampire who could predict things, just someone you'd call sensitive, but I'd noticed she felt things almost as acutely as I did at times. In fact it had been happening rather a lot lately, and I was beginning to wonder about her.

The pressure was building rapidly at this point, and within a few moments the sense of something terrible about to happen seemed to reach a peak.

From the corner of my eye I saw a flicker in the trees and a pool of light wink off, and then on, as if someone or *something* stepped back into the shadows the very moment I looked in their direction.

'What's up, Moüsch?' asked Sansonnet who had popped up next to me.

'I'm not sure,' I replied in a half-whisper.

The forest around us had got darker, and we began to feel as if we were standing in a tunnel. Suddenly it was blindingly obvious to me. 'We've walked into a trap!' I shouted at the same moment I thought it. Peregrine and Chassignol immediately took to the air and the rest of us formed a circle again. Nothing moved and no one spoke for a minute or so.

'Ahem.' Grue cleared his throat. 'What exactly did you see?' he said, looking nasty. 'If you're wasting our time, as usual, jumping at your own shadow, I suggest you toddle off back to the ship, and take Sansonnet with you as well. You're only slowing us down – you can make us a cup of tea for when we get back – if it's not too much trouble.' But I was hardly listening to Grue. There was that buzzing sound inside my head and my eyes ached. As I half-turned to Sansonnet, I noticed her top lip was beaded with a fine sheen of sweat.

Definitely, without a shadow of doubt, I felt the entity I had sensed on the beach moving closer, rushing down the mountain to meet us.

Any light coming through the canopy then disappeared almost entirely and there was an eerie hiss and an inhuman-sounding chuckle. The others heard it too. No one spoke and everyone huddled closer, except Chassignol, who took to the air to get a better look around. 'Can you see anything?' he asked, looking down toward me from where he hovered.

'Gnargh, no.' My voice came out as a croak.

And then *They* stepped into the light and we all jumped out of our skins.

Ghosts! First up, Vampires believe in them. We really do. It's partly because, as the supernatural goes, we're pretty supernatural ourselves, and the idea of a ghost isn't exactly all that astonishing. It's also partly because we see ghosts.

It doesn't actually mean we *like* ghosts. Phantoms and the like still give us the heebie-jeebies, same as anyone. They have this bad habit, for starters, of popping up in unlikely places when your mind is on other things and making your bones go all jangly. And they do it on purpose, I swear. Secondly they never look in good shape. Fundamentally far too transparent, unwell-looking and generally dusty, if I'm being honest.

And then ghosts like to *tell* you things as well and it's never, ever, good news. They'd do themselves a huge favour, once in a while, if they turned up on a sunny day, whilst you're sunbathing or drinking something cool and refreshing. It would give you a good chance to get used to them, as opposed to their usual trick of popping up behind you when you're looking in the bathroom mirror at night, or you're down in the cellar bending over something covered in cobwebs. And instead of saying something like, *Woo, woooo, your head's going to fall off* or, *You know your auntie Ethel? Well, she'll end up falling down a deep hole in her nightie,* instead they *could* say: *What a nice day, how are you, see you soon, etc., etc.* Even if they don't really mean it, it would still be nice. Just once in a while – that's all I'm saying.

Anyway, these weren't the usual class of spirits. The leader, or at least the first one that stepped into the light, was tall and very beautiful. Her long silver hair billowed, as if moved by invisible underwater currents, catching the light that shone through it like a halo. Shadows began to gather around her. These seemed to be her companions, mere shapes really, vaguely two-legged but indistinct – so hard to make out that I could only see them if I looked sideways – viewed directly, they melted into the background of leaves and creepers. When their leader spoke it was softly, the trace of a whisper, and the shadows about her wavered and flickered in tempo, in a way that reminded me of the tips of bird wings. It was as if the sound of her voice was all too much disturbance for them to bear in the heat. She stared unblinkingly at each of us in turn and then spoke directly to Chassignol, who had landed directly in front of her and was the only one of us tall enough to look her in the eye. They would have made a great-looking couple, if she wasn't dead, and I noticed Sansonnet scowl.

'Who are you?' the silver-haired apparition whispered.

'We are Vampires,' said Chassignol, bowing deeply. I noticed that Peregrine had moved around to protect Chassignol's back from the shadows that still stirred and moved in the bushes as the tall ghost spoke again.

'Where are you from?'

'We've come from across the sea,' replied Chassignol. 'From the Keep.' There was a long pause, so drawn out that Bud began to fidget.

'I've heard of you,' replied the ghost, eventually.

'Don't tell her any more,' I said, from right at the back, where it was relatively safe.

Then Grue, and I'll never forgive him, stepped forward into the light. 'Don't worry, I don't think they're here to harm us,' he said firmly. The ghost bowed at Grue and smiled and then turned her head in my direction and gave me a sort of funny look down the side of her nose, as if she was doing a complicated sum. In time she turned back to Chassignol as he spoke again.

'And may we know who you are?' Chassignol asked, bowing again, politely enough, although the tone of his voice suggested that he expected a straight answer. There was more stirring at the back and the tall ghost turned her head as if she was listening to what the others had to say. The voices all seemed to be saying different things at first, then, almost out of the corner of my mind, the whispers grew more uniform until they became one.

'*Safe*,' they said in chorus.

The ghost turned back to face us. 'My name is Orieste,' she said. 'We were once the Faie that inhabited this forest when the land had no sea and the woods stretched for thousands of leagues from the setting sun to where it rises and was known as *All Earth*. We are the ghosts, cut off from the rest of our Nation by the slowly rising waters and the parting sands, for even we die ... by and by,' she smiled sadly.

Chassignol stepped forward and bent down on one knee. 'If that is so,' he said, 'and I believe that it is, then this island must be yours and I humbly ask permission to cross it and climb the mountain at its centre.'

There was another movement behind her and more whispers blew through the jungle, like dry leaves in winter.

'You are not the first.' Orieste said eventually.

'Who came here before us?' interrupted Grue, pushing through rudely to stand next to Chassignol.

'I cannot say, for he never spoke his name, not even in his thoughts, but he asked about you,' she said, and I noticed her tongue, small and very red, flick across surprisingly yellow and pitted teeth. Funnily enough, I'd always imagined that dead Faies had better dentistry. 'And he asked about the Chalice.' She paused again, presumably to see what effect these words had on us and, I must say, we all rose to the occasion by standing there with our mouths open. 'I can take you there,' she said, and the shadows around her trembled with what seemed to be anticipation.

Now, everything had been going fine until this point. Everyone except for me seemed to be relaxing and enjoying how it was all going. Quite frankly, getting the Chalice back seemed incredibly easy, barring a bit of seasickness and wet shoes. But this buzzing I told you about earlier just kept getting louder and, to make things worse, I was beginning to feel decidedly sick. At first I thought that it might be something I'd eaten recently – you never can be too careful what you stick your teeth into abroad.

Her companions remained hidden in the trees and heavy undergrowth, yet as they fanned out around us I felt my head begin to spin, and when I shut my eyes I saw crows' feathers – the horrible black and oily sort – and felt even worse.

Just then Milan and Faucon came back carrying the crystals, and we discovered something else they did: a small breeze lifted the canopy above our heads and a shaft of light found a way through to the forest floor. It happened to shine directly through one of the M.E.C.s and then onto Orieste.

The refracted blue light seemed to go right through her. I hesitate to go into details, in case you are eating, but instead of the usual stuff – heart, bones, ribs – we all saw what Orieste was really made of. At a glance, this seemed to be mainly a writhing mass of lice, worms, spiders and strange centipedes that were literally crawling and bulging under her skin. And as if that wasn't enough to make us run behind the nearest tree to throw up, everything now became clear inside my head – the shadows now gathered about her like black wings, the visions of beating wings, yellow canines, the still-sense of a trap.

'Well, I think we've found our Hag,' said Grue, echoing my exact thoughts.

⤝⤞

Now our kind can move on the ground at lightning speeds, but it's nothing compared to how we fly in the air: except, that is, for yours truly. In a single movement we had drawn our swords and used them to slice through the heavy jungle canopy above. We flew upwards in close formation, with Peregrine carrying Bud. *Her Hagness* was too surprised to move for an instant, but her shady friends were right on our tails. As we cleared the uppermost trees of the jungle, the shadows lifted from the forest floor and gathered into a shape of a noose at our feet.

Everyone reacted very quickly to this new danger.

Everyone, barring me.

It is a hard thing to live with fault but harder, even after so many years, to own up to it in writing. I cringe now, as I write these words, but the truth is we would have been up and away to safety that day were it not for my un-Vampire-like slowness and oddly-wired brain. Grue was right to want to leave me behind, after all.

Perhaps it was the fogginess that still clouded my head, the unfamiliar weight of my new armour or – I am still ashamed to admit – fear. However, my wings could beat no faster, and as the others pulled away from me in close formation heading for the *Sprite*, I felt the icy blackness of the Hag's hoard encircle my ankles and start to drag me slowly back down to the dark jungle below.

Milan was the first to notice. Without hesitation he wheeled around and came after me. In an instant, a tendril broke off from the raven-clawed shadow that gripped me and took hold of Milan, who barely had time to look startled before he was dragged down past me into the boiling black cloud. Peregrine, throwing a surprised-looking Bud to Grue, came next but he was captured too. The haze and the sickness returned with such ferocity that my eyes closed. Within a few moments we were all caught up within the black cloud that bound our hands, wings and feet and when I tried to draw my sword I succeeded only in uselessly wiggling the tips of my fingers, so I lashed out with my only available weapon, my teeth. The cloud tasted of rotting flesh. I retched. I felt branches whipping my legs and face, and hit the ground, hard enough that I felt my left leg dislocate at the knee and I had to clamp my teeth together to stop myself from screaming. A few more bumps of bodies landing nearby told me that the cloud had probably got us all. I felt like crying with shame. Thanks to me, a few days into the QUEST and all we'd got for our trouble was a really crap ship, one brief conversation with a lunatic and certain death.

⤝⧉

Annoyingly, I didn't have much time to really bask in self-pity.

'Moüsch! That you?' It was Faucon. He actually seemed quite perky.

'Yes. I think so.'

'Great.'

'Oh *really*?'

'Hello, hello?'

'S-S-Sansonnet?' Milan coughed out, clearing his lungs of the black mist.

'Yes, I'm here.' The fog began to clear, drawing back into the forest, filling the dark spaces between the leafy bushes and the pampas grass.

I made out six lumps lying close by. The one nearest me looked like Peregrine, his sword lying a few feet from him. As the remaining vestiges of the cloud flowed away another shape, tall and graceful, approached in silhouette. It was the Hag. She didn't look too happy.

'This isn't all of them,' she said to no one in particular. From the undergrowth a parched, indistinct whisper came back in response. I did a quick count of us. She was right. Chassignol was missing.

'Ha,' I said. 'Chassignol escaped – he's the best of us! He'll come after you and chop you into tiny pieces. ''

'Yeah, when he's finished there won't be enough left of you for a square meal.' said Faucon.

'Well, perhaps just a s-small ha-ha-*haggis*.' Milan snickered.

"Milan?' It was Grue and he sounded especially menacing.

'Er, yes Gr-Grue?'

'If you make another joke like that, anytime during the rest of your life, then forget Miss Creepy Crawly here, you'll have me to deal with.'

'Sorry, Grue,' said Milan. 'It wer-won't happen again.'

'See that it doesn't. Now,' said Grue, turning awkwardly where he lay, to face the Hag, 'I don't care about the rest of these idiots but I suggest that you apologise and let me go. I am apt to become unpleasant.'

Whether anything we said to her was getting through, I am not sure but she thought about Chassignol for a moment and then shrugged. 'He'll turn up sooner or later,' she said. 'In fact, I daresay he'll make good sport on the island, wherever he is hiding. After I've finished with you.'

I didn't like the sound of that.

The Hag smiled and once again we were treated to the sight of her truly terrible teeth, of the sort that give vampires, who set a lot in store by good dentistry, the heebie-jeebies. Slowly, almost theatrically, she drew a long knife from the folds of her robes. It was very old and tarnished but the point looked sharp enough. I struggled to get up but realised that my hands and feet were bound. I looked down and saw a black sticky substance growing from the ground, corkscrewing around my body from my feet up to my shoulders, pinning me down. I felt like a fly in a web.

'You wish to be released – by all means,' she said, squatting down by Grue to cut his bonds.

The instant they fell away, Grue leapt up and reached for his sword. As he drew it from the scabbard strapped to his leg, the blade became a long-stemmed flower.

'Why, thank you!' she exclaimed, taking it from Grue's surprised hands. 'He warned me you would come looking for the Chalice. But He never said you'd bring flowers. How absolutely charming!'

Grue let out a cry of fury and went for her neck, his teeth fully extended. The Hag merely blinked and Grue's mouth filled with a mass of lice, similar to what writhed inside her. He gagged and fell to his knees as they spewed out onto the jungle floor.

'Who is *He*?' asked Sansonnet, kicking at an especially long-legged creature that had crawled down Grue's chin and was blindly making its way towards her.

The Hag stepped over Grue's prone form and tapped Sansonnet playfully on the nose with her flower.

'Silly thing. The Thin Man, of course!'

'And I suppose you're keeping the Chalice for Him?' Sansonnet gave her a look you could shave with.

'The Chalice, what makes you think I've got what belongs only to Him? I would not be worthy to hold the cloth that polished it!'

'So who's got it then?'

'Who knows?' she said, 'Who knows? Perhaps He's got it already and He's simply toying with us. He's very playful, you know. *Such* a scamp.'

'I'm guessing that this was a trap then?' Grue had got his voice back.

The Hag pirouetted. 'Why how clever. Yes! Snippety snap, a trap – set by Corbeau and those nasty smelly Weres, all those years ago. Let the Vampires think it's here, and they'll come, tum ti tum!' ' She paused as a new emotion seemed to stop her in her tracks. Her clear blue eyes flashed with uncontrolled rage. 'I will eat your *hearts!*'

The last word came out sounding like something between a snarl and a howl of madness. The closest I would come in this life to hearing the roar of flames in Hell. Then she breathed deeply and seemed to calm herself.

'But what to do first?' she murmured, stroking the tip of the blade. 'I know,' she smiled brightly, eyes sparkling again with joy. 'I will drain their bodies and feed my garden with their blood. My lovely flowers will blossom ... crimson and scarlet!' I noticed, with alarm, that she had begun to dig the point of the knife into the exposed palm of her hand, gouging the flesh.

The smell of her blood brought me back to my senses. It seemed to affect Peregrine too, who stirred and involuntarily flexed his muscular shoulders. His tongue flicked briefly across his teeth.

The Hag still seemed to have things to say. 'Then they won't be able to look anymore, and He'll reward me. I'll finally be able to leave this miserable island, with nothing but these Shades for company.'

Shades! I had wondered what the fog was. Shades, I remembered vaguely from stories my father used to tell me, were long, long dead ghosts – so tired and ancient that they couldn't keep form anymore. They needed someone like the Hag to coax them from the shadows to take shape. They weren't necessarily evil, just weak.

Nothing to do with the Hag, then, though she could obviously control them. Now that I knew what they were, I began to listen more intently to their sighs and their muttering. It took a few moments but gradually their thoughts became distinct.

LEAVE THE ISLAND! they choursed, LEAVE US, THE SHADES, SO FORLORN, SO SAD, SO CAREWORN. WE WILL BE ALL ALONE! SOLITARY ... SILENT.

I concentrated hard. 'Er ... hullo?' I said in my head. This had happened to me before – perhaps another symptom of my *condition* – but up until now I'd only been able to catch snippets of words and phrases in my own mind and only at certain times. I'd put them down to the inner voices we all have, however, I had a feeling that if I could hear the Shades in my head, I might be able to talk to them. It was a long shot, to put it mildly, but I had a feeling that even if the Hag could read thoughts, she had her full attention on other things. Right now, she was still banging on about how nice it would be to get off the island for an extended holiday.

At first I didn't think I was getting through. Then I noticed the shadows begin to pool and gather closer to my side of the clearing.

You know she's barmy, don't you?

SHE'S ALL WE HAVE!

Fair point. Now, if I could get my knee to pop back in, I thought. I concentrated on moving the joint by rotating my ankle. It hurt like hell. I gritted my teeth. *If you help us, I'll make sure she stays.*

STAYS ... SHE STAYS?

Yes, I'm really not sure she's ready for the outside world.

There was a long pause whilst they seemed to be debating something amongst themselves that even I couldn't hear. I gave my ankle another go. I needed it to go back in if this plan was going to work. I felt the cartilage and bones in my knee grind together and I had to bite my tongue so as not to cry out. Nothing doing. Damn!

The Hag had moved over to where Sansonnet lay and was bringing the point slowly towards her rapidly blinking eye.

'One quick jab, and it will pop like a fat grape.'

Time seemed to have run out for Sansonnet, but at that very moment the Shades came to a decision. WE WILL HELP ... SHE WILL STAY ... YESSS! they cried in a collective shout as they rushed in a solid black wave to envelop the Hag, just as my throbbing knee clicked back in its socket. She screamed. As did I.

'What are you doing?'

'NEVER LEAVE USSS!' they cried as she was dragged off her feet, twisting into the air.

With my knee back in its joint and reasonably straight I was finally able to get enough leeway in my bonds to twist and kick Peregrine's sword within his reach. He grabbed the hilt and grinned at me. 'Mind out,' he said, and using the tips of his fingers flicked the razor-sharp blade across the bonds on my legs. They fell away.

Within seconds we were all free and ready to fly. Grue, still coughing terribly, was supported by the cousins.

As I took to the air I noticed the Hag's knife lying on the ground. Something told me it was important, so I picked it up.

We flew up into the welcoming sunlight, back towards the *Sprite*, zipping over the tops of the trees and out to the reassuring azure of the sea. To my surprise Chassignol stood there on the deck, looking completely unharmed. As we approached, the small crease he always got in the middle of his forehead when he was worried disappeared and he broke into a broad smile.

'Thank the Chalice! You're alive. I thought I'd lost you all.'

Sansonnet flew up to Chassignol and thumped him hard on the shoulder, more in relief, I suspect, than anger.

'Ow! *Ow?*'

'Where have you *been?*' she said.

'When you all got caught by the black fog, I followed you down to the jungle but I was too far behind and when I got through the canopy, you'd all vanished into thin air. I looked everywhere, working my way upwards, towards the mountain. I don't mind admitting I was getting pretty bushed, but then, just as I thought I couldn't go on any further, I ran into a goat – it appeared to be tethered to a tree.'

'Mm, goat blood,' interrupted Bud who'd try anything once, 'very ... goaty.'

'Um ... yes, quite right,' said Chassignol, shooting Bud a glance. 'Anyway, when I started to drink, something strange happened – I found I couldn't stop. My jaws were locked and my fangs wouldn't retract. I drank and I drank until I thought my stomach would burst. Then I noticed that it didn't taste like goat's blood at all anymore.'

With Chassignol seeming to falter at the memory, Sansonnet put out her hand and touched his cheek. 'What did it taste of?' she prompted.

'Vampire blood.'

'Oh yuk.'

'Blargh!' Even Bud looked unimpressed.

'I know. However, I didn't have long to think about it. When I looked down, I saw that the goat had disappeared and I was feeding from someone's exposed forearm.'

'Whose?'

Chassignol looked decidedly ill. 'My own.'

'What happened next?' I asked.

Chassignol squirmed and seemed embarrassed. 'In truth, I think I must have passed out.'

'That's nothing to be ashamed of,' Sansonnet said loyally, looking at us all with an *I dare you to laugh* expression on her face.

Good grief, I thought.

'Anyway, when I woke up, I was holding this.' Chassignol fished about in the pack he'd been carrying since we left the Keep and pulled out a knife, which was exactly the same as the one I still held. This one also looked razor sharp on one side, yet oddly grooved on the other. Wordlessly Chassignol took the knife from my hands, and after a couple of attempts fitted its dull edge against the groove of his own. The two halves slotted into one another with a barely audible hiss that reminded me of the Shades.

'How on earth did you know it did that?' I asked.

Chassignol didn't look up. 'I'm not really sure – a hunch, I expect.' he said absent-mindedly, absorbed by what he now held. Slotted together, the two blades were no longer tarnished and dull. They now shone, as if newly made. Turning the burnished metal in his hands, letters appeared, picked out in gold and bronze, as the sun caught grooves in the silver surface.

'It's written in Weirish.'

'Old Were script,' murmured Sansonnet, and she was right. For centuries none of us believed the Weres could read, let alone have their own writing system. It was basic to some but I always admired its brutal simplicity.

However Grue, mostly recovered, seemed unimpressed. He cleared his throat testily. 'Great … whatever … anyway, look, this isn't exactly the most pressing matter right now – I think that we'd better get a move on. Whatever Moüsch managed to pull off back there was probably more to do with fool's luck than any real skill and I can't imagine it will last long.'

'Thanks for the vote of confidence.'

'Yeah,' said Milan, still pulling bits of the black webbing out of his fur, 'let's cher-chalk this one up as experience and hope that it never, ever happens again. I don't suppose we've ger-got any sp-spare sails?' he added.

'It's alright, I've had our crew on standby for the last half an hour,' replied Chassignol. 'Look, those Wight chaps are on their toes, for once – we're already moving.'

A brisk wind was indeed blowing us east, away from the land. Everybody started to run around ordering each other about. Exhausted, I leant against the side of the ship, looking back at the island.

The crew and my companions were all so busy that nobody, except for me, noticed that a tall, thin and almost entirely black vessel slipped anchor from a far-off lee and followed us.

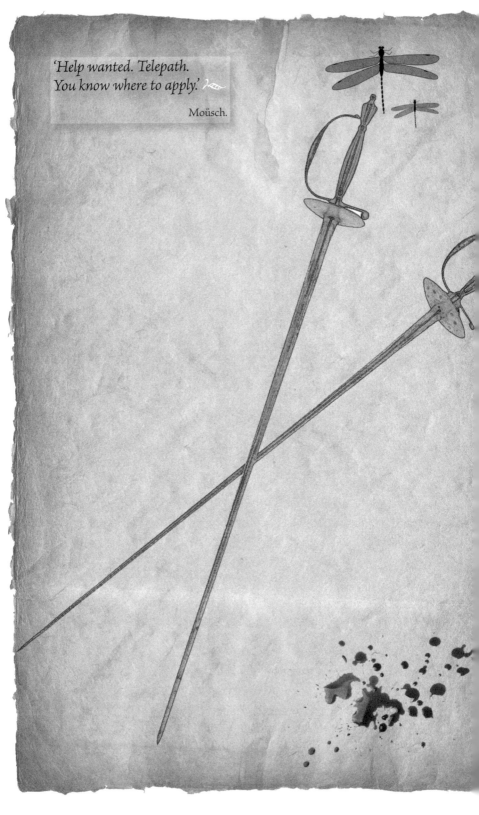

'Help wanted. Telepath.
You know where to apply.'

Moüsch.

Chapter 5

Swordplay

Grue was looking pretty sinister the next day when we all came down for tea and toast in the *galley*, which, I am told, is the word you use for a sort of titchy, inconvenient kitchen where you eat when you're floating about at sea in the middle of nowhere. He seemed to be coming down with a nasty cold after his insect-eating ordeal, and he also had a point to make. 'But what are we going to do now? That's my point,' he moaned, between buttery mouthfuls of toast.

'I'm sure the Hag was telling the truth and was guarding nothing,' said Chassignol, carefully brushing bits of Grue's breakfast off his lap.

I think we'd all come to the same conclusion, namely that she was an evil old bat, intent on torturing us, as her reward for leading us into a trap. She did know about the Chalice but that may only have been from whoever had come to the island before us – whoever was sailing the black ship. I looked out at the horizon and saw nothing. I would have liked to find this reassuring but I felt sure that it was still there, lurking below the curve of the Earth. Something also told me that whatever I had seen, I should keep to myself – for now, at least.

'If she really had the Chalice,' Chassignol continued, 'then she could have easily defeated us and I also don't think there's anyone on the island strong enough to have hidden it from her for all these years. Anyway, last night Moüsch managed to decipher the Weirsh on the knife.'

'What did it say?' half a dozen voices chorused, meaning more bits of breakfast sprayed about, getting in the butter.

Chassignol paused. 'Quite a bit, but most importantly, not all of the Were army went to Truant Island.'

Now their ears fairly pricked up at this.

'It mentions a secret force of Weres who made their way to Alahamba'dara in Persia.'

'*Ala*-what?' asked Milan.

'You say it like you're falling backwards down a well,' I explained.

'Rightyho.'

'Anyway, this was merely a feint to put anyone following off the scent. From there, the text says they were seen going to England with the Chalice, but the writing stops.'

Now this bit of, admittedly sketchy, information was interesting.

For one thing, it was the first time anyone had actually ever used the word *seen* when talking about the Chalice in a proper context since the Were Wars. To hear this was a big relief, as I was beginning to suspect it had gradually become one of those symbolic thingamajigs that we could have spent the next decade or two looking for and still be none the wiser.

Secondly, Chassignol obviously knew more from the start of this thing than he was letting on: even when I had stayed up half the night deciphering what was carved into the dagger, it was pretty vague, and what he was telling the others now definitely wasn't all on there. It's my experience that when people have secrets about something as important to us Vampires, then that secret is steeped in Lore and very old and generally worth knowing – plus Chassignol was your basic honest type of Vampire and he wouldn't keep secrets from us unless it was *for our own good*, and it was nice to know someone was looking out for us.

'Oh marvellous, the English summer.' Grue. Again.

'Yup! So we better steer north then,' Chassignol smiled, 'and pass the marmalade, would you? Thanks.'

⚘

Now, Vampires are a little funny about places like England. There are plenty of ghosts knocking about the place and castles and history in great platefuls – in fact all the sorts of things that

Humans would call supernatural – but rarely Vampires. At the time I had a personal theory that it was all because no one ever really took us all that seriously in England and we're easily offended. England's the only place I know of where ghosts don't even believe in themselves – it's as if they're embarrassed about finding that they're the Undead and would rather not make a fuss. This is very funny (curious funny, not ha ha funny), really, considering that England is more full of ghosts, Faies, witches and all sorts in the magical kinship than practically anywhere else on the planet.

As any young Vampire fiend who paid attention to their tutor will tell you, the list is endless but the three main groups are the Faies, Wight-types they call Brownies, and Goblins. None are especially evil or good but basically you have to watch out for the lot of them: they don't like strangers or people wandering about on their patch, though a fully-armed Vampire with his wits about him or her can deal with most of the so-called supernatural species. These days, certainly since the Were Wars, we have all seen a lot less of other members of the magical community. The Hidden Kingdom is finally living up to its name.

Faies are perhaps the most dangerous because they have more magic in them than most. Plus they really don't like us very much.

Hobbits don't exist.

But to the English, England is all about green fields with white clouds, recently skythed lawns, cows, lots of outdoor sports and now, it seems, the Chalice. Chassignol explained everything over a second slice of toast. 'So, as we all know, after the battle at Truant Island the Chalice was lost and nobody knows exactly where it went.'

'It doesn't help much that none of us here knows what it looks like either,' added Faucon cheerfully.

'Shut up Faucon,' we all said.

' ... anyway,' Chassignol went on, ignoring the interruption, 'most of what we know is no more than legend and gossip but I – well, actually, the Eltern – agree that there's no smoke without fire, which means we need to pretty much follow the legends that we know of, at least the ones that seem the most likely and I think this is right.' He looked thoughtful. 'I suppose we are following legends to find a legend, the most important one of all, at least to us Vampires and who knows who else, and in a sense it means that we are living in a legend. In years to come, whether we fail or not, people will talk about our story in the same way that they talk about the other great stories of the Chalice. It all becomes one. Milan and Faucon, Peregrine and Bud will become part of the story, it's why this isn't merely a journey, it's a *quest*. We're not only looking for the Chalice, we're adding our stories to the legend to keep the story alive and that's why everything we do must be done with honour and courage. If we don't behave properly on this quest, we let not only the Eltern down but the whole tradition behind the Chalice and centuries of sacrifice and the lost lives of our ancestors.'

Impressive stuff. Chassignol could really turn it on when he needs to and it was at moments like this when I could see why the Eltern chose him to lead us. All this stuff about honour and quests takes on a whole new potency for us Vampires who just love anything like this. Most of us sat there like a row of kittens watching a mouse on a string. On cue, though, Grue did his best to put a spanner in the works.

'What I don't understand,' he said, doing his best to look bored, 'is why it's become so important all of a sudden. It sounds to me like the Eltern are getting upset over nothing.'

Just for a second I saw Chassignol look uncomfortable. As quickly as it came the look was gone. He turned to Grue and replied as equably as possible. 'First of all because Corbeau is back and that should be enough to get any of us worried. The last time he came he nearly destroyed the Clans and he has made no secret of the fact he wishes to use the Chalice as a weapon to subdue his enemies. We may need everything we've got to defeat him, especially if the rumours are true about him trying to summon the Thin Man.

'Secondly we're entering a new cycle now, the Age of Aquarius, the age known as the Time of Truth and the texts all agree on one thing – that this is the epoch when the Chalice will finally reveal itself for what it is. The texts also speak of The End of Days. And this is it. But it doesn't mean the end of the world, unless the Thin Man wins. If we find the Chalice before him, we can reveal It to the world and this Age of Truth begins – this Age of Aquarius. If the Thin Man gets to it first he can use the Chalice for whatever purpose he chooses and it's not likely to be good. The End of Days will probably mean the end of us.'

Everyone went unusually quiet.

'And it's not simply the Weirsh on the dagger. Many of our own legends and even those of the other species like Faies and Humans, say that the key to finding the Chalice lies in England,' Chassignol went on, almost to himself, 'perhaps even the Chalice itself, so that's why we're sailing there.'

'Where do we start?' asked Sansonnet as Chassignol looked down at his hands and recited the following words to no one in particular.

'*There was a King, who was no King, crowned on a hill that was no hill, round at the base and round at the top and surrounded on all sides by a sea, that was no sea, in a kingdom, which was no kingdom at all.*' This was all completely new territory to me. No one moved or said anything for a bit; all I could hear was the creaking of the boat as it rocked to and fro on the waves.

'Well, with directions as sensible as that, I imagine we'll find it straight away,' said Grue.

Nothing much happened for the rest of the voyage until we approached the shores of England. As we went north, the weather got colder and on some mornings there was even frost on the rigging when I got up to take over the watch. We spent our days learning from the Wights how a ship like the *Sprite* worked and I almost began to like the old wreck – until the last day, as we sailed out of the Atlantic and started navigating the

English Channel. After that I swore I wouldn't get on another ship, boat, dinghy or peddlo unless I was drowning. And perhaps even then ...

It started like this.

Peregrine, Chassignol and Grue had been taking it in turns, when the weather was fair, to give us lessons in swordsmanship. That morning Grue had tried to pair off with Sansonnet but she had managed to get her way and had Chassignol teaching her, though not much fencing seemed to be going on from where I stood. Grue's long nose was well and truly out of joint and, as usual, he was taking it out on someone smaller and weaker, namely yours very truly.

I can fight with a sword as well as most as long as I don't have to move about on my feet too much; but Grue's a real specialist, easily as good as Peregrine, although not as mad. Because my legs are untrustworthy, my arms have grown strong and I can parry and attack with good speed.

Anyway, then he started on all this vampiric stuff, 'I thuck your blahd,' etc. etc. Now, if I make him seem stupid please forgive me, for Grue is in fact clever and dangerous – his whole Clan has a reputation for ruthlessness. When Corbeau went bad, it was touch and go as to whether Grue's Moldova Clan would join him – and things may have been very different if they had. But fortunately for them, the Clan stuck with the Eltern, which is usually the best course, as any student of history could tell you. And the Moldiva Clan practically invented the term *swot*.

I was in the midst of my own duel with Grue, and although this one was meant to be friendly practice, it felt anything but.

Each time I dropped my guard to shift my weight from my worse side (my right), Grue stepped around me nimbly and rapped me across the knuckles or along the length of my arm. After about ten minutes of this both my hands were bleeding and Grue, wouldn't you know it, had started to cheer up no end. Unlike most people, smiling didn't mean that his temper was softening – if anything he started hitting me even harder and more often.

I'm not putting up with this, I thought, and as luck would have it I had an idea. Now, I don't usually go in for this type of thing, it's like the *abuse of power* one hears so much about, but Grue badly needed to be taught a lesson and if I didn't stand up to him now it seemed more than likely that he was only going to get worse as this Quest of Chassignol's went on.

Anyway, I read his mind.

Not complete *delving*, as I like to call it. I need peace and quiet for that and I had no wish to know exactly what a nasty piece of work like him was thinking about in too much lurid detail. All I really needed to know was where he was going to move next. The first few seconds was a bit tricky as there was a lot of noise on deck, what with the others either fighting or watching and shouting encouragement from the rigging.

'Take that, and ther-that, then that … aargh!' shouted Milan as he fell down a hatch that Faucon had left open on purpose.

Swordsmanship is a point of pride with us Vampires: it's a part of our upbringing and we take it very seriously indeed. For my Human readers here, the best swordsman of your kind would be no match, even if they were the right size, for the most elderly and decrepit Vampire you could dig up (literally). Imagine how fast a hummingbird's wings move and you'll get the picture. Anyway, after a few moments, I managed to blank out what was going on around me, and Grue's thought patterns began to emerge. As I suspected, he was working on a series of set piece moves because he thinks I'm a bit of an idiot when it comes to fighting – for instance, parry once, parry twice, side step left, feint right, lunge; and not much more complicated or imaginative than that. This all happened in his head a split second before he moved. The first time I wasn't quick enough and he got through my guard again, bringing the flat of his sword down across the back of my hand, breaking the skin. It stung like mad.

Milan and Faucon sensed something interesting was happening and stopped their fight to watch ours. 'St-steady on Grue,' said Milan, 'it's only practice.'

Grue said nothing and I kept my trap shut too. I was busy.

As I looked at him in the face, I scanned his thoughts and was shocked. Grue really meant to hurt me this time. Like all your garden-variety bullies, he was out for blood. Literally.

'No Chassignol to hide behind now.' Grue sneered. 'I bet that last move hurt – feels like your whole arm is on fire, does it not?'

It did but I faked a smile, which made him look angry all over again and to annoy him even more I added, 'Sansonnet's not even watching, Grue, you're wasting your time.'

'Why are you even here?' Grue had moved around to my left, trying to force me down the same hatch Milan had fallen into. 'We've already got one fool – Milan.'

'Hey!' said Milan.

' … we don't need another.'

'The same could be said of you,' I replied, still smiling. Not exactly brilliant, I know, but I was currently trying to step around the edge of the hatch onto a safer piece of deck. 'Peregrine's better with a sword, Chassignol's got the brains and Sansonnet's better looking … everyone agrees.' By way of an answer, Grue jabbed his blade easily through my defence and drew it across my exposed forearm. Blood started to drip onto the deck. It was a deep cut this time.

Concentrate! I told myself, as Grue's thoughts swung into range again.

Grue permitted himself a wintry smile. 'I suppose you think that it's your so-called *gift* that got you here and not the fact that Chassignol merely feels sorry for you?' His blade flicked dangerously close to my face as I retreated. 'Merely because you get a funny feeling once in a while doesn't make you special. There's another name for that – it's called cowardice. So now, let's see what you're really made of, shall we?'

With that he came in fast again, like a praying mantis going for the kill. This time, however, I knew exactly where he was going.

His body language and his eyes said he was going right, but he skipped left with blinding speed. I ignored the right feint and before he was through the movement got myself in position to meet the left attack and brought my own sword down on his hand before he had a chance to defend himself. When dark crimson blood welled up through the broken skin and onto his white silk sleeve, I knew how much it would have hurt.

'Well d-done!' shouted Milan.

'Bravo!' Faucon clapped.

It must have seemed to Grue as if I'd just been lucky because he got himself in position again and said, '*En Guarde*,' through gritted teeth, his eyes narrow with malice.

Fair enough, I thought, and settled into his thought patterns. Grue was angry but he wasn't going to let getting his revenge stand in the way of a good fight. He had another set piece mapped out in his head. I saw that he planned to push me back towards the rigging, using his size, hoping my sword would get caught up in the ropes that hung down this side of the deck. By parrying and riposting and edging forward after each riposte, he slowly forced me back. If he got me tangled in the rigging I wasn't exactly dead meat, even Grue wouldn't try to kill a fellow Vampire; but I'd seen enough duelling scars on people's faces to know that he meant business. Now, I'm not what you'd call a *delicate beauty*, in fact, even in my youth, I doubt I made any of the Duchess Vampires swoon at parties, but I didn't relish the prospect of Grue making my face look any worse than it does already.

By now we had been fighting for around ten minutes, which meant I was getting pretty tired. However, being able to read Grue's moves in his head meant he couldn't get past my guard and I could see this was beginning to upset him.

Knowing I couldn't last too much longer, fighting a bigger and fitter opponent, this had to be the last move. The deck had gone strangely quiet. Everyone had stopped what they were doing and was watching intently. Even our Wight crew, their leathery, hooked faces leering with keen interest, hung off ropes or climbed on barrels to get a better view. But I was exhausted and I *had* to finish this now.

I glanced up at the rigging behind me and then I slipped. Not so much that I fell over but my head went down and I dropped my guard dangerously low.

I saw it all in an instant: Grue meant to lunge and slice at my exposed neck and cheek. As I suspected, it wouldn't kill me but there would be blood everywhere and he would have scored a victory over me that would damage what little reputation I had as a respectable Vampire for the remainder of my long life. The scar on my face and neck would bear testament to that daily.

He came forward again, with a look of triumph beginning to form on his usually morose features. Sansonnet, Milan, Faucon – everyone, in fact – drew a breath.

However, I knew exactly where he was going and although no one else had spotted it, my slip had been a fake, a bogus fall to let him think he'd won. Everyone has one good leg and one that is weaker; my best – or should I say, *better* leg – is the left one and the one, as it so happened, that still had a firm footing on a piece of nice dry deck. So, pushing up with all my remaining strength, I barrelled into a very surprised Grue, and hit him squarely in the stomach with my head.

He went down like a bag of laundry, which isn't surprising as it hurt my head like hell and my skull is harder, by some degree, than Grue's stomach. Whipping my sword up with all the speed I could muster, I then spun around and brought the needle sharp point to within millimetres of Grue's pulsing jugular.

For an instant I saw real fear in his eyes. Given what we both knew he'd been intending to do to me, I was well within my rights to take my revenge. Fortunately for the quest, though, I didn't get a chance, as the deck now erupted with applause and whistles. Vampires love a good piece of swordplay, and the chance to do a bit of swashbuckling on the high seas, exactly like real pirates, practically made them delirious with joy.

Even now, when I venture out of my chambers in the Keep, the young Milk Imps will follow me up the road, teasing me – good-naturedly, I like to think – about my limp and my poor eyesight. Little do they guess that I once defeated the great Grue in an open sword fight. But the anonymity is preferable to me these days. At the time, however, I basked in the glory.

Not for long though.

A cry came up from the Crow's Nest high in the mast. 'Storm coming, *ssstttooooorrm!* ... and it's a bloody big one, too from where I'm standing,' added the disembodied voice.

Chassignol stepped forward. 'Well fought, Tærgu Mar,' he said holding my sword arm. It was impossible not to smile, as Chassignol only used my real name when he was proud of something I had done. He went on, grinning broadly. 'I think you've surprised us all, and perhaps Grue can now see why you're here after all – but we have to get below now, I think, batten down the hatches? Well fought, too,' he added diplomatically, turning to Grue, 'let me help you up.'

'Get away from me!' snapped Grue, slapping Chassignol's hand away and struggling to his feet. His narrow eyes had taken on a weird glassy look that I didn't like one bit. As he passed me he turned and hissed in my ear, close and low enough so that no one else overheard. 'You shouldn't be here, you're a burden, the sooner everyone sees that the better. Oh, and you'll pay for that stunt you pulled, cripple.'

'Charming,' I thought, and shivered as a vicious wind whipped across the deck and sent us all below, seeking shelter in the belly of the boat.

'Our dreams are there to guide us. They are the
backwaters and the byways on which our subconscious
soul follows its own course.
        If a meaning is not clear at first, then be patient.
Ignore dreams at your peril.'

Sansonnet, *Letters*.

Chapter 6

Storm Warning

As I have already said, Vampires really don't like sailing. That being the case, we'd all started to feel pretty much at home on the *Sprite* over the last few days, and most of us had even begun to swagger about a bit – discussing sails, and charts, and behaving like the old sea dogs we were most definitely not. Now, however, the story was quite different with everything becoming bumpier by the minute. Bud's round face had already gone greenish at the mere thought of a storm, and Grue had excused himself to go to his cabin and change, and I somehow doubted he'd be coming out anyany time soon. When Chassignol stuck his head out the galley door to look at what the sea was doing, it looked, for all the world, as if someone had chucked a bucket of water over him when he pulled it quickly back in again.

'It's raining,' he said, as if there was only a gentle shower outside and then went and sat beside Sansonnet, which he always did when things started to look dangerous. I went over to Bud to offer him a peppermint leaf for his stomach.

Fifteen minutes later the *Sprite* felt like it was flying in the face of a fierce wind that was propelling us like a giant surfboard from one crest of a wave to another. I looked out of the porthole and noticed a thin smudge of coastline in the distance through the rain and spray. Peregrine saw it too. 'Looks like the crew are steering us toward the coast,' he commented. ''Ope they know what they're about, the English Channel is a main shipping route for Human traders and warships.' He left it there, but I shuddered at the thought of crossing the path of one of those sailed monsters. I had seen one in the Mediterranean a hundred thousand times the size of the *Sprite*. Close up, it was really just great cliff made out of huge planks of trees, ploughing through the blue waters, leaving dirty foam in its wake. Horrible.

By now the wind was howling like pack of Weres on a cold

night, and the crew had quite sensibly taken down all of our sails to stop them shredding to rags. This meant we were no longer being steered but bobbing about at high speed in ten different directions. At this point most of us took the opportunity to get reacquainted with our breakfasts. So much for being hardened sailors, I thought miserably, sticking my head back in the leather bucket between my knees and wishing Grue *had* actually killed me.

Time passed. The wind blew and I did my very best to stop thinking about being sick as the boat bobbed about, waiting for her fate, with all of us trapped on board.

It was a long, slow day.

As it began to get dark, the feeling crept up on me that something was wrong. Sansonnet seemed to think so too because she raised her head and looked towards the cabin door.

'What's happening?' inquired Grue, who had just appeared in that weird creepy way of his without anyone noticing. He looked fine. Now if anyone can spot trouble at twenty paces behind a good stout wall, it's Grue, so that was when I really started to worry. Sansonnet got up and moved towards the cabin door.

'Don't open it!' shouted half the cabin, looking up from their buckets. Too late, as the door was already open and for a few instants the full fury of the storm waded in around the cabin, banging cupboards about, knocking over buckets, which really wasn't pleasant at all, and generally making its presence well and truly felt. It was like having a short, freezing cold shower. When Milan and Faucon had finally got the door closed again we all looked at each other for a long, worrying moment.

'Er, did anyone see the crew?' I asked hopefully.

There was a longish pause and then a sudden rush to the cabin's single porthole. Just as I got to the window a wave dipped and a temporary valley appeared. Outside, the sea was grey and tipped with dirty white edges that looked like sludge. The dusk and the rain made it hard to see perfectly but, unless they were hiring boats out by the hour on the coast, there was every reason to believe that the rowing boat that we could all see through the spray was the only lifeboat we had, and the scurvy dogs rowing her away were our good for nothing, treacherous crew of ugly Wights.

'We're buggered,' said Grue with something almost like satisfaction and disappeared back to his cabin, presumably to find his water wings.

'That's just your opinion,' I said (quite the Vampire of the Hour in the last day or two), and was very pleased to see Sansonnet smile encouragingly at me. 'Whose for a spot of sailing?' Now I had something to do I began to feel marginally better and so I did my best to look dashing as I got into my oilskin coat and tried not to slip up on any of the numerous puddles of sick.

'Good man,' said Chassignol, who'd taken a while to react to my unexpected optimism. 'We'll have to sail the boat ourselves. Any volunteers?' A few moments later we were on deck (even Grue), running about, pulling on this, letting go of that, and keeping busy by and large until we drowned, which seemed pretty much a foregone conclusion. It was almost totally dark now, except for flashes of lightning from the raging storm.

I came across Peregrine on his way up a ladder. 'What are you doing?' I yelled into his ear.

'I'm learnin' to play the Ukelele ... *what* does it look like?'

'Ha, ha. Seriously, why don't you fly?'

'I tried that!' Peregrine bellowed back over the noise of the storm, 'and the wind nearly pushed me over board!'

'You'll never get up this ladder, you're too large!'

'We'll someone 'as to!'

'I'll go.'

'Be my guest, Strigoi.'

I put my foot on the first rung as a wave crashed over the bow and soaked us. 'By the way,' I shouted. Peregrine put his hand to his ear and moved closer. 'What am I meant to be doing when I get to the top?'

'Good question!' he roared back. 'There's a light sail up there, wrapped around the mast. If we can get that down we'll be able to steer this 'eap of junk, if not chances are we'll drift in and be smashed like raspberries against those pointy rocks!'

'What pointy rocks?'

He jabbed a battered finger at a jagged outcrop on the horizon. 'If we can get past that, assoomin' we're really lucky, I think we might make it into an 'arbour I just clapped me eyes on. But at this rate we'll hit the rocks in the next few minutes and we won't stand a chance of swimming to shore with these waves.'

'I'd better get a move on then.'

'Good luck, son!' Peregrine thumped my arm as I started to climb past him. At this point I think it is worth reminding you that we're talking at least a three-foot climb in Human terms. That's the equivalent of a Human reader going up the side of a cathedral in a force ten gale. Using nothing but a soggy rope ladder. Peregrine stood at the bottom, seemingly impervious to the movement of the boat, legs apart, bellowing orders I couldn't hear above the noise of crashing water and screeching wind.

Anyway, by the time I was about half way up I was beginning to regret my decision. It's pretty hard to kill a Vampire, and even in this wind my sodden wings would break my fall but the deck was getting smaller by the minute, and the chances of missing it completely and tumbling into the furious, boiling sea below were looking distinctly high. The further up the mast I climbed, the more the swaying of the boat meant I spent most of my time concentrating on not being sick again. If I fell into the sea I'd struggle not to drown. I really had no choice now but to carry on climbing.

Then, without being aware I'd done it, I was at the top, looking at the sail just above my rain-plastered hair.

I looked down to see the blurry forms of Peregrine, Bud, Chassignol and Milan staring up at me and began to feel less nauseous and a bit more heroic. I locked my arm under the rope ladder, twisted it around my elbow and did the same with one of my feet, to make sure I wouldn't slip. With my free hand

I stretched out and began to untie the sail. It must have been fear or the fact I'm half blind, that meant it was only then I realised the minute the sail came down it would drop directly onto me and I would fall. Of course, this only occurred to me as the last fastener was coming loose in my freezing fingers. The sail unfurled with a torrent of trapped water, for added weight.

And I fell.

I had time to open my wings and aim for the deck before my head hit something hard. I turned as another lightning flash lit up the ocean like a picture. About one hundred yards away there was the black ship again; its sails were intact and the water all around her seemed flat and eerily calm. But my eyes closed and my mind shut down before I had time to tell anyone.

⤷⟋

Reverie I
The Key in Argent

⟋⟍ *I dreamt that I once lived on a high hill that was so steep and whose summit was so remarkably pointy that, from far away, it looked just like a huge needle. My name, in this life, was Baule.*

The hill we are talking about was miles away from anywhere and, at its base, you would find a tiny staircase, cut into the rock long ago by some helpful soul. The staircase wound around the foot and carried on upwards until about halfway it passed a small bush that grew next to an ancient stone well. The well itself was surrounded by a stumpy wall, which for some long-forgotten reason was shaped like the fortifications of a miniature castle. The staircase disappeared abruptly after the well, the next part of the journey being completed by an ancient rope ladder. If you were very brave and had decided that now that you'd come this far you might as well finish the job, the ladder would carry right on up the hill, taking you unbelievably high, to the very top. On the way up, the rope ladder passed a bird's nest, currently occupied by a short-tempered stork – long ago retired from the business of delivering babies to grateful parents – and then on to a tiny cloud, no bigger than your average pillow and very white.

And after the cloud, surrounded by a small spiky hedge was
Baule's hovel.

᠀᠄ On the morning of this story Baule was busy throwing metal
pots and pans out of his kitchen window where they clattered and
clanged down the side of the hill, narrowly missing the surprised
and indignant stork. He was distracted because he'd misplaced his
one treasure, a small silver object he liked to think of as a key.
Or 'The Key'.

The cloud, more than usually upset by the racket and hating any
form of conflict, had begun to rain, which didn't do much for
improving anyone's temper, especially Baule's, who found it hard to
appreciate the cold little drops that made his cheeks sting and
distracted him from looking for his precious Key in Argent. The final
straw came when he stubbed his little toe on a large rock. This made
him hop about on one leg, clutching his damaged foot with one hand
and shaking his fist at the heavens with the other. Then he lost his
balance and banged his head on a wheelbarrow.

The cloud started raining all the more and, as far as Baule was
concerned, there was nothing for it but to put his head in the air and
howl against the terrible injustices of a heedless world that hid his
things, rained on him and made him fall over onto sharp and
unforgiving objects.

This terrible racket drifted down from the steep slopes of the
mountain, past the stork, past the bush, past the well and then
tumbled across the plain where the first human ears to hear it were
those of a blacksmith who happened to be hammering at the time on
a particularly hot and obstinate lump of pig iron. The shock of the
noise, which sounded, for all the world, like someone had set a
firework off inside his head, made him hammer his middle finger
almost completely flat. He too howled and cursed so much that his
skinny wife, who perpetually looked like she was chewing wasps,
kicked over a bucket of goat's milk and screeched, which woke up
the alderman who lived next door and worked nights.

He, in turn, stuck his head out of the window and started yelling
that he hadn't had so much as two hours sleep in the last week

because of the blacksmith and his shrew of a wife. Unfortunately the next-door neighbour on the other side was a little deaf and, reasoning that anything he could hear must be serious, deduced that there was a war on. He ran to tell the priest – a birdlike, panicky old soul – who flew up the belfry steps and started ringing the great bell for all he was worth. People came running from all directions, yelling and shouting and asking what the matter was, only to be told that there was a full-scale invasion on its way from the neighbouring town.

This was the vote-winner the town mayor had been dreaming of. Proclaiming that attack was the best form of defence, he promptly used all this as an excuse to mount his own invasion of another neighbouring town that owned all the best fields and had far prettier oxen. The ensuing rumpus caused all the other towns in the Five Valleys to prepare for war, which in turn gave their neighbours the jitters, some of whom decided life was getting a little too strenuous what with living next to warlike neighbours and so they built fleets of flat-bottomed ships that allowed them to sail off and invade other, more distant and peace-loving people, all in the name of progress, or sometimes ideas.

The war raged for five years, each conflict spreading out like ripples of sound, reverberating through towns, valleys, forests and whole countries. Five terrible years, which was about when Baule stopped howling for long enough to realise his precious key had been in his back pocket all along. For the first time in a very long while he smiled and said nothing at all. Quietly, he walked down the path and put it in the well for safe-keeping.

Silence drifted down the hill like mist, across the plain and to the blacksmith's door. Abruptly the blacksmith and his wife felt, for some unknown reason, a profound sense of relief. They stopped their constant bickering and considered each other in silence. To the blacksmith, his wife no longer looked like a pinched old witch with a face like a spanked bum; he noticed, instead, her fine high cheekbones and her girlish waist. Gently he took her hand and kissed it; her heart, in turn, fluttered like a caged bird.

Next door the alderman got the first good night's sleep he'd had in ages; and his next door neighbour, noticing that it was peaceful for once, went to inform the priest the war was finally over ...

Halfway up Baule's hill the stork uttered a single crisp note, which hung in the air.

Baule fell fast asleep and so Moüsch dreamt still deeper ...

༔— Moüsch's next dream at first carried with it only sound and a vague sense of extreme cold, of bright spots of searing heat and of metal scraping on metal or bone. Somewhere at the back of his retina a series of flashes made his eyelids flicker and wince and he stirred as his mood in the dream registered panic. Then the dream shifted and he had the impression of a face calmly looking at his. The stranger's features gradually settled as if they'd long ago lost their form and were only just now finding their rightful place, to reveal a being of such extraordinary beauty that Moüsch felt like crying for joy. Behind the stranger's shoulders, like a shadow, he could make out wings hunched in a shrug. The face mouthed something he could not hear and the eyes cast themselves downwards. Extraordinarily for a dream, Moüsch found he could follow the gaze and as he did so realised he was looking out over Baule's plain, from about halfway up his mountain, except that the flatlands were now strewn with corpses. Some were small, almost like children, others huge, like the carcasses of whales washed ashore in the spring tides. The carnage seemed to stretch for miles, beyond the edge of the horizon.

Moüsch's companion turned his face to his ear and Moüsch smelt the stench of cadavers and something else more sinister that made him retch. 'I,' whispered the stranger in his dream, leaning forward until their faces almost touched. ' – am the Thin Man.'

༺

'Vrykolakas or Vampires adore garlic. A gift of a clove will render any Vampire your friend for life. That's usually about thirty seconds – for garlic is also deadly to their kind.'

The Wisdom of Faies, Albion Edit, 1453.

Chapter 7
fields of avalon

I woke up to Bud shoving a lump of rotten apple up my nose.

'Gnargh, blagh! What on earth are you *doing* Bud?'

'Sorry Moüsch, doctor's orders – well Sansonnet's – she said I should find you something to eat. I got this out of a ditch.' He offered me another sticky, sandy lump from his podgy hand. 'Do you want some? I chased most of the ants off with a stick.'

'Oh, cheers, really are you sure?' I said. I was starving though. I paused and gave him what I hoped appeared to be a heart-melting look. 'I don't suppose ... ' I started.

Bud sighed and rolled up his sleeve. 'Don't let Grue catch you,' he said. 'He doesn't think Sanguines should do this sort of thing anymore.'

'Do moo mimnd?' I asked.

'Actually no,' he shook his head. 'I suppose I wouldn't be here on the Quest if it wasn't for this.'

I broke off. 'Don't ever say that,' I said. 'Seriously.'

Bud looked grateful. 'Thanks Moüsch,' he said.

There was a pebbly, crunching sound behind me.

'Ah, the hero awakes.' It was Sansonnet and I was glad to see her. If she'd arrived earlier she might have even been in time to stop Bud from trying to poison me with old fruit.

'What happened?' I asked, in the time-honoured tradition of people with bumps on their heads.

'Depends what you remember really,' she said, flopping elegantly down beside me on the sand. I raised my head and looked about. We were sitting on a curved beach, forming a crescent bay with a broad expanse of corn-coloured sand running down to the tide line. Tussocked grass banks lay on one side of the bay and what looked like a pebble breakwater ranged out to our left. The sea was flat and blue and everything looked pleasant in the sunshine.

'I really don't remember much,' I replied, and after a moment's thought added, 'I fell off the ladder.'

'You certainly did.'

'We all thought you'd be dead.' Bud remarked with a mouth full of my apple.

Sansonnet went on. 'After your amateur heroics getting the sail down, Milan and Faucon managed to get control of the wheel, though it took all their strength, and we were able to steer the *Sprite* towards this bay and avoid the rocks.' She pointed delicately towards a group of evil looking crags poking out of the water. 'Chassignol did his bit by tying himself halfway up the mast and shouting directions to the cousins.'

'Where's the *Sprite* now?'

'We hid it further along the coast, up an estuary. Chassignol and the rest of them are there now. We thought it best not to move you too far until you'd woken up and I could check that bump you got hadn't made you go stupid or mad.'

'Stupid-*er* or madd-*er*,' corrected Bud, which I thought was rich coming from an only recently evolved species.

My head still felt sore, and so did my bum, where I landed on the deck, but I wasn't in any hurry to broadcast that. 'I'm fine,' I said, getting up shakily, 'what next?'

'We're eating,' said Bud.

'We're *meeting*,' corrected Sansonnet.

About an hour later we were all sitting in the shade of a large leafy tree listening to Chassignol and Grue argue about where we were going first. He pulled out a map I'd never seen before. 'We're about three days walk from the village of Glastonbury, by my reckoning,' said Chassignol, ignoring Grue who was suggesting we stay put or now and wait for some more information. Five minutes earlier he had even been suggesting that I go back on my own to the Keep and ask the Eltern for guidance. Not for the first time did I have my doubts about Grue, so I tested a theory.

'You do know we are being followed.'

Most of my fellow Vampires looked suitably surprised, even, I was disappointed to note, Grue. Chassignol moved from where he was standing right behind me. 'By who?' he asked.

'*Whom*,' Sansonnet corrected.

'I'm not sure,' I said. 'I saw a ship, that's all. Twice.'

'A boat? At sea? Well *really*.' Grue's sarcasm is very irritating. Everyone else looked appropriately concerned though.

'Tall, black and sinister looking,' I glared meaningfully back at Grue. 'Hidden Kingdom, not Human, before you ask.'

'Alright, we'd best push on,' said Chassignol, probably sensing another pointless argument. 'Whatever you saw, it doesn't seem to have landed, perhaps it sank in the storm?'

We all followed Chassignol as he picked up his pack and headed north across the fields.

It was a lovely day for a stroll after all. Flying was voted against – we didn't know who might pick up our magical traces, and anyway Bud had put on a fair bit of weight during the voyage and no one felt like carrying him more than a few feet.

Dry land did indeed feel good and after a day in the fresh air my head (and other tender and cherished parts of my anatomy) stopped throbbing and I began to feel more Vampire. I still had a nasty gash across my forehead where the rope from the sail had whipped downwards but it was healing nicely in the warm dry air and it made me look pretty rakish and dangerous – or so I liked to think.

Some gypsy Vampires I spoke to once assured me that there's nowhere to beat England in the summer. There weren't many Humans about, so as we strolled along I took in the leafy lanes and sunny hedgerows, all bordered by pea-green fields and murmuring streams. We had taken very little from the *Sprite* apart from the clothes we stood in, the M.E.C.s and the last of the gold dust. I also had a small cache of diamonds hidden in the hilt of my sword for emergencies, though I doubted we'd find much to spend our money on here. Mostly we lived off wild strawberries and blood harvested from sheep, a species that seemed to be everywhere you looked.

On the first evening, just as we were starting to look for somewhere comfortable to spend the night, I fell into step with Bud. Unlike the rest of us he was relatively old by Vampire standards, and at over five hundred years, very old compared to most Sanguines.

'You knew Corbeau when he was young, didn't you?' I had heard the rumours.

Bud's normally good-natured features clouded and he pursed his lips, as if wondering how best to answer. 'Yes,' he said, 'when he came to the Keep with his father, Raben, and stayed with the Moldova Clan's cousins – the Brasovs.'

Well, well, I thought. 'The mysterious Nosferatu Picus, he's the Clan head, isn't he?' More frowning from Bud followed, ultimately, by a nod. 'What were Corbeau and his father doing there?'

'No one knew,' answered Bud, 'the Ducesa was always … ' he paused, 'secretive.'

'I heard she's still alive.'

'She was exiled. The father, he died.' Bud said it quickly, with an air of finality.

' … and this Picus, he then became the Clan head?'

Bud's features relaxed. 'Yes, and the Brasov Clan is better for it.'

'So how come he's not at the Keep?'

Bud opened his mouth to reply but I never got my answer, as Milan suddenly turned dark blue and fell over.

Faucon and Sansonnet got to him first and started loosening his clothing, looking for signs of an injury. Milan responded by clawing at his throat and his heels began kicking the earth around him flat. His eyes bulged, bloodshot, looking fit to burst.

'Quickly! He's dying!' Faucon stared at Sansonnet and me in fear and wholly understandable panic. It was at that moment that I think we all realised that losing his cousin would be the worst thing that could happen to him. Ignoring Milan's distress as best I could, I started rummaging around in the undergrowth where he'd been standing.

Sansonnet looked at me. 'What are you doing? He's been bitten or stung by something, we've got to find out where the poison went in!'

I ignored her as she carried on with her frantic search of Milan's body whilst I started to search around the base of an old horse chestnut.

Milan's face had now gone a pale grey and in the back of his throat he uttered a dry 'gah gah gah,' sound over and over.

'He's looking worse ... please!' Faucon stroked his cousin's forehead and thick, sweat-matted hair. We're very hard to kill, so watching another Vampire dying so rapidly is extremely un-common and the severity of what was happening and speed had taken everyone aback. Even Grue seemed at a loss. If we couldn't get him breathing, we only had a few moments before we lost him. I plunged my hand into some soft earth between two of the larger roots and, by some miracle, found exactly what I was looking for first time. Blood luck, I thought as I spun around and jammed the muddy nubbin of tuber into Milan's mouth. The effect was instantaneous and highly satisfying, I must say.

From being on the point of death, Milan's colour came back instantly and his breathing started up again with one huge gasp for air, like a swimmer who has been trapped underwater. He was still trying to say something.

'Ga-ga-*garlic!*'

Well, he got there eventually.

'I know,' I said, smugly, 'and that's an old hangman's tree.' I pointed at the horse chestnut.

Sansonnet nodded, slowly at first, then more certainly as the penny dropped. 'So that's a mandrake root you force -fed him.'

'Certainly is. Was.'

'I thought that was just an old wives' tale,' said Chassignol.

'It is,' said Grue, 'it's more likely the effect of the chalk stuck to the tuber counteracted the effects of the poison. Everyone knows chalk is one of nature's most effective antidotes.' He smiled at me in a way that made his lips all but disappear. 'Lucky again, that's all.'

'Well, well, 'ere's the culprit,' remarked Peregrine, pointing a twig at some white-tipped bulbs with tapered green stems. 'Wild garlic. Some of it must have brushed against your noggin.'

There was a pause and Milan looked sheepish. 'To ber-be honest, it smer-smelled rer-really good … I couldn't resist trying some.'

'You total moron!' said Faucon and he cuffed Milan about the head. 'What were you thinking?'

'I know, I know,' said Milan, looking foolish and still a bit sick, 'it sounds dense but I thought the wild stuff here in England might not have the s-same effect. It smelled so inviting that I began to think it couldn't possibly be ber-ber-bad for me. I only tried a ber-ber-bit.'

'I'll give you a *ber-ber-bit!*' Peregrine looked like he would hit Milan too. 'You dismal little Vampire,' he growled. 'You do realise that one clove of that stuff can kill ten Vampires in a sitting. Chalk … or mandrake,' he added diplomatically, glancing sidelong at me, 'you're bloody lucky to be alive in my book.'

'Well,' said Sansonnet, 'after all these fun and games, I wouldn't advise we spend the night here. Milan obviously can't control himself in the nibbling department.' She gave him a stern look. 'Let's go down there by the river.'

⌁

Thankfully the rest of the journey passed without incident. Chassignol's estimate was about right and on the second evening at sunset, Glastonbury, or to be more precise, the *Tor*, slid into view as the surrounding woods thinned out to reveal a weird isolated knoll or hillock, standing quite alone in the middle of a dead flat plain.

The hill was round and looked oddly familiar. It also seemed altogether too symmetrical, as if someone had drawn it or made it up. And just to make it look even more singular a narrow tower (the *Tor*) had recently been built right at the top. The sunset behind the hill had now gone from orange to a deep plasma crimson.

I was limping along as best I could beside Chassignol. He was in a talkative mood. 'All this used to be surrounded by an inland sea. Legend has it that Arthur, the first King of England – who was never really a king, more a warlord – was buried here over six hundred years ago. He sent his knights on a quest to find something called the Holy Grail, which is said to be their name for the Chalice. Arthur knew that to find the Grail was very important and believed with all his heart that it would unite his Kingdom forever, the same as our Eltern. The Grail was said to contain the blood of the son of their God, Iesu.' Then, almost to himself, 'Funny how it always seems to be about blood.'

'Sounds like he nicked our act, if you ask me.'

Chassignol smiled. 'Can I ask you something, Moüsch?'

'Yes, of course.'

'You can see forward in time, I think we all know that.'

'To a certain extent,' I agreed. Warily. People talking about my gift – even Chassignol – made me jumpy. Experience had taught me that these conversations rarely ended well or to the other person's satisfaction. You'll see why.

'So, is it possible to do the same in reverse?'

'What, see into the past?' I asked, smiling, almost relieved.

'No, to go into the past. Or to re-shape it, I suppose that's what I am trying to say.'

I would have laughed but he seemed in deadly earnest and I also suspected I knew what this was all about. 'No,' I said, as gently but as firmly as could, 'it's not possible. Or at least I can't do it.' Chassignol looked crestfallen. 'There are too many paradoxes, I doubt if anyone can unravel the past.'

'Oh,' he said, doing his best to shrug it off. 'I read something about it somewhere, that's all.'

'You've been reading a lot lately,' I remarked. 'It's unlike you.' I remembered his words back on board the *Sprite* a few days earlier. 'There was a King, who was no King, crowned on a hill that was no hill, round at the base and round at the top and surrounded on all sides by a sea, that was no sea, in a kingdom, which was no kingdom at all.' Now, where had that all come from, I wondered.

'Yes,' he said, 'I suppose I have.'

'From what you're saying it sounds like we're the valiant knights and you're this Arthur.' Chassignol laughed, displaying a humour I just didn't feel at that point in time. The reason was simple enough: this last hour I'd been having on and off visions of drawn swords, reflecting silver and darker patches of spilled blood by moonlight, and of arrows flicking silently through silhouetted trees. And Chassignol was taking of my condition as if it were a gift I could do something useful with but, in truth, I was beginning to come around to Grue's point of view that whatever is was it had lately become a hinderance and no good to anyone around me. What did it help if I saw things I couldn't make any sense of? Chassignol was talking again.

' … quite so, Moüsch, quite so! Right, let's stop and set up camp. We'll investigate the Tor in the morning.'

Tell you the truth, I was pretty relieved when Chassignol suggested we stop for the night, because the thought of poking around these parts with night coming on made my flesh creep. Anyway, we were all tired, so without any hesitation we stopped where we were, which happened to be under a large hawthorn bush and curled up to sleep. Milan and Faucon took the first watch.

When I opened my eyes again the Moon was still quite low on the horizon: heavy, like a giant stone. A very few stars shone out of the night sky and the air was cold. Dead cold. Still half asleep, I started delving my mind in and out of the shadowy areas under the trees and almost immediately picked up about a dozen *things* lurking behind the hawthorn. I was about to raise the alarm when I felt a hand go to my mouth. My eyes went very wide.

'Gmph brrrgngh!'

'Shhhh.' It was Faucon. 'I heard something, then I saw you wake up.' Milan also came over, moving silently, as only a Vampire can, and squatted beside us. If they were still on watch it meant we'd been asleep less than four hours.

'What can you s-sense Moüsch?' he asked. It was a fair question – Vampires have about the best night-vision around, apart from some of the weirder-looking fish. We are also blessed with hearing at least as good as any cat, but whoever was out there knew how to disguise themselves very well indeed. I wondered what else they were good at. I concentrated for a few heartbeats.

'About ten or twelve of them, over there,' I said pointing to a small ditch around the base of the hawthorn. 'They're watching us for the moment. I'd say we've about three to five minutes before they turn nasty and, from what I can pick up, these boys can make themselves pretty unpleasant if they have a mind to.'

'What are they?'

I closed my eyes. 'Faies,' I said, after some thought. 'Although I think they still call themselves Fairies in England,' I said. 'I'd bet the Chalice that's what's lurking under those bushes. You'd better go and wake the others, and quick. This lot will attack soon enough.'

If it was any other creature, we could probably have paid them off with a few pecks of gold dust, especially if they were Pixies, or uncut diamonds, if they were Trolls. Faies, on the other hand, are almost as rich in gold and precious stones as Vampires – the big difference is that they are always leaving it lying around for Humans to stumble upon. This is never a good thing. Faie treasure always, without any exception, brings misery. Perhaps that's why they do it.

'Righty-ho,' said Faucon and slid off, his bony body snaking through the grass, keeping to the shadows. Whilst we knew more or less who they were, they couldn't say the same for us. If you're going to attack a Vampire and live to tell the grandchildren about it from the comfort of your favourite chair, you have to do so with speed and complete determination or else pretend you haven't seen them. Not having Vampires in

England explained their hesitation. They simply hadn't a clue who we were. They did mean to attack us, though. Waves of malice were rolling across the camp from their direction. Faies are pretty tough customers, especially if you stray onto their patch uninvited. They are good with the sword and have a natural flair for magic. Never sleep under a hawthorn, I thought grimly as Faucon came back. 'We're all awake, Chassignol will give the signal any second now. We go straight at them, although Peregrine is going to try to get around the back. Chassignol says not to kill any of them unless we really have to. We strayed onto their patch, so we're at fault. The last thing we want is to spend the next few weeks dodging swarms of Faies instead of looking for the Chalice, but we also have to stick up for ourselves and show them who's boss. With any luck, they'll leave us alone if they know we're not to be messed around with.' He was grinning so broadly, I'm surprised the Faies weren't blinded. When all's said and done, most Vampires just love a good fight. 'You ready?'

'No.'

As the waves of ill-feeling and indignation coming from the bushes reached a crescendo, Chassignol jumped up and shouted, 'Akuzati!', and not for the first (or last) time I had to admire Chassignol's timing. Put yourself in the Faies' position: one minute you're all upset and angry that someone dares to cook up sausages and then go to sleep under your favourite tree, and you're just about to teach them a lesson they'll not forget in a hurry; and then the next thing you know, the sleeping lumps you thought were going to be a pushover, leap up and start waving a sword under your nose.

The first Faie I got to was a little taller than me, wearing a scarlet tail-coat trimmed with fur, which could have been dormouse. In the Moonlight his features seemed hollowed and too sharp, and yet he had the sort of wicked beauty that always gives me the creeps whenever I'm forced to have any dealings with their kind.

I caught him off-guard, so he barely had time to look surprised before I cut across his sword arm, forcing him to drop his weapon with a squeal. The second Faie was bigger, thick-set, with tufts of electric blue hair that spiked in several directions at once. He was more on the ball and even got a couple of parries and lunges in before I disarmed him by taking off the top of his thumb and most of his forefinger. His piercing blue eyes met mine briefly and he gave me a look of deep loathing before he melted into the night. I shuddered. Perhaps I see some of us in them, but there is something cold and somehow prehistoric about a Faie and they don't make easy enemies.

Just then, an arrow hummed past my nose and sank itself into a young ash tree behind me. I glanced up to see that the dozen or so Faies had now been joined by six more, three of them carrying fairly hefty bows. Six against eighteen is not a comfortable margin for error and a Faie with a bow or indeed any kind of projectile is deadly accurate. There was still no sign of Peregrine and Chassignol either. To my left Milan and Faucon had disarmed three Faies and were now cuffing them around the head with big bony hands, as the hapless Faies ran for the safety of a rabbit hole. Sansonnet was trying her best to fight two at once and Bud was up a tree chucking rocks. Grue had injured one very badly and now stolidly held off four others, but even with his skill it was looking like hard work. We had to disarm the archers but I had another Faie in a ruby and thistledown waistcoat advancing on me and there was no clear way through to where the bowmen were getting ready to loose another volley. If something didn't happen soon, at least one of us was going to be badly injured or worse.

Luckily Peregrine and Chassignol decided it was time to join the fray.

In a heartbeat the three Faie archers lay prone on the floor and the three remaining Faies who'd come as reinforcements were fighting a losing battle with Peregrine who swept through calmly but with the ruthless efficiency of a professional knight. Milan and Faucon had disarmed one more and I was pleased to see that the Faie who'd been making for me with a nasty look on his face now lay unconscious under Bud's tree. A few more flicks of the sword and those remaining, who were still able to run, melted into the night.

We all looked extremely pleased with ourselves, except for Sansonnet, who seemed furious about something. 'I'm not sure that was necessary,' she said to Chassignol. 'Couldn't we have tried to talk to them first?'

Ignoring Sansonnet, whom I'd never before heard criticise him, Chassignol flicked the blood off his sword and whipped it back into the sheath strapped to his leg. He was breathing hard. 'Everyone OK.' It was more statement of fact. In fairness we all did look fine – all, that is, except Grue, who sported a nasty-looking bruise over one eye. He shot a baleful glare at Bud, who did a very good job of looking completely innocent.

'I've got a good idea,' Grue said, stepping over an injured Faie. 'Let's stay away from hawthorns in future.' He cocked a long bony finger at his Sanguine, who gulped. 'And now I want a word with you.'

We spent the rest of the night sitting miserably under a hedge whose field lay at the foot of the Tor itself. Chassignol had posted lookouts in the form of Milan, Faucon and Peregrine, although none of us could sleep.

It was midsummer and, before long, a grey streak signalling dawn appeared on the horizon, far off to the east. It's a myth, by the way, that Vampires crave darkness – I'm fairly sure our enemies made that one up to make us sound peculiar. So, once the sun had risen, Sansonnet and Bud lit a fire to warm us and we all fed on some nearby sheep. It promised to be a pleasant day.

Anyway, there I was, sat away from the rest, looking across the fields and chewing on an elderberry. Daydreaming, really. Without warning I heard a noise right behind me, as if someone had cleared his throat. My nerves were still frayed after the night before, so I may have squeaked as I jumped to my feet. I tried to turn and draw my sword and, as is sometimes the case, my legs let me down and I fell backwards into a ditch. When I eventually emerged, smelling of wet leaves, I looked up to see a very large brown and white bull peering down at me.

'Hello', I said, non-committally. The bull twitched his eyebrows. I noticed that he had a curious tuft of hair growing over his upper lip that gave him a military look. My first impressions were confirmed almost immediately.

'My name's *The Colonel*', he boomed. 'I'm the local soothsayer. Dashed pleased to meet you!'

'The *Colonel of Truth*, then', I quipped, playing for time – even in our world cattle don't usually talk. Colonel-what's-his-name glared at me.

'Cheeky young pup', he muttered into his cow-moustache, then did a good impression of a bull looking sardonic. He directed a long hard stare at me. 'You seem to have the mark of the soothsayer about you too. D'yer have the Gift?'

Up until now I thought that he was probably a bit of a fraud, but he'd spotted something in me so I gave him a *B minus* and the benefit of doubt for now. I nodded.

'But you're not the leader of the troop are you? I don't sleep much these days, too many memories, so I've been watching you lot since before dawn. Are you on the run? What sort of operation are you on? It seems pretty *covert* to me.'

'Um, I really can't say.' And I gave him my Cunning Look, which seemed to keep him happy.

'Ahh, covert op it is then!' And I swear, if he had had anything resembling a decent set of fingers he would have tapped the side of his nose. 'Same as that other chap, then.'

Despite the warm morning air my ears abruptly felt chilly. 'What other chap?' My voice sounded squeaky, like a startled mouse.

'Strange cove, looked to some extent like your lot but not quite. Did a good job of being friendly but had a nasty glint in his eye. I didn't care for him much. He said I might bump into you, though —'

'Hello *bovine*. What else did he have say?' It was Grue. He had somehow snuck up on me again, and now stood there, looking bleak as a funeral.

The Colonel looked up. 'Hullo! Didn't see you there. Now you must be the comedian of this outfit? Ha!' The Colonel looked immensely pleased with himself, and Grue did a pretty good impression of someone trying to smile whilst being kicked hard in the bottom.

'You could say that.'

'I think he's seen the Thin Man,' I said, turning to face Grue.

'Fascinating,' Grue replied. 'And how would this Sunday dinner on legs know the difference between the Thin Man and a dead badger, I wonder?'

'Whaat?!' The Colonel went purple-ish in the face and his eyes watered. 'This is outrageous, let me speak to your commanding officer this instant!' He turned to me, 'You, Young Pup, go and get him on the double, I'll keep an eye on this … this *bounder*! Up to something, I'd wager. Who let him join the unit, anyway?'

Who indeed? I thought and I turned to walk away, I still hadn't had the rest of my breakfast and I was too tired to deal with talking bulls and Grue.

With no warning, my legs buckled. I felt a sharp pain across my forehead, the roof of my mouth went dry and I had a feeling of tumbling down a steep slope then into a void. A few moments passed in a limbo.

Then I saw a pin prick of light, far off in the distance. There was nothing else to do down in the hole or whatever it was, so I waited patiently. The light got larger and materialised, not into an image, as I was half expecting, but a voice. 'Sorry about that, old chap.' My God, it's that bloody cow! I thought. How did he do that?

'Needed to speak to you alone, this is a little mind trick I picked up in special training. I've got an important message. It's one we *Bovines* have been guarding for over 90 generations.' I tried to do a complicated sum in my head, 'That's nearly 3000 Moon Cycles,' the Colonel finished it off for me. Blimey, I thought, He really can read my mind. The next thing he said was in a different tone altogether. 'Your Eltern contacted us to contact you, Moüsch. The Quest is in peril,' the Colonel intoned. 'The secret you seek pertaining to the Sacred Blood and the Chalice lies to the east in a great city called Sarum. Seek the tomb of Longspee. The Chalice is the key. Beware the Thin Man and a threat from within. The Chalice is True Love.'

'Have you quite finished?' I asked. I felt unusual.

'Hurrmpph ... yes, sorry about that. You'll come round in a few minutes, and when you do, speak to your commanding officer, oh, and follow the signs in your dreams, whenever possible.' The voice faded and I was left looking at a pinprick of light surrounded by darkness. A feeling of falling *upwards* followed and, when I opened my eyes, the Colonel had disappeared.

Grue was staring at me down his long nose. 'You're an idiot,' he said simply, and marched off.

I got up and started to walk down the path. The sun was shining and birds sang in the hedgerows and thickets but my head ached. Chassignol was folding his things away into his rucksack. He looked up, 'We need to talk.' I said, and sat down heavily on the grass.

'Shoot,' said Chassignol, in his best Commander of Vampires manner.

I looked at his handsome profile and realised that he was the last person in the world I wanted to hurt. I took a deep breath. 'When you mentioned Corbeau and the Thin Man to me at the Keep, you were holding something back.' Chassignol said nothing, so I ploughed on. 'And when I mentioned that I thought he was following us, two people in the party barely registered surprise.' Chassignol rubbed his hands together and stared at the Tor to the west of us. I probed as gently as possible. 'Grue seemed annoyed that I'd noticed and not him but you wanted to change the subject. Why was that?' Chassignol winced, and I could sense some internal struggle taking place.

'Now look here, Moüsch,' he said finally. 'There are certain things about the Quest I can't tell you for your own sake, for your own protection, if you like.' And even as he said it I knew he was lying again. He was my best friend, but I felt a surge of anger that I didn't have the good sense, at the time, to control.

'Sounds like you're simply playing along with the Eltern. That's all very well but just remember who's on this trip with you. I didn't notice any of them risking their lives to volunteer for the Quest.' Chassignol's face darkened, and I immediately wished I hadn't said it. I knew I'd played it wrong. So much for being the brainy one.

'Well, luckily for us it's not really important what you think,' he said, and stalked off towards the others.

'Maybe not,' I muttered, and marched off the other way to sit under a tree.

The next few days weren't exactly a picnic. That Chassignol and I had stopped speaking filtered through to everyone within a few hours. Sansonnet tried to patch things up but we weren't in the mood. Vampires can harbour a grudge for a couple of centuries if they try hard enough. I didn't mention what the bull had said. If Chassignol could have his secrets, well, then so could I.

My thoughts festered, though. If Grue reckoned that I was a waste of space, the others probably thought so too – and now even my best friend was holding things back. He'd never done this before and I had to admit it hurt.

So, I sat around sulking, watching everyone closely, brooding about the possible traitor on our midst that the bull had spoken of, whilst Chassignol sent out search parties around the Tor. Needless to say, I took immense satisfaction in knowing these were a complete and utter waste of time, if Sarum really did hold the Chalice.

Two days later I had made up my mind and, in the dead of night, when Bud was on guard, I slipped out of the camp and headed east, like the bull had suggested. I went alone.

'The problem with prophecies is that there are quite simply too many of them amongst Us. The first time I met the Vampire they call Moüsch, the truth was, neither of us had a clue about anything.'

Raptor. Dispatches.

Chapter 8

Meres

Tired of walking, and wanting to put as much distance between me and the rest of the crew as possible, I took a chance and flew for most of the night, skimming over the tops of the smaller trees and hedgerows and skirting around the side of any woods.

Flying, after weeks cooped up on a boat or walking on my bad legs, felt absolutely amazing. For the ten leagues or so, I raced across open countryside at near supersonic speeds until I came to a forested area.

Going through a wood at night, I reasoned, would be tricky and the chances of being snapped up by an owl or a bat with ideas above its station was a risk I'd rather not take. It took a little longer, but it was nothing like the vast forests of our homeland. Some of the trees I saw were ancient enough though, and I wondered what they must have seen in their long lives. Battles fought and kingdoms rise and fall, no doubt. Not for the first time, the thought struck me that if you stood still in a field for long enough the world would ultimately come to you.

Ahead of me, no more than a mile or so down the hill, a large Human town spilled out into an open countryside of neat hedgerows and rectangular copses. In the dark, the houses gave off their individual dabs of firelight, each contributing to an overall orangey glow on the horizon. It should have been comforting, like the embers of a fire in a hearth, but I didn't see it that way. One Human is big enough on their own, but there is something about their need to build things on a grand scale – be it their churches, monuments or machines for moving objects – that I find somewhere between awe-inspiring and downright scary. It's as if they want to fill every corner of the planet with themselves.

To my left, a cart laboured upward through a wooded lane, iron clanking as it crested the hill and began its curving descent towards the distant town. As it sped away I couldn't help reflecting how, for all their faults and their apparent willingness to turn their backs on magic, Humans were still incredibly inventive. I remembered Bud saying that one of the best things about Humans was their invention in the East of the dip for eating finger food. 'You can have one bite of hot chilli, followed by another with honey. It's just like having a small meal, followed by a tiny pudding every ten to fifteen seconds!'

Vampires can certainly move quickly but our power of flight is limited and, over the last four or five generations it was actually beginning to desert us. To the utter dismay of the Eltern and parents, some Vampire babies had even been born with wings far too small to carry them more than a few feet at a time. The carts and chariots that Humans charged about in, criss-crossing the planet on roads they made of stone, were getting more numerous every year after a brief respite, when their Romans had gone away.

In spite of feeling guilty about leaving Sansonnet and the cousins behind, it felt pretty good to be off on my own private quest without the rest of them clanking about, bickering and getting in each other's way. The air was cool but not too gusty, and a huge midsummer moon gave the English landscape nice sharp lines in silver and black. My head felt clear and untroubled for the first time in ages. I was following up a lead, I told myself, and it was quicker to do it on my own. And if I unearthed something really interesting, Chassignol might start treating us all like responsible adults and tell us everything he knew. Yet a nasty little voice at the back of my head told me that I really just wanted to worry him sick and then rub his nose in it when I found the Chalice on my own. I silenced it by revelling in the night air and losing myself in the stillness around me.

As dawn started to wake the birds, I was exhausted but still in much better spirits than I'd been in a while. I landed with a bit of a bump in the corner of a field that I'd carefully checked for hawthorn and within minutes I was fast asleep, unable to fly another wing beat.

It was around midday when I was rudely awoken by the unmistakable smell of greasy, sticky food. I looked up and sniffed the air greedily. Sausages! This was my first waking thought; then, 'Crikey, is that the time!' I stared, horrified, at the sun, which was almost at its zenith. I had originally planned to sleep for two or three hours at the most and then get some more distance in between Chassignol and me. Even being generous, I'd slept for more like six or seven hours and, if the rabble I left behind guessed the right direction, they'd have found me by now and I'd be sitting on the grass surrounded by angry and disappointed faces, not enjoying the prospect of having some explaining to do. I looked about shiftily but the coast seemed clear enough. They've probably decided not to bother even looking for me, I thought – good riddance. Now where was I?

Sausages!

Vampires have an excellent sense of smell. In front of me there was a pile of refuse absolutely heaving with the run-of-the-mill Human goodies I rarely got my fangs into – and not only sausages. I could smell bread and cake – something appley – and the remains of someone's ale. Sugar and fat fuel – precisely what I needed for some long-distance flying. I looked around and guessed I was near someone's garden and that I was looking at where they threw things away. I'm not proud. Best be quick though – Human children have a habit of appearing when you least expect them, and the last thing I needed was to be captured whilst stuffing my face in a bin and made into some five-year-old's *Special Friend*.

I was busy chewing on an especially tough piece of meat, keeping an eye out for shrill voices and sticky, grasping fingers when something caught my eye. Call it fate. Lying amongst all the rubbish was a broken wooden cross.

The form of it was strangely comforting but the carving itself – of a man dying, his hands nailed to timber and his thin body broken beyond endurance, made me shudder. Iesu Christe. In the last few hundred years, his name cropped up in both Human and Vampire stories relating to the Chalice.

Most Vampires found it a little creepy that Humans should worship the form of a man in agony. Some Vampires even hinted that it was all part of a Human sacrificial cult. Typically barbaric, they said, of Humans to worship that.

Sacrifice – certainly, but Chassignol's dad had always said the point was that Iesu had sacrificed himself for others.

This was something else though. It was a sign, every sense in my body told me so – of what or why, I didn't know but I'd learned long-since to listen to my instincts and I knew it would be significant in some way when I got to this place – Sarum – and found the tomb. I loved this kind of thing, so off I went, zooming over the tops of trees at full speed.

'Yipeeeeeeeeeeeee! Take that … and *that*! You fear the bite of the blade, the sting of cold steel, no? Well have some of this! Ha!' My imaginary enemies fell away in terror and the murky outline of what I took to be Sarum grew larger as I zoomed up the small river valley super fast. However, it was all particularly cheerless because the weather had just got foggy, as I'd noticed it was apt to do in this country, and with my eyesight I couldn't see anything further than a few dozen yards away.

Eventually I decided to give the poor willow fronds a rest and concentrate on my next move. Glad to be left in peace, the trees resumed their mooching about in corners of the river, trailing their branches in the ebb and flow of the current.

Now, rumour has it that we Vampires spend most of our time lying about in coffins waiting to be discovered by girls wearing expensive frocks. Chance would be a fine thing, I say. But you can't beat a night out on the town – especially if you've been at sea for three months, been half-drowned and then dragged ashore in order to spend the next three weeks sleeping in ditches and eating refuse. Anyway, I bet they had some really great rubbish in a great big place like this.

However long I may live – and I am now pretty decrepit, even by Vampire standards – I don't believe I'll ever forget that first night in Sarum, when I first met the underfed and filthy Strigoi who became probably the greatest Vampire knight of them all.

Now ancient, and looking more and more like an elderly prune with each passing summer, I can look back on a full life. I have had adventures in all the continents of the world, and more; I have ventured deep into the *Unterlander*, the very core of the world, and I have seen the faces of Death and Hope in all their costumes and disguises. But I will never forget meeting Raptor, who became the greatest general and leader who our Small Vampire Nation has ever known. And I saved his life!

But I am getting ahead of myself.

So here I was, a young Vampire, with a mission to find a hidden clue as to the whereabouts of the Chalice in a Human tomb that belonged to a chap called Longspee. So how was I to start? Naturally, I did what any self-respecting tourist would do: I wandered around aimlessly until something happened.

This took all of several minutes.

The day had been warm and windless, so the foggy evening had settled into that curious stillness that makes the night seem hotter. Humans bustled to and fro – *hither* and *thither* – looking sweaty and slightly on the wrong side of irritable.

There was a market below me whose main ware, by the smell of it, appeared to be fish. It's another thing I never could understand about Humans, how they could stomach sea creatures.

But watching them up close was fascinating. As ever, the incredible poverty and occasional embarrassment of riches was shocking: poverty and hunger is something that Vampires hardly know but Wights, Weres and even some Faies do. Hunger does not effect us because our chosen food source – blood – is so abundant. Poverty because, long ago, we found we all had quite enough money to get by, provided one or two of us weren't allowed to hoard everything for themselves. So, whilst there are rich Vampires it is mainly in land and objects of great beauty, not cold cash – even the poorest have access to enough gold and silver to make their lives perfectly comfortable. There are no

Vampire beggars, but here, amongst the Humans, I saw dozens in one street alone: covered in sores, missing limbs – their children whimpering with hunger, squatting in the dirt, their hair crawling with lice.

But the market was also frequented by merchants and knights of such obvious wealth it was almost obscene by comparison: fat men swathed in silks and velvets, dripping with jewellery that hung from jowly necks and pudgy fingers; knights who swaggered with swords, looking for violence, talking in over-loud voices, kicking the beggars if they happened to be sitting in their path. Is this how we seemed to less fortunate in our Kingdom – the orphaned Faies, simple Trolls, unskilled Wights? I certainly hoped not.

It was still unbelievably foggy but after bumping about short-sightedly, I found a window ledge above a tavern called *The Gutted Mackerel*, from which to watch them at a safe distance. I fell into a sort of waking daydream, half of me thinking how do such great big lumbering people fit into such a small area without getting on each other's nerves all the time, and the other half thinking about supper.

If Vampires had to live in such close proximity there would be fights pretty much all the time. Outside of The Keep (whose public areas are kept pretty spacious), when more than say one hundred of us are gathered in a relatively confined area, we have a tendency to *swarm*. By that I mean we strut and fly around in circles generally getting more and more offended by each other as we collide and then, without warning, we'll attack something unsuspecting. It's in our natures, which is why older Vampires, especially the Nosferatu, tend to live in very big houses up hills on their own most of the time. For now, though, I was in no particular hurry, so I sat there and allowed myself to become semi-hypnotised by the flow of the Human traffic around me, concentrating on channelling my subconscious towards letting something relevant happen.

All very holistic and it must be pointed out that this is not so much part of my Gift, more of a trick I've learnt over the years.

Focus on a goal (Longspee's Tomb), but only in the corner of your mind and pretty soon, if you don't focus on it too directly, or try too hard, someone or something will come along sooner or later. Usually this is a sign, a cosmic hint.

In this case it was more a cosmic smack in the face.

Weres!

As usual, you could hear them about half a mile before they appeared. A Were is about as quiet and unobtrusive as a gorilla in full armour, rolling down a stony mountain, trapped in a steel drum. It's their voices, which are the vocal equivalent of having your ears ground between two rocks. Shape-shifters, Weres originally came from our neck of the woods – quite literally those surrounding the woods around the Keep – where we hunted them for sport, I'm ashamed to say.[1] So I was surprised to discover them in one of England's main cities. The Humans, trying to make their way home or to get into the inn to drink flat, warm ale, didn't notice them since the Weres, at ankle height, kept themselves well-hidden amongst the litter clogging up the cobbled gutters. Anyone really looking could easily have mistaken them for an oddly-shaped rat, which was pretty much the shape they had assumed. If seeing them here was unusual, I was also very surprised at who was with them. So much so, that I very nearly fell off the ledge.

Wearing a ragged pair of trousers, and the remains of had once been a woollen sack, was a young Strigoi Vampire about fifteen years old. A chain was fastened around his twig-thin neck and his feet were bare and covered in cuts.

Undernourished and filthy as he was, even from a distance his deep blue eyes showed that he was unmistakably of pure Vampire blood. A Vampire in a supposedly Vampire-free country was surprising enough, but one who seemed to be a slave was a real shock. The Weres were walking along the road, arguing, bumping into rotting fish heads and soggy wrappers. They were bumping into things because they were very drunk,

---

[1] The only use I'd be fighting Weres is as *bait*.

which I had never seen before. There was something else – even bigger than the largest Weres I had ever seen myself back home – they had a *rawness* about them, as if barely tame. They weren't right. They also seemed physically stronger than usual: A Human cart that was partially blocking their path was pushed aside by two of them as if it weighed nothing. I doubted if ten fully-grown Vampires could do the same.

The alcohol made them smell worse than usual and their eyes flashed red as they growled out their guttural, rasping language to one another.

Every so often the largest Were – a real monster who was carrying a knobbed cudgel – would remember the Vampire boy and give the chain a good tug. This would make the Strigoi fall over. The first time this happened I was surprised that he didn't put his hands out to protect himself, instead he landed flat on his face on the wet pavement. This would enrage the big Were, who for some reason took it as a personal insult, and he would hit him across the back with his cudgel so hard that a similar blow would have broken my back. When the boy stood up again, I noticed his hands and wings seemed to be locked together, not with rope, as whatever held them fast was invisible. I suspected an enchantment. Vampires are in general immune to this sort of thing but a fairly strong spell will keep a young Vampire in check, and he was very young, very brutalised and totally outnumbered. A thin trickle of blood ran down his forehead.

As I looked into his eyes, however, I was impressed to see he wasn't cowed or crushed yet, in fact, not by a long way. As he lurched between fall and beating, he kept his eyes fixed on the Were's throat with a curious intensity that I recognized as a fellow Vampire. Once or twice the Vampire almost smiled, and when his lips parted I saw his canines glint under the red glow of a street torch. You're in for a nasty surprise when he gets out of his bonds, I thought, looking at the Were, who had now stopped and was taking a long drink from an earthenware flask he carried. When his companions moved on without him,

I decided it was about time I stepped in. Silently I dropped down to street level.

'Bad doggie!'

The Were stopped what he was doing and looked at me through bloodshot piggy eyes. In his momentary confusion at being unexpectedly addressed by a stranger, he did nothing but blink at me, and I knew I had a few precious seconds of surprise.

His captive turned to me. 'Break the cudgel,' he said quietly.

As fluidly as possible I took my sword out and hacked the blade down on the cudgel's smooth middle section making it snap with a load *crack*. Immediately whatever held the boy's wrists and neck sprang open. The enchantment must have been in the lump of wood itself. His hands were free but I didn't see what happened next. The ragged Strigoi moved in a blur, faster than I'd seen anyone move in my entire life – even Chassignol or Peregrine would have been at a loss to follow. When I refocused, the huge Were lay dead on the floor, his throat ripped out.

The Vampire turned. 'We go.' But it was a bit late for that. Four darts skipped off the pavement, falling a few feet short of where we stood. I looked up to see a Wight running towards us, a blowpipe for poison darts at the ready. I might have known it – the Weres were bound to have a handler nearby. Right now his charges were taking on their largest, scariest wolf shapes: Extended muzzles, razor teeth and huge, clawed talons. One of them punched a rock aside, which splintered under its iron-hard fist. I drew my sword again and prepared for business.

Something wasn't right though; my arms felt heavy and my left eye wouldn't focus properly. 'Weeep waarp waarmp?' said my new companion, eying me oddly, as I looked down to see that a dart had stuck into my leg, through the top of my boot.

'Uh oh,' was my last utterance as my knees gave away and I passed out.

Reverie II
The Four Maids

꙳ *Early one morning, four bright and beautiful girls sat on the top of a hill overlooking the village where they lived. A gentle slope, covered with soft green grass, fell away beneath them towards a small stream where an apple tree grew in its own quiet way and water lilies lazed …*

The girls had nothing to do until breakfast, so they sat there in the sunlight, chattering like sparrows. With their white dresses spread out beneath them, their faces shone with that radiance only seen when beauty is unaware of itself.

As it so happened there was a secret path, which ran close by, where a Faie King would often take his morning walk.

That day, as he walked along with head down in thought, he heard the gay laughter and looked up. The scene was exquisite and he was deeply moved. So much so that he promptly turned all four young girls into snowdrops so that they would remain there, dancing in the breeze and nodding to one another, as if still in conversation. 'I have done a good thing,' he declared, 'to preserve the beauty of this spot.' Like most Faies, he prided himself on being a conservationist, if nothing else.

However that afternoon there was a sharp summer storm. It washed across the surface of the stream and battered the poor flowers, who were quite helpless against the onslaught.

The next morning, the Faie King was mortified to find them dead, their delicate green stems broken by the downpour. When he realised the terrible mistake he had made he wept bitter tears of remorse, vowing never to be so meddlesome again.

꙳ *As time passed and more lichen grew on the apple tree, the Faie King grew a little older, a little more selfish and somewhat forgetful. One morning, he was passing along the same path when he troubled to look up. Before him lay the same scene of four young girls laughing in the sunlight and the same apple tree growing by the stream. Once again the beauty of it all filled his heart and chords of admiration hummed in his chest. But mindful of his mistake the last time, he paused and thought gravely for a few moments.*

Then he turned them into four pure white marble stones.

'In this way their beauty will be preserved forever,' he said out loud, 'or at least until long after I am gone. The idea was right last time but the method was wrong. After all, there are no perfect ideologies, merely fortuitous situations.'

⟩— The statues weathered as clouds raced across a flickering sky and the Moon danced around the Sun over ages of Vampire, Faie and Man. Once again, the perspective shifted and Moüsch was in a place he recognised. Stonehenge. The Standing Stones. He'd seen engravings in books and remembered that the site was near where his friends were. Three figures stood by the four stones that had once been the young girls. They were talking. One was hidden completely from view by a hooded cowl, the other was Corbeau. The third had his back to him and yet, at the sight of him, his stomach knotted and something older even than his soul said R U N !

He thought the fear would wake him, but he felt trapped within the dream itself. The third person was now turning towards Moüsch, ever so slowly, and as he did so Moüsch had the strong impression he would be spotted. Then Sansonnet stood there, before him, obscuring his view of the third mysterious figure. She smiled at him and Moüsch felt calm again. She reached out, touched his arm and he woke.

'Your enemy is the bloke who winds up getting you killed. At the end of the day, it 'ardly matters which side he's on.'

Peregrine. The Open Coffin Tavern. Late.

Chapter 9
Sansonnet's Story
battle at the standing stones

As I was lying, half-dead, my body fighting the effects of the poison, another drama was unfolding a hundred miles away. Years later, I read an account of it in Sansonnet's journals. She'd left them mouldering in an attic, where I found them one afternoon whilst looking for something completely different. Of course, I'd heard the story many times from other people, even from those who were there, but I don't think any capture the spirit of the events quite as well as Sansonnet. Anyway, here it is word for word:

⤝

No one discussed why Moüsch left but, at the time, I suspected Chassignol knew more than he was admitting … perhaps even to himself.

Well then, it was three days after Moüsch had disappeared that Milan and Faucon noticed the Faies gathering amongst the dark shadows in the distance.

We also started to hear their pipes and drums in the night and our sleep became fretful. The Faies were gathering for the Hunt. We were the quarry. The survivors of their first attack had spread the word far that there was a Vampire party at large in their ancient kingdom and no Faie Lord would stand for such an incursion into their territory. I still believed that Chassignol should have tried to make peace with them that first night we camped under the hawthorn.

Chassignol may well have been worried but he was also determined. He stated that he refused to leave the area in order to escape the Faie threat whilst we were still waiting for Moüsch to return. If we did leave, he said, Moüsch would not know where to find us and if he came back here alone he would walk straight into the Faies – alone. He would almost certainly be killed. Grue pointed out that even Moüsch wasn't that stupid. I just thought that Grue was trying to save his skin. To my shame, I accused him of cowardice, though now I think he was right. Any Vampire is more than a match for a Faie and he would spot them if he he was on his guard, long before they even suspected he was there.

However, my outburst carried the day and we travelled a relatively short distance nearer to the Standing Stones, placed by the Humans on an old Faie site. Old People. Though we did not stray far from the area where Moüsch left us, we were careful to move our camp a short distance every night. It was like a game of chess but eventually so many Faies had answered the call to arms that they were able to trap us. It was in the grey half-light before dawn that Bud, who happened to be on watch with Peregrine, came to wake me. I had been dreaming of Moüsch. He had been there, with us, at the Standing Stones. I felt he was in danger and I needed to warn him, so I reached out to touch him. When I did, he turned and looked at me and then he was gone. The dream lingered and I was cold. There was the promise of rain in the chill pre-morning air.

'The Faies are here,' Bud repeated in a whisper.

'How many?' I asked, looking around at the dark outlines of trees and hedges that bordered our small camp. They looked menacing in that light – like silhouettes of people in pain.

'About thirty,' he said and then I noticed his lip was trembling. 'Peregrine is sure we're surrounded. What's going to happen?' Poor, easy-going Bud was terrified, so I put my arm around him.

'Don't worry,' I said. 'Chassignol will know what to do.'

'Sansonnet.'

'Yes?'

'It's not for me to say, and I know I'm often wrong about these things … but I saw Chassignol talking to someone last night.' At that moment, Peregrine came up with Chassignol himself. I looked away from Bud. Chassignol's face was grim but he seemed confident, considering. He crouched down.

'Look here, we've been surrounded by one of their advance parties.' He turned to Peregrine. 'Is everyone awake?' Peregrine nodded but said nothing. 'Good, because we've got to act now,' Chassignol was scanning to horizon, 'before any more of their lot turn up. If we're caught out in the open by their main force they'll cut us to pieces. We'll use the stones as a natural defence. They make effective cover, and the Faies won't be able to attack us head on. Peregrine, take Grue and see if you can draw some of their force away. Make as if you've seen them and that you're trying to escape. With any luck, they'll split their force to follow you. Then double back as soon as you can without them seeing you and come and join us – that means we should have less to deal with – perhaps only twenty.' He grinned, his teeth very white and long in the darkness. 'Good odds, I say.' And I reflected that I was heartily glad at that precise moment that he wasn't my enemy. Surrounded and outnumbered or not.

'What do we d-do?' Milan and the rest of them had now crept up and joined us.

'Stay put for the time being,' replied Chassignol, getting up and brushing wet grass off his knees. 'I've got a plan.'

⟩⟨ The Earth revolved and the sky before us went from grey to a pale pink. We could clearly make out the sound of Faie pipes from the dawn chorus of birds. Judging by the directions of the various melodies, Bud was right ... we were surrounded.

'We've less than an hour before the rest of 'em turn up.' Peregrine commented. 'Faies don't like an early start any more than the rest of us but I get the feelin' they'll miss their breakfast for a spot of revenge.' He strapped his sword belt a notch tighter and turned to Grue. 'Shall we, sir?'

Grue nodded once and flew sharply into the air. Peregrine followed, and, as they made their way towards the rising sun at the foot of the slope, I noticed half a dozen shapes break cover from a thicket to head them off.

Peregrine and Grue were too fast for them, though. At the last instant they veered off their course and headed sharply south, instead of east. The Faies, taken by surprise, veered too and nearly caught them, but by now the fleeing Vampires were heading further into the valley, towards a large wood that covered a nearby hillside.

'They'll try to lose them in that,' said Chassignol, looking relieved that the first part of the plan had worked. 'Time to take cover, what?' He nodded towards the waiting stones.

꙳ Although we had camped by the Standing Stones for the night, I hadn't ventured into the circle. When I did, I noticed a subtle change of atmosphere, as if we'd passed through a thin mist. An invisible doorway. Looking out from inside the ring of stones, the light seemed different, somehow more opaque. It had started to drizzle a few minutes beforehand but I could feel no rain here, or at least, less rain. Surprising, I reflected – Humans had built this and they weren't known for their magic but there was definitely something of it here.

My thoughts were interrupted by an arrow rushing out of the trees, across the tops of the long grass. I had turned far too late, it darted straight at me. For what seemed like an age, I just stood, frozen to the spot. However, the moment the arrow crossed the outer stone circle and entered the perimeter it veered sharply, as if refracted in water, and fell several feet short of where I stood. More arrows followed, silently leaving the cover of the hedgerows, darting across the open ground towards us. The Faie archers were well within range and each reached the stone circle zinging through the air, fast and true but, just as the first had done, they crossed the invisible barrier made by the stones and fell harmlessly at our feet.

Bud, Milan and Faucon were all now crouching behind separate stones looking mystified. Chassignol seemed unconcerned. Instead he was poking about in a giant hole with a long stick. Then, a large rat's nose appeared from the hole. Chassignol gave it a smart whack and stepped back. The rest of the rat appeared, looking rather cross. Chassignol hit him again. 'I can't believe it,' remarked Faucon, scratching his unruly hair. 'As if we haven't got enough on our plates, without him picking fights with rodents.' Chassignol was standing in front of the rat, dangerously close, as it reared above him on its hind quarters. It must have decided that he was in range, for it gave a screech and leapt forward, its sharp incisors aiming downwards at his throat. But Chassignol was expecting it, and in one movement he dropped the stick and drew his sword. In another heartbeat he had lunged forward to meet the rat halfway and skewered it neatly through the eye. The rat gave another screech, kicked twice, its back ridged, and slumped. Then Chassignol did a strange thing. He cut the beast's throat. The rat's heart must still have been pumping, as arterial blood sprayed across the grass and the scent of fresh blood was caught on the morning breeze.

'Have you g-gone per-potty?' Milan hissed. Chassignol was looking rather pleased with himself. 'You know what the smell of b-blood will do to the Faies. They'll go round the b-bend!'

And sure enough the scent must have reached the Faies' cover, for when we looked up they were streaming across the grass in ones and twos, yelling and waving their swords in the air. They seemed to have been taken by a collective madness.

'Exactly,' said Chassignol. 'With a bit of luck they'll come at us in a blind rage. They won't listen to their leaders and their attack will have no proper discipline. We might have a chance of getting out of this alive, if we keep our heads.'

⌇ Both Milan and Chassignol were right. Faies are much like Vampires. First of all they are both very vain and secondly they are very sensitive to the smell of blood. If caught unawares, as they had been, it drives them into a frenzy before they know it.

They must have also guessed (wrongly) that one or more of us had been hit by the volley of arrows they had sent over. They were now very near us indeed and they didn't seem to be looking where they went. 'Steady,' said Chassignol between clenched teeth, 'wait for my command ...' he raised his arm and brought it down in a brief, chopping motion. 'Akuzati!'

The first Faie that came through into the enclosure was one I recognised from our earlier skirmish with them. He fell on Chassignol's sword before he even noticed Chassignol was standing there, dying with his battle cry still on his bloodied lips, pierced through the lungs as Chassignol turned and cut the throat of another Faie carrying a light, platinum axe. Milan and Faucon had somehow fared even better, as I looked up to see five bodies, all lifeless, at their feet in a matter of a few moments. Chassignol's plan was working better than any of us expected. Milan was stern-faced with concentration as he took on two identically-armoured Faies at once and forced them back to the outer circle. The rest of us stood with our backs to the stones, so we could not be attacked from behind. More Faies had arrived by this time and we had all joined in the fray. I had time to see Chassignol wound a large Faie who was wearing a very fine shirt of silver chain mail, before I found myself fencing two determined assailants carrying long, curved swords. One tried to outflank me but I was quick enough to edge my sword under his guard and pierce his leg deeply, just above the knee. He squealed in that oddly childish voice they have and pulled away, as I turned to face the second Faie who had drawn a dagger. With an abrupt movement of his hand the dagger left his fingers and tumbled through the air, making a strange keening noise as it spun in my direction.

The world seemed to stop.

Everything around me moved with painful slowness and I instinctively knew at that very moment that I was experiencing the Quickening.

The Quickening, for us, is a trance-like state we sometimes slip into in moments of danger or fear. It's very rare, being a sort of elevation of the senses and most Vampires will never experience it whilst, for others, the true warriors of our Nation, it happens each time they go into battle. I have only experienced it once and I found it hard to describe even at the time. It is happiness and rage, in one emotion. I was only distantly aware of anything but a rushing sound in my ears and four Faies lay dead by my own hand. I looked up to see about a dozen left standing, the rest being dead or wounded. Milan and Faucon were fighting two apiece, Chassignol had four and was struggling. However, I felt a stab of fear when I looked to see Bud, some distance from the rest of us, desperately defending himself against three Faies who sensed easy prey. Bud's face was contorted in fear, but as I went to help him the large Faie who had been wounded earlier by Chassignol blocked my path. Blood ran down his mail shirt and his face was twisted in pain and hate. Wounded or not he was still quick as an adder and as his sword met mine I felt the anger and strength in his arm. The Quickening had now passed in me and it was going to take all my concentration to kill the brute. I felt another stab of panic as I saw Bud stumble and cry out in fear as the Faies moved in for the kill.

Then I heard a shout of victory from Chassignol. Grue and Peregrine had shaken off their pursuers and entered the fray. With a brief clash of swords, Chassignol's opponents turned and ran – Grue and Peregrine gave chase, aiming to cut them down as they fled. With the bulk of the Faies fleeing for their lives, wounded or dead, the battle was won but Bud was still in grave danger. 'Chassignol!' I shouted. He turned to me and a look of alarm spread across his face as he half flew, half ran towards me. 'No!' I yelled, 'not me, help Bud!' He glanced in Bud's direction, seemed to make a decision and carried on towards me. I heard the unmistakable sound of a sword thrust hitting its target, tearing through flesh and bone.

'No, please!' Bud's strangled cry suddenly cut through the morning air. Bud, who never hurt anyone. I turned in horror. Bud, who was the best of us. I felt my knees start to give way with grief.

Bud, who lay dead.

Something not unlike the Quickening then overtook me but with no joy, just cold fury. I turned to face the large Faie who was most probably their leader. My sword arm flashed past his guard and under his neck, where the chain mail stopped. He fell, bleeding heavily from an artery, and I hacked him down with no emotion and, later, scant remorse .

When I got to where Bud lay on the grass, Milan and Faucon had already killed the Faies who had cornered him. Chassignol crouched by the body. His face was white and taut, a fleck of blood stained his cheek and I thought I saw a look of guilt sweep across his features.

'Why didn't you save him?' I shouted.

Chassignol turned to me, alarm colouring his cheeks. 'I went to save you, you were closer and that large Faie … '

'You left him on purpose! I was fine. You might as well have killed him yourself!' I was yelling. But Chassignol only turned and stared over my shoulder.

Someone ragged stumbled into the stone circle and fell. His mouth worked but no sound came out. He was filthy, and his face was grey. Moüsch! Milan gave him some water. Moüsch drank deeply and then looked straight at me. 'The Chalice,' he said and started coughing. As great shudders wracked his body I felt a new wave of panic, at the thought that he might die too. The coughing subsided and he looked around with a hint of the old spark back in his eyes. 'I know where it is,' he rasped, and then passed out.

'Moüsch's powers, at the start of the so-called Quest, were more of a burden for him and the rest of us. They played on his mind and slowed him down. Just to survive, he would have to learn to use them more to his advantage.'

Grue. *Miscellaneous Letters*, unedited.

Chapter 10

moüsch

Unaware for the moment of the unfolding events at the Standing Stones, and still feverish from the effects of the Wight's dart, I looked up to see the Strigoi whom I had just helped rescue heating something gooey on a small fire. He was young, but his movements as he stirred the food and brought the contents over to me were strangely assured. You have to go a long way to find a genuinely clumsy Vampire (me), but there was a grace to this boy's actions, which spoke of an uncommon agility even in one so young. More like a fully mature Nosferatu. A huge, ungainly rat scrabbled into my field of vision, sniffing along the wall. It reeked, almost as bad as one of the drunken Weres. This didn't seem to bother the Strigoi, who spun around with a flick of his wings, sank his fangs into the beast and started feeding from a large vein that pulsed behind the rat's ear. Like the Weres earlier, there was something untamed about him: I felt vaguely revolted and extremely hungry at the same time.

'Who are you?' I managed to croak.

The boy paused briefly at the sound of my voice but did not turn. 'Raptor.'

'Er ... OK.' I squinted around me – we were in a tower, with an enormous mechanism in the centre of the room. Concentric wheels and pulleys turned, seemingly at random, a metal arm made a clicking noise. I peered at it, impressed: the device was obviously some kind of clock. I really had no idea ... these Humans – they weren't as stupid as they sometimes looked. Outside, through a small window, trees swayed in the breeze against a night sky. It was no longer foggy. 'How long have I been out?'

'Hours.' He looked at me and, as if realising he could be more talkative, added. 'Are you better?'

'Probably as bad as I look.'

He stopped feeding and gave something approaching a bloody smile and, for the briefest moment, I saw some warmth in his thin, dirty face. 'Pretty bad then.' His smiled vanished. 'I have to go now,' he said, now handing me this horrible looking concoction in an earthenware cup.

'What? I'm still sick. I may actually *die*,' I added with emphasis. I gave the concoction a quick sniff. 'Especially if I drink this.' It smelled of pee.

'Our jobs are simply different,' he replied, 'and you'll be fine, the drink will do you good.'

'What makes you so sure? You're only a Strigoi.' He turned and looked at me for a few long moments, sizing me up.

'And you're just a cripple,' he said.

Years of practice had got me used to insults but I hadn't expected it from someone whose life I'd just saved. 'And your point is?'

He shrugged. 'Your name is Mutsh or Moosh or something like that and you can see the future sometimes.'

I was genuinely startled. 'How did you know?'

'It's one of our prophecies,' he said glancing out of the window. He seemed to be in a hurry. 'What you are looking for is over there. In *that* building.' He pointed to something I couldn't see from where I lay.

My head hurt but I was more than a little curious to find out I was famous. 'Whose prophecy?'

'Corbeau's.' he said and I began to feel much worse again. The boy moved towards the door. He really was going.

'Where are you going?' The Strigoi looked out of the window for a while then drew a breath.

'Corbeau came to England in exile. He spent many years building an army of Weres, masterless Faies and enslaved Vampires stolen from the Old Country who he's brainwashed to fight for him. My parents and I were captured when I was a Milk Imp and taken into slavery.' He paused. 'They both died under torture before I could walk – they had refused to kill other Vampires to further Corbeau's cause. I was saved by a Vampire from the Keep. He holds an enormous power within him but will not use it, he once told me, until the time is right. Then, a few years ago he simply disappeared. I must find him.'

'What is his name?' I asked.

'Picus.'

Him again. I propped myself up. 'And once you do?'

'My job is to lead the Vampires out of bondage and to fight Corbeau before he becomes too strong. Picus can ... no, *must* help. Corbeau plans to lead an army back to the Old Country and take the Keep and rule as a warlord. He will kill anyone who opposes him. You are here looking for the Chalice, so you will have to fight the Thin Man himself. This is *your* job.' I thought of the Eltern and wondered, once again, how much they knew and didn't tell us. I wondered if they knew who had been the mysterious figure talking to Corbeau and the Thin Man in my dream.

Raptor stared at me again and, not for the first or last time, I felt disconcerted by this half-child's steady gaze. 'Corbeau has to be killed,' he said, his voice deadpan. Not stopped or defeated, I noted, but *killed*.

'He murdered my parents, too.' I pointed out. 'And my brother, Moineau and my sister, Alouette. She wasn't much older than you, when he stuck a sword through her heart. If anyone is going to kill Corbeau, then it will be me. I've waited over sixty years for the opportunity.'

Raptor lowered his gaze briefly, then brought it up again.

'In that case, when the time comes,' he said, 'I will make sure I deliver him to you. You have my word,' he added, quietly but firmly.

'So what do you plan to do?' I asked.

Raptor gazed out the window again, as if he hadn't quite learned the art of eye contact for all his self-assurance. 'Corbeau is more feared than loved. He has his followers but there are many more who just need someone to give them the courage to face him in a straight fight.'

A day before, I probably would have found the idea of a mere fledgling leading Vampires into battle against the most ruthless opponent they had faced, far-fetched – even completely ridiculous – but barely an hour or so in Raptor's company was making me think otherwise. 'Corbeau says he despises Humans,' he continued, 'but he wants us to be like them. He doesn't believe in freedom, in individuals. He wants us all to work together, to build like the Humans build, to labour underground day and night. He wants to build a new Vampire Nation that will wipe out all the other magical creatures for good and then rule the Humans. He says they will be the new Sanguines. Everything that is done by his army and his followers is controlled by him and anyone who disagrees, he deals with personally.'

'How, exactly?'

Raptor turned and, kneeling down, brought his face very close to mine. I could smell the rat he had fed from on his breath. 'Corbeau has taken to feasting on the blood of those who oppose him – he feeds until they are nothing more than dry husks.'

I felt about nine years old again, standing in the attic as my family lay dead around me. I shook my head, fighting the urge to vomit. 'That can't be,' I said, 'no Vampire, however depraved, would drink another's blood against their will.' The law against drinking the blood of Vampires was absolute, unless it was to save a life. Any Vampire who broke a commandment so fundamental to our species was committing the worst crime imaginable. It had other drawbacks, too: feasting on our own species would give the Vampire great insight and even strength but the texts were clear, the price would eventually always be too high.

In the old days, it was said that if a Vampire committed a terrible crime – like treason against the Eltern, or say, the murder of a child – then his blood would be drained and thrown into the sea and his body burned. His dried corpse would then be buried in a pit outside the curtain wall of the Keep. To be interred without a drop of blood in your veins, for all time, was considered by Vampires to be condemned to Hell for eternity.

'No, Corbeau is not depraved,' Raptor shook his head, turning to slip out of a hole in the woodwork. 'Corbeau is insane.' And with that the Strigoi melted into the night.

I didn't see him again for another four hundred years.

><co-

For the time being I lay there, thinking partly about what he had said but mainly about what he hadn't. Our paths were different, yes, but they both revolved around Corbeau.

The background to the terrible events that destroyed my family all those years ago was the civil war between the rebel Vampires under Corbeau, and those loyal to the Keep and Duke Barsop. Corbeau had been a court favourite of the Eltern long before that, and it was easy to see why. Like Chassignol now, he had been the most talented Vampire of his generation: a brilliant fighter, a natural leader, vastly intelligent and vain as a cat. By the time he had reached his eightieth year he had outgrown the Keep and had begun to think that he should be the next elected Eltern. This worried the Eltern, for whilst they admired and respected Corbeau, and had indeed harboured great hopes for him as a military commander, perhaps even a general, he wasn't born from a noble enough family to become an Eltern. And his father, Raben, had been a traitor. To make matters worse, Corbeau's family had refused to acknowledge the father's crime. Corbeau's mother languished in the Keep's prison, although some said this was for her own protection, that she had a terrible illness with no name, a pressing burden of sadness that reduced her to little more than a shell. So a young and vulnerable Corbeau had been brought up by an unusually cold and cruel series of aunts and uncles.

It's not surprising, really, that he had quietly turned into a maniac under everyone's noses. Anyway, because of all of the above, the Eltern felt that they could never trust him fully, and told him that he would never rise above the rank of public servant. Not being known for their tact, they were probably more than a little undiplomatic about how they went about dishing out the bad news.

At first Corbeau seemed to take it all pretty well. But the reality of it was worse, much worse, than anyone had imagined. He went away and wrote this tome – he called it *The Book of Truth*, whereas it was, in fact, just a pack of lies aimed at appealing to anyone who felt hard done by under the Eltern. Secretly and rather skilfully, he had spent his next few years at court plotting and recruiting misfits and malcontents to his cause.

It was about this time that he also became obsessed with controlling the Chalice. I am not sure that someone like Corbeau believes in magic, but this would ensure that he had everyone's attention and that he got control not just of the Keep, but of the Vampire Nation the whole world over.

By his ninety-first birthday, when a Vampire is said to reach the first stage of adulthood, he had spread enough discontent against the ruling Blood Chamber of Eltern to raise a secret army from within the Keep itself. They struck without warning, during the longest night in winter. The snow around the Keep and Palace grounds turned red as they went from house to house looking for the Chalice.

Worst of all, *they targeted the children where they could.* They reasoned, quite coolly, that if there was no line left to inherit, the old titles and families would die out, and anyone could become an Eltern based on ruthlessness and a willingness to stab others in the back. Corbeau would have had his revenge, his beloved Chalice and a nice neat political solution in one terrible act.

The truly noble families were visited by Corbeau himself, which included mine.

By the time he had got to our house he was lost in a frenzy of hate and vengeance, unaware that his followers were already losing the battle that raged in the town. Why he hesitated to kill me, I may never know. It might simply be that he had no time and, in a moment of characteristic decisiveness, he decided that he must run before escape became impossible. Chassignol always says it was because of my deformity – that recognized Corbeau recognised something in me that reminded him of himself; we were both outsiders, he by birth and a legacy he could never change, I by the handicap of my withered legs. That may be so, but I have always suspected it goes beyond even that.

Whatever the reason, Corbeau's duel with my father cost him precious time and, most probably, the crown itself. In the end, he barely got away with his own life. His supporters were not so lucky, and by dawn they had all been executed and hanged from the Keep battlements. No doubt Corbeau, fleeing through the woods, could turn and view the remnants of his Great Revolution kicking and twisting in the frosty air.

No one had heard of him again directly ... until now, that is.

⤸

And so here I was in Sarum, tearing my thoughts away from Corbeau and back to the job in hand.

Dawn was not far off, and I had the deeply unsettling feeling that time, somewhere or other, was running out. I hadn't seen precisely where Raptor had pointed out as my goal but when I closed my eyes I had a vision of a striking tower, hollow in the middle and vast.

So I struggled over to the window.

Rising up, taller than anything I had seen in my short life so far, was a Human cathedral, previously obscured by fog. So immense, it robbed everything nearby of perspective. The spire looked as if it was built in an attempt to lay a vertical bridge to Heaven itself.

It didn't take a huge stretch of logic to know that in here was where I would find Longspee's tomb.

The streets were almost deserted now and I guessed that it must have been about four in the morning by the Human way of telling the time. I had another hour or so under cover of darkness. Feeling to some extent revived, unbelievably thanks to Raptor's cooking skills, I crept out of the tower that stood on the northern edge of the great square and approached the building with some trepidation.

The huge doors leading to the western portion were firmly

shut, but I could make out a gap in the vast mosaic of stained glass above the arch where a shard had been broken. I flew up groggily and had to grab hold of the leering face of a statue to stop myself falling backwards. The poison from the dart was still making me nauseous and dizzy. Best not fly for a bit unless in short bursts, I decided, as I peered through the gap.

Creeping into the church I noticed there was a change of atmosphere, as if time slowed by a couple of degrees and all sound was deadened. It smelled of chilly air, damp stone and candlewax.

Two long corridors ran up both sides of the interior and met with a junction that then continued towards what I remembered was the important bit. In keeping, the layout thus formed the all-important cross I was looking for. My sign from the day before.

I glided down.

It didn't take much time to find Longspee. About halfway along the southern aisle was a tomb with his name on it but I was nonplussed when I got there. The tomb's base was wooden, which was unusual in my experience, but aside from that there was nothing remarkable about it. The effigy was that of a knight decked out in gaudy blue, gold and red. Matching shield – very nice.

I stood there for a while, looking up and down, as if a guide might suddenly pop up and start explaining things. Then I took to clambering all over the wretched thing, pressing knobbly bits of stone and tweaking things in the hope that something might be a switch. I even tried the old trick of knocking for hollow panels – except all of it seemed pretty hollow – and generally I began feeling more and more idiotic. I jabbed long-dead Longspee in the nose with my sword, more in malice than actual hope it might do something.

He stared up at me, impassive and utterly disengaged by my antics.

So I glared back at him. On second thoughts, he wasn't actually looking at me at all but rudely over my shoulder, like a fellow guest at a party who would rather chat with someone more interesting or important.

I followed his gaze.

About ten feet up I saw what he looked at so fixedly: one of the ornate stones that formed the floral decoration at the top of the roof arch was missing. Instead, a highly suspicious-looking hole in the stonework opened out into the gloom of the church.

Up there.

⟩☙

The inside of the sloping spire was filled with wooden scaffold beams the builders had apparently simply discarded when they'd finished with the stonework, because none of it seemed to be fulfilling the purpose of holding this incredibly tall, spiky structure upright. If anything, it was the other way around.

I alternately climbed and flitted for a solid half hour before I reached the top.

Although my head was clearing, my wings and legs ached and I wondered where the others were. I knew that if I had found what I was looking for here, then it was time to go in search of them.

I decided to take a breather and have a look around. To be perfectly honest, the fact that I was only there thanks to a talking cow and the hazy-at-best predictions of a Strigoi, should have made me feel uneasy. But it still *felt* right being here. Sort of.

I was now perched inside the very top of the spire, looking down at the huge cavity below. The capstone was just above my head, and to my left was another hole where I could make out the grey light of pre-dawn, gloaming through the gap. Something told me to keep going up; so I did.

As I clambered out into the fresh air, I had an unexpected feeling of vertigo before remembering I could fly. I steeled myself, and holding on tighter than was strictly cool, I crawled up the final miniature pyramid of dressed stone until there I was – at the top. Well, practically anyway: for at the apex of the structure, glued in with crude cement for good measure, was a huge iron cross. That symbol again, so Human, yet linked somehow to the Chalice. My head swam again. This pig metal isn't exactly a favourite of our kind – after silver, it ranks as the material we least like to be near – and the poison had weakened my defences.

Shinning up the last few feet over the painful, jarring sensations iron always produces[2], I slipped and nearly fell. My wings buzzed like mad and I grabbed hold of the iron at the last instant. I gritted my teeth very hard.

Onwards and upwards until finally, the hairs over my body standing on end and flashes of white light flicking across my vision, thanks to the iron, I made it. I stood atop Sarum Cathedral, wings extended and humming faintly, vibrating to steady myself. I looked east towards the dawn.

Something scratched on the surface of the metal at my feet caught my eye.

My heart skipped – the writing was very faint – but unmistakably very ancient Vampirik Runes. Most Vampires use a simplified form of the old lettering, but even to this day, young Vampires are taught the old writing in our version of school. Luckily, unlike Chassignol, I had worked hard at this sort of thing. There was no poem, no riddle to unravel, no cipher to unlock, and the old language came easily to me. The message scored on the ironwork was simple enough – the text simply read. *Some toe-rag has nicked the Chalice, you'll find the old guy who knows where It is in China. He is called,* The Dragon.

I flew as fast as I was able. At first I gained height – corkscrewing upwards until the wind coming hard in from the east picked me up and trebled my speed as it buffeted me westwards in a constant freezing draught that threatened to tear my wing membranes to shreds.

---

[2] I'm told Humans have the same sort of feeling thing about metal on their teeth.

The poison from the Wight's dart still coursed through my veins and each mile sapped my strength dangerously but I carried on. I knew I had to reach the others as fast as I could. The feeling of needing to find them had been growing steadily since I had entered the cathedral, and it was beyond doubt now that they were in mortal danger.

It was nearly three hours before I began to pick up their traces. I had come to a broad plain as the sun rose above the horizon, and I saw the Standing Stones, and the four, smaller stones – the maids – the same I'd seen in my dream, arranged like sentinels looking out to the rising sun in the east. Even without the strong magical footprint, I knew that this was the place. I also sensed a large number of Faies nearby. With the last of my strength, I rocketed towards the Stones.

And suddenly I was there and so was Sansonnet, her face bathed in tears. In front of her, Bud lay motionless on the ground, and I could smell his blood on the wet grass.

'These two cows were standing in a field. One went, 'Moo!' The other one had a little think, then turned around and said, 'I knew you'd say that.'

Bud's favourite joke.

the road of bones

We had all heard the stories. As soon as the *Dragon's* name was mentioned, we knew where we were going. None of us could face going back to sea for now, so we journeyed overland all the way to China. Months passed as our party hopped from cart, to mule, to foot; as slowly, mournfully we headed east.

Sanguines, like Vampires, very rarely have more than one child. The loss of any is a tragedy and we had all loved Bud, especially Grue, who took his death particularly badly. Chassignol did not speak much and never mentioned my running off on my own. Nobody spoke much at all, in fact. It took me a few days to recover my senses and when I explained what I had found to the others, they mostly just accepted that we had another long road ahead of us and prepared for it without comment.

We had left the Standing Stones within an hour of the pitched battle and flew to sanctuary about ten miles away in a wood near a busy Roman road. It was there that we buried Bud, under a Rowan to protect his resting place from Faies, who avoid these trees for some reason. I was still unconscious, carried there on a litter by Milan and Faucon but we had to get away before the main force of Faies caught up with us. Chassignol sent Milan, Faucon and Peregrine into a nearby town to scavenge supplies, whilst Sansonnet took care of me. The effort of flying so far and fast had caused a sort of relapse and the poison burned once more through my veins.

Grue and Chassignol worked out a route together and kept guard. We left by nightfall, catching a ride to the coast in the back of a cart pulled by an old ox who leaked cow fumes into our faces all the way.

A horse then took us to a fishing boat and over the sea to France, and more carts then rattled us over the course of a long month through Europe. In Germania we found a trading caravan that was heading overland to Muscovy and then yet another that went further east.

In time we travelled what, a few generations later, would become known as the Road of Bones – the rutted Siberian highway, strewn with corpses of the enslaved Humans who were to lose their lives in its making. The area was so potent with the terrible events to come, images of slaughter came to me unbidden. They were to perish through sickness and starvation and cold. As we moved along what was in those days little more than a patchy trading route, through freezing rain or sleet, I thought of Corbeau and his plan to enslave his own kind. As free Vampires we had been brought up believing that only Humans could stoop to such cruelty – that our Nation may kill in the heat of battle, but always with honour and that Vampires would never condemn their own to a slow death in servitude. Now I wasn't so sure.

Looking at the desolation around me, I felt a new fire in my belly searing through my despair, cauterising my tears. We had to find the Chalice to stop the Thin Man and Corbeau. The Quest took on a new sense of urgency, no longer simply because we had been sent by the Eltern, but to save others from the same fate as the dead Humans who were destined to lay in piles of wind-dried bones along the terrible route we now trod.

And yet, I wondered how many others had died in their own quests for the Chalice. So at times I hated this trinket, blaming it for the death of our friend Bud and the purpose of my burning desire to find it was to destroy it for good.

I tried not to think about the Age of Aquarius Chassignol had mentioned, the End of Days and what Raptor had said would happen if Corbeau won. I just wanted to go home. Gradually, though, I realised it was the only thing that would give meaning to Bud's death. In my heart I knew that if we didn't find it, then his dying would have just been a pointless episode in the middle of a series of misadventures.

I, for one, was not going to let that happen.

It was now late autumn and it rained almost constantly. If it wasn't for Milan and Faucon – the only ones amongst us who still retained any good humour – we may all have given up several times on that terrible journey. They still laughed amongst themselves and had a smile for everyone, even Grue, and thus we endured thanks to them.

One night, I saw the ghost of a young suicide.

We were camping by the side of a lake, having travelled through open countryside with a Russian trader carrying bottles of potato vodka across the vast Steppes.

It was dusk, and leaden clouds rolled across the landscape, breaking momentarily to allow an improbable shaft of sunlight to illuminate the surface of the lake. Nothing but wind-blasted bleakness surrounded us. The surface of the water was still, save for a steady stream of ripples that shuddered from one end of the lake to the other and made the black-ended reeds on the eastern shore line topple to and fro. Then a bitter wind set up a low keening sound as the light began to fade, like the cry of a child, and a lone figure came out slowly from under the trees to stand by the water's edge.

The figure was that of a very young Human, head bent, making no sound as the wind whipped at her dress as she walked barefoot across the dead beach. The longer she stood on the bitter shore line, the darker it became; an unearthly murk, that seemed to creep up on the lonely figure from the clammy marshes behind her and now gathered at her shoulder. She held herself perfectly still.

It was now completely dark, and the wind seemed to take strength from this, gradually increasing from a whine to a high-pitched whistling sound. The girl advanced a step and let her thin shawl drop. She stood, a bent figure, with her feet in the water and her shoulders shaking. She was crying.

By the time she had moved forward again, the wind had increased to an almost human shriek, running from one side of the desolate lake to the other. Then she slipped below the surface.

Moments before she disappeared from view, the girl turned

her head. Her face was white against the dark background of the sky, and she stared directly at me.

⁂

Unlike most Vampires I don't recover from illness easily but, little by little, I began to get better. Thanks to Sansonnet's attention my strength was coming back and each day I felt more and more like my old self. We slipped into the habit of talking a lot during the evenings, and once or twice I caught Chassignol giving us a bruised look – for Sansonnet had still not spoken to him, and when he had tried she had simply ignored him or walked away. I assumed that their rift would heal in time. Instead we talked of the Keep, the Chalice and sometimes about of Bud. By now I had decided that she was almost certainly developing a gift similar to mine and, to take my mind off the bleakness of our situation, I set about showing her some of the techniques that I had learnt over the years to control and focus the visions. One evening I decided to set her a test. We were camped by the side of a road, beside a muddy stream, and I placed four of its large pebbles side by side on the frozen ground. 'Which one will turn to sand first?' I asked.

She looked at me. 'You're kidding aren't you?'

'No, they all dissolve to gravel, then sand, and naturally one of these will do it first, eventually.'

She raised an eyebrow in my direction then squinted at the four pebbles, half-serious and half in mock concentration. 'I give up,' she replied in the end. 'Which one?'

'I've absolutely no idea.'

'Then why did you ask me?'

'Give me a minute.' I scrabbled down the slope and came back with four almost identical icicles, collected from some of the lower branches overhanging the brook. I held them up. 'Which of these will melt first?'

Sansonnet hardly paused. 'Easy, the one on the far left.' She pointed a long slim finger in its direction.

'What makes you so sure? It's bigger than the others.'

'I just know.'

I looked at the icicle. She was right. 'So how come you couldn't do the same with the pebbles?'

'I guess it's something that will happen too far into the future.'

'Yup, its one of the Rules – the further something is into the future, the harder it is to predict, so something that is hundreds of generations away, like the lifetime of these pebbles, is almost guesswork. Something that is just around the corner,' I glanced at the icicles, which were almost half their size already, 'is relatively clear.'

'Fair enough.'

'It doesn't end there. You can predict things that happen to others who are close to you, but hardly ever to strangers, unless it's really serious. It's almost impossible to see into your own future but when you do, it'll be important, so it's worth paying attention. Similarly, you can predict violence but hardly ever death itself.'

'You didn't see Bud's death then?'

Damn, I thought. 'I …' my voice caught, '…when I read the inscription on the cross, I immediately knew that something terrible was about to happen, that's why I flew back from Sarum so quickly.'

Sansonnet reached out and brushed my cheek lightly with her fingertip. 'We all miss him, you know,' she said, her eyes softening.

'Even Chassignol.'

There was a faint crunch of compacting snow behind us. I turned and saw Chassignol himself emerge from the line of trees that bordered the stream. Sansonnet's face clouded.

'Milan and Faucon have found a road that heads due south. Tomorrow we'll take it. We should be in China in three more days – with any luck.' He nodded at us, then turned and walked stiffly away in the direction he had come.

In the end, Chassignol's own prediction was wildly wrong. The only traffic heading south at that time of year was nomads on horseback or people goading donkeys loaded with cheap trinkets to sell to Chalice-knows-who – the whole, miserable place seemed to be completely deserted.

In the main, it was just another long, bumpy and rather smelly ride. However, as we left the frozen wastes the landscape began to turn into vivid expanses of fertile-looking grassland and the weather even did us a favour by improving a little. Then, late one evening, the donkey train upon which we had hitched a lift with came to an abrupt halt. Grue and I poked our heads out of a saddlebag and had a look around.

It wasn't much but it was the first one we'd seen in a month and a half: a town.

Well, more a sort of wretched miserable collection of warehouses, really and about thirty mud-splattered hovels and a large grey and white stone building claiming to be an inn. But the settlement also had something else far more interesting to us. There was a staging post for messenger ponies and caravans.

'I'll inform Chassignol,' muttered Grue, although I could tell he was almost as pleased as me at the prospect of making the rest of the journey in relative warmth and comfort.

Half an hour later we had found a deserted wagon carrying bundles of post. It had warm straw. There was even a small burner and the remains of someone's lunch to steal. It all presumably belonged to the guard who was at that moment marching up and down the one street, blowing a horn, looking important. 'Do we even know where it's going?' someone asked.

'South,' said Chassignol curtly, 'and that's where we want it to go.'

The wagon made a funny clunking noise, the horses pulling it huffed as if upset about something and the whole shebang set off slowly towards the gathering darkness. For the first time in weeks my feet and wings began to thaw out, and one by one we all fell asleep.

The cold beams of moonlight shining through the canvas and

into my face woke me a few hours later. Inside the heated canopy, though, I was warm and felt blissfully sleepy and secure.

The rocking of the wagon must have made me drift off once more, for when I next woke I saw that Chassignol was already up. His face looked drawn and pale. His usually placid features were oddly animated, almost jumpy, and he was whispering to himself, in a constant stream of words, which I strained and failed to hear from where I lay. His mind was a tangled mass of thoughts I could make no sense of, so I tried a more conventional approach. 'Chassignol?' I whispered. '*Chassignol.*' His head whipped around, and in the harsh moonlight, he appeared to snarl, his long teeth bared. For a moment I was genuinely alarmed, but then with an almost visible effort his features slipped back into the face I had known since childhood.

'Hullo Moüsch. How did you sleep?'

'Peachy, thanks. You seemed out-of-sorts?'

Chassignol looked furtively at his hands, which trembled. 'No, I'm fine. A little tired still, I imagine. Dawn's hardly an hour off.' He turned and plumped up a bit of saddle wadding he was using as a pillow. 'I think I'll try to get some rest before the others wake up.'

'Sure.' As I lay back down, I looked over the sleeping bodies and saw that someone else was also awake.

Grue stared at Chassignol for some time, his dour face cold and impassive and then turned to me as I suppressed an involuntary shudder. I still hadn't forgotten our fight on board the *Sprite* and nor had he, I was pretty sure.

To take my mind off thinking about the terrible things Grue would probably like to do to me, I lay still for a while, piecing together what I knew about the Dragon and his Clan. Apart from swords and a smattering of old Lore, in theory, at least, Vampire education is patchy. A young mother will usually feed her Milk Imp with hummingbird blood mixed with honey and tiny, non-threatening, amounts of her own blood. Vampire blood is very potent and contains not just protein but all the memories and experience of the donor. From an early age, then, an infant Vampire is born with the experience (including the memories) of generations of past Vampires in their family, plus the ability to talk, fly, walk and, in most cases, even read.

When we are about fifteen, those of noble families are often given a tutor. This will be a Vampire from another part of the Keep, and one who is a few years older, not some old shuffler. The thinking behind it is that they will introduce you to other Vampires you may not get a chance to meet, and take you to places you might not have gone. It's like being given an older brother you never knew you had, and normally it works very well. Mine was Milan, which was interesting, to say the least.

Whether or not I had been told, or whether this knowledge had been passed onto me when I was merely what older Vampires call a Milk Imp, I knew that far back in our history the wandering Kings had circled the land mass, now referred to as Pangaea as nomads. They were in exile, from what or by whose hands our histories do not tell us; even this is too far back in pre-history to have be been recorded and kept as anything more than rumour and historic tittle-tattle. *Pangaea* means *One Earth* and indeed this was before the continents had been pulled apart by earthquakes and the oceans' ebb and flow. All land, lakes, forests, mountains and grasslands were one, like a great big island, fifty times the size of anything now, sitting in the middle of the world, surrounded by ocean. It was our Eden, which we shared with all other animals and, by all accounts, we lived in harmony, with no fighting, except perhaps a bit of bickering once in a while. Then again, people always say it was better in the old days, so you can use your own judgment on that score.

As the huge great plates of rock that make up the outer core of the Earth's crust began to move about, we all started to lose touch and become separated. Geography or, indeed, geology isn't exactly a Vampire's strong suit, so it took us a while to work out why bits of sea kept appearing where there hadn't been any before. Quite a few of the Wandering Kings decided that this would be a good time to settle down and so they set up shop in what we know today as the Craggy Peaks and the Keep was founded. So this was how the majority of the Wandering Kings stopped gadding about and became the Eltern, and got into lie-ins and their weird thing about parlour games. But some others decided not to settle down immediately.

What happened over the next few generations is a tad unclear, but the ones who kept their nomadic ways began to change as the land split up and things like the weather and the food became different. Some became distinctly un-Vampiric and perhaps turned into Faies and Fairies (still a theory), whilst others just modified to some degree but essentially remained Vampires, more or less. The Dragon Clan is a good example of this. The Clan, in fact, settled about the same time as our lot but they decided, for their own reasons, that Asia Minor suited them better. Over millennia their wings got smaller and the fur on their bodies changed gradually from black and white to swirls or stripes in a kaleidoscope of colours.

Over the last few generations, like a lot of distant cousins, we had lost touch. I'd seen pictures but I was looking forward to meeting one of the Dragon Clan in real life, assuming we could find them. The place they were last seen and thought to have as their stronghold, was south, high in the foothills of the Himalayas. In keeping, they called it the *Eyrie*.

For an old civilization, very little was actually known about the Dragon Clan. Thinking about it on the journey, I guessed that there couldn't be that many of them, otherwise we would have had embassies, exchanges, tourists and all sorts like we get from the few other Vampire Clans all over the world.

Anti-social or not, if they really had the Chalice, I still couldn't understand why they hadn't, at the very least, told us. This didn't make me very hopeful about being able to march up to the front door and ask them just to hand over what was supposedly the most important artefact in the Vampire Nation. Nor did I fancy picking a row with them. One thing that we did know about them was that they were every bit as good as us at dealing with people who upset them. They used different swords from our own rapiers. I'd seen an ancient example at the Keep – a long sort of cutlass, narrow but incredibly sharp.

When I was much younger, the Sergeant of Arms at the Keep had given us a demonstration of one of their swords by cutting an apple thirty-six times, each section so thin you could see through it. He then cut a piece of silk cleanly, and as a finale sliced a large rock in half. The blade showed no nicks or dents. It left you with the abiding impression that anybody who went to all the trouble of making one of those obviously took their weaponry, and most likely their warfare, pretty seriously.

If we were going to have to be diplomatic, then, we needed a plan, and worryingly Chassignol still seemed unwilling to discuss anything with us. So, instead, I lay there fretting.

'We should talk.' A sinister voice I recognised all too well, whispered into my ear. I aged about ten years on the spot.

'Grue!' I hissed, and Peregrine, who slept nearest me, stirred but didn't wake. 'Are you trying to give me a heart attack? And anyway, how do you *do* that?'

'I am sorry if I alarmed you,' he said, looking anything but. 'I didn't want to wake the others and you looked worried about something.'

'So what?'

'I think we're concerned about the same thing, that's *what.*'

'Go on.'

'Chassignol doesn't seem to be his usual self, wouldn't you agree?'

'How would you know? He ignores you.'

'Oh, but he ignores everyone these days.'

'He's got a lot on his plate.' After my desertion to Sarum I found I was pleased to have the opportunity to defend Chassignol. 'And unlike you, he's probably more concerned with others.' Cheap shot, and Grue just ignored it.

'Do we know how to find this Dragon Clan? They haven't even been seen for over a thousand years. And what do you suppose we do when we get there?'

I knew Grue's doubts were not unreasonable but I wasn't going to give him the satisfaction of even partially agreeing so, instead,

I stared coldly at him for a long while. 'Go back to sleep Grue,' I said, and turned over. 'If the Eltern wanted you as leader they would have said so.' When I looked back after a few minutes, I saw, to my relief, that he had slipped away again.

✸

I didn't think that I would fall asleep again but when I next opened my eyes I found that the hazy dawn had been replaced by bright sunlight. Streaming through the dirty canvas covering, it showed the dust moving about the cart in lazy swirls. Peregrine had been exploring and had found a knapsack full of food, stowed deep in the straw. He and Milan heaved out a skin of fresh water and soft crumbs of bread the size of my head. We poured the water into the battered silver cups that we all carried, then we dug into the soft breadcrumbs with our hands. They felt warm, pillowy and tasted utterly delicious.

After five minutes of stuffing our faces in silence, we were all in relatively good spirits, even Chassignol, who gave no indication of what had passed between us in the early hours. Grue, on the other hand, kept shooting me long meaningful looks that I did my best to ignore. Peregrine finished eating first. He wiped his mouth with the back of his hand, sat back with a satisfied grunt and stared across at me. 'So, 'ow do we find these Dragon blokes, eh, Moüsch?', then started picking his long, diamond-capped teeth with a rusty-looking dagger. I was taken aback, as up until now all questions like that had been addressed to Chassignol. Chassignol didn't seem to have noticed.

'Er, um … ' I said, feeling unusually tongue-tied. Peregrine began to look disappointed and out of the corner of my eye I saw Sansonnet stifle a smile. I re-grouped. 'The last place they were seen was Liijang. We'll need to get our paws on a map sometime today but Chassignol was right last night,' I turned and offered him a smile but he was still staring out of the window, ignoring the whole conversation. 'We are headed in the right direction for now but we may have to change transport soon-ish.'

Milan stuck his hand up like he was in class. 'I heard that the Ker-Keep has had no contact with the Dragon Clan f-for centuries.'

Oooh, I was beginning to enjoy this. I nodded. 'At least.'

'So w-what if they're not a-around when we ger-get there?'

'Do you mean they might have popped out to the shops?' Sansonnet laughed, and I felt a little of the tension ease off, even if the joke was weak.

'They may have mer-moved on.' But even as he said it, Milan looked unsure: Vampires, especially those in Clan strongholds, rarely just push off unless they've got a very good reason.

Chassignol stirred. 'They'll be there,' he said with certainty and the tone of his voice was, as usual, pretty convincing. 'The tough bit though,' he carried on, 'is locating the Eyrie itself. I remember looking at a map of the Dragon Clan's lands and they are fairly extensive. We've a lot of ground to cover ... '

' ... and not much time.' I added.

Everyone turned and looked at me again, so I finally started to tell them all about Raptor, and what I knew about the army Corbeau was raising. I left out the prophesy about me but made sure I emphasised the slavery and attacking the Keep. For once everyone listened without interrupting. I ploughed on: I reminded them about the dark ship I'd seen following us during the storm, about my dream of the Thin Man on the battlefield and I spoke of the hordes that would engulf the Vampire Nation, using the Chalice as a weapon. I also told them of my dream about the Standing Stones, and of Corbeau and the Thin Man in conference with another Vampire I could not see. In fact I pretty much talked non-stop for an hour until the back of my throat went dry. 'There is no reason to believe that the Thin Man is hot on our heels now but I'm not sure and, importantly, I don't know how he always knows where we'll be,' I finished.

'O,'

'K,' said the Milan and Faucon in unison and we all sat there, lost in our own thoughts.

It was Grue who broke the silence. 'Bereck's Muster,' he said.

'What the what?' asked Peregrine looking aggressive, as he always did when basically he was just confused.

'Bereck's ... *Muster*,' replied Grue as if repeating the phrase would help.

Chassignol looked up, interested. 'Do you know how to do it?'

'I do.'

'That's rubbish,' I said, 'no one, apart from one or two Eltern, can perform the Rite and even then they've probably never done it – it'll all be theory and out of a book.'

Grue looked at me and smiled in an oily way. 'But I've done it.'

And sometimes you think you know someone.

'Would one of yous like to tell the rest of us what you are talking about,' Peregrine sounded distinctly testy by now. I was still croaky, so I looked over at Chassignol and raised my eyebrows. He cleared his throat.

'Bereck's Muster is one of the more obscure rites in our Lore. It was named, unusually, not after the person who invented it – no one knows this, unless Grue's got any more surprises up his sleeve – but after the first and last person who tried it and got themselves killed.'

Sansonnet clapped her hands together. 'It all sounds so tempting.'

'G-go on,' prompted Milan, leaning forward with a grin.

'Well, Bereck's Muster is a complicated procedure by anyone's standards, even for Vampire Lore, which is half practical magic and half mumbo jumbo in my experience. The mumbo bit of the jumbo is hard to weed out, so practitioners of old Lore generally follow the instructions and hope for the best. Bereck's Muster requires three skills. First, mastery of the fantastically complicated procedures to set it up and get it going. Second, enough knowledge of the lunar calendar to predict the exact time of a New Moon. And third, the ability to run very fast indeed, and usually on a dark night.'

Grue, provided he was telling the truth, seemed to have point one under his belt, and point two was covered as everyone has calendars these days. It was point three that worried me personally.

Chassignol carried on. 'Essentially the Muster is a very powerful Summoning Spell. Whereas most are designed to work on specific creatures – summoning a Troll for a laugh to do your bidding, or a Vampire who owes you money, Ghost or whatever – the Muster will summon *all* magical creatures within a given area. Now here's the problem. The magic it uses acts like a virus on creatures such as Faies, Pixies, Trolls etcetera. Too strong and it will kill them, too weak and it will summon them, no problem. But their own magic defence systems, like an immune system that stops you catching a cold, will kick in, and before you know it you've summoned a pack of Weres who break the Muster and then decide to make you their next warm meal. That's exactly what happened to poor Bereck, hence the need for point three in the above list.

'But, if you get it right, you can summon all magical creatures in one area of about forty miles and the point is they will do your bidding, *no questions asked*, until the Moon rises again. Your very own private army, ta, da! One of them is bound to know where this Eyrie is.'

Peregrine smiled. 'Cor, as magic tricks go, that beats a bunny out of an 'at or an exploding 'anky any day.'

'Basically it's incredibly risky,' Chassignol finished up.

'What are our options?' Sansonnet asked.

'Well, we could wander around a bit when we get there, put an ad in the local paper, tie a balloon to a tree. That sort of thing ...' Grue flicked an invisible speck from one of his silk sleeves, which still showed a faint bloodstain from our duel all that time ago.

'I hear the mountains around that part of the world are full of Trolls and worse,' muttered Faucon, looking morose.

Chassignol stood and turned to face us all. 'If Moüsch is sure about what he read on the cross ... ' I nodded emphatically at Chassignol, and then at everyone else for good measure, ' ... and Grue is sure he knows the Rite ... ' Grue, arrogant git, merely inclined his head, ' ... then we've no choice.'

'Question is, if you don't mind me askin' it,' said Peregrine, 'when's the next New Moon?'

Grue squinted and muttered under his breath. He looked up. 'Two days from now.'

'Two days?'

'Two days.'

The wagon began to slow, tracing the curve of the rutted track ahead, as a large town, a city almost, came into view.

We were soon passing through shanty suburbs, each shack linked to its neighbour by a line of ragged washing and an open gutter. It all looked less than salubrious, but to be fair the people squatting in doorways seemed happy enough. Further ahead I could see a small group of taller, more solidly built structures and even a spanking new building or two, with at least five stories, each one marked by an attractive curved roof.

'Let's get off here,' said Chassignol. 'We'll look for a map and try to find out where we are.'

Twenty minutes later we were all sitting on a window ledge, looking out at the crowded market below. We all had our mouths open in frank amazement. Even in Sarum, I'd never seen so many Humans. Hundreds, or possibly thousands, of people milled and jostled each other for space in the myriad streets. It looked like a market day; Sansonnet pointed at a stall below us. 'Ah, look, little *puppies!*'

Personally I'd never understood Sansonnet's obsession with small dogs and cats. They may be cute to Humans but anything I'd had to do with them had been a total nightmare. I'd lost count of the number of stories I'd heard of terrified Vampires having to run for their lives whilst being chased by enthusiastic kittens.

'They're selling them for food,' stated Grue, who was probably as tired as I was of hearing Sansonnet wish that there were tiny versions of toy poodles to play with back at the Keep.

Milan was stunned. 'You're ker-kidding?'

'No, really, it's true. Half of these mutts will be served up with boiled rice by the weekend.'

'That's … *horrible*.' Sansonnet looked like she was going to burst into tears on the spot and I began to feel a little guilty. Grue must have regretted telling her as well because he offered to fly down and let them out.

'No,' Chassignol cut in abruptly, seeming to tune into the conversation. 'We don't have time.' He looked annoyed. Sansonnet half opened her mouth to speak and for a moment I thought she was about to argue. She hesitated and then seemed to decide that she wasn't going to get far if Chassignol took that tone.

We had a good vantage point, and being high up meant we were out of harm's way and the risk of being pulverised. Faucon's sharp eyes had also spotted a map stuck to a wall inside. Closer investigation revealed we were looking into a scholar's chamber and that it was a parchment map of the whole country. This was just what we were looking for. We knew the name of the town (I forget it now) from a sign as we came in. Careful inspection of the map, which was in Chinese so took some working out, showed that we had only travelled across about one hundredth of the country overnight. We still had at least two and a half weeks travel left, even if we were to find a direct caravan to where we were going in the south.

'We're never going to mer-make it,' said Milan.

'Not in two days for the New Moon, anyway – bad luck!' added Faucon.

Grue shook his head. 'Oh, I think you'll find we just need to change the method of transport.'

The vulture was not exactly the most inspiring sight in the world. *Flea-bitten* would have been a good description. *Decrepit* was another one that sprang immediately to mind. We'd come across it chained to a post in a dusty compound at the back of some houses. It looked like they used it as a type of guard-bird-come-rodent-repellent. 'Well, it's the only bird around here big enough to take us all, so we may as well get on,' said Sansonnet.

'After you then,' said Grue. And I don't think he it was being gallant.

'Well ain't this all nice and cosy,' said Peregrine a few minutes later, doing his best to be optimistic as we settled into the evil-smelling feathers. A bunch of chickens sauntered over. One of them fixed me with a nasty beady eye. It looked hungry, so I gave it a poke with my sword, just to make it clear who was boss.

'Pa'aaaark, puk, puk, paa'aark!' it yelled and ran off to the other end of the yard.

'Stop tormenting the natives,' said Chassignol, and continued writing something on a piece of paper.

'Oh, really ... why?' Just to annoy him I clambered further up and settled down next to Sansonnet. I glanced back. 'What are you scribbling anyway?'

Chassignol did not look up at first. 'I'm checking the lunar calculations,' he said eventually. 'Once we get that chain off, if you can control the bird's thoughts enough to get it to fly in roughly the right direction, we should land sometime this evening, which gives us a whole day to make preparations and for Grue to get himself ready for the rite.'

So, to be useful, I started delving into the bird's brain and came up trumps. It was a simpleton. Really stupid. 'This should be easy,' I said.

꞊ꘌ

Half an hour later, looking at the receding city below as the vulture's huge wings picked up a thermal and we soared higher, I realised that we must have been going very fast indeed, though if you closed your eyes it almost felt like standing still. The gigantic bird gained altitude and then, thanks to some mental coaxing from me, started to head south. Although the air was a bit brisk up there I eventually settled back and began to doze, lazily wishing I had brought something to read.

Time passed and I was beginning to think that the journey

would be uneventful, even a little boring. However, about six hours into our flight, Sansonnet called out to no one in particular. 'That's odd. You'd better come and look at this.'

We looked over at where she was pointing. Night was falling and the sky had taken on a worrying aspect. Storm clouds raced across it, twisting darkly at their peaks, like airborne mountains. I couldn't help noticing how their underbellies were stained dark red by the setting sun. Like blood. The next thing I saw, however, really made my mouth go dry.

Flying, or rather, sailing between the clouds was the forbidding vessel I had last seen off the coast of England. Black sails flapped, ragged and frayed in the wind and the bows tossed in the currents of turbulence.

A dark figure stood alone on the ship's deck, facing us.

'It's Him,' I murmured. 'The Thin Man.'

'*What?*' Chassignol sounded almost as panicky as I felt. A clap of thunder and a bolt of lightning seared across the sky in a jagged line, like a scar. A *thump* made the great bird twist in the air. There was a rushing sound and my ears went *pop*.

'We're going down!' Faucon yelled and, sure enough, when I looked into the bird's mind, it was out cold. The lightening hadn't actually hit us but the senile old vulture had had a kind of seizure, out of fear I supposed. If I hadn't felt so frightened myself at that moment, I'm sure I would have felt a twinge of pity for the creature. By now there were clouds tumbling past us as we corkscrewed down towards the ground. I could still make out the silhouette of the ship high above, sailing on through the twilight sky, watching as we plummeted to our deaths.

'We need to get off right now,' Chassignol shouted. He grasped my arm. 'Can you do something?'

I closed my eyes and immediately saw that we had only one choice – I needed to wake the bird, to get it to slow down. If we jumped off now, our wings would shred in an instant and I doubted any of us, even Peregrine, would survive a fall like that.

Then Sansonnet was by my side. 'Concentrate,' she said, taking my arm.

'It's no good. It's practically in a coma. There's no way I can get through.'

'Let's try together,' she said.

It felt weird, going in with someone else – a little like being stuck in a confined space without any trousers on with someone you don't know that well. But after a few tries I got over my squeamishness. Yet each time I almost got inside the bird's mind, my roving thoughts found hers and became distracted.

'Wait,' I said, 'we're blocking each other. It's like two people trying to walk through a door at the same time. We're getting in each other's way. I'll go first.' I closed my eyes and within seconds had it. Good: the bird wasn't dead, just catatonic. 'I'm in, you go,' I said and felt Sansonnet's mind join mine and start to prod about, searching for some brain activity to kick start the vulture's senses.

'I can see the t-tops of trees, we're all going to der-der … *cark* it,' I heard Milan shout.

'Sansonnet ...' Nothing. 'SANSONNET!'

'What? I'm a little bit busy right now.'

'It's not going to wake up in time. We'll have to go in really deep and control it ourselves.' This was going to be like taking over its whole brain function, effectively turning it into a zombie. I turned to Chassignol, speaking very quickly. 'If we get the bird to put the brakes on, don't wait for us, all of you just jump!' I sensed his hesitation. 'Stay put when you land. It'll be easier to find five of you if you don't split up.'

He thought about it for an instant but could see I was right. 'OK,' he said. We had minutes to go before the bird hit the ground and we were all turned into a horrible mess on the side of some rock.

'Now for the tricky bit,' said Sansonnet.

'Ladies first.'

'On the contrary, *laddies* first!'

'Suit yourself.' Going in this deep was something I'd not done before. I found I had to squeeze my brain to fit inside the bird bird's – the mental equivalent of sticking your own head in a vice and turning it until your eyes popped out of their sockets. On the upside, I suddenly could see how this was going to work. 'Sansonnet, we're not going to be able to do this together, but I need you to stay on the edge of the bird's subconscious. If – when – you can see I'm controlling the wings, grab me. I won't be able to come out of its mind quick enough to fly. You'll have to get me to the ground.'

'Got it.'

Jumping really deep into the recesses of the bird's brain was the same as finding myself in a dark cave with hardly any time to work out where the exit was before something terrible happened. Luckily the vulture had only a few main functions, so the cave in question was a small one. Much of the brain was given over to food – rotten meat, to be precise – so I moved elsewhere ... *squawking*, no ... *staring at things malevolently ... perching* – ah, this was more like it ... *flying*! Gotcha! Now, *wings* ...

'Hurry up!'

'Shut up Grue!' said Sansonnet.

Now *flap!* ...

There was another flash of lightening and the vulture's brain jolted as if electrified. There was a searing, white-hot pain behind my eyes and my skull felt like it was going to crack open. I shook my head ... I'd been thrown out. The trees and rocks really were ridiculously close now. Damn! If anything we were going even faster. The others were holding on to various bits of the bird as it tumbled out of the sky, Chassignol looked grim, Grue worse. Only the cousins looked like they were almost enjoying themselves.

'Try again, we've still just got time.' Sansonnet yelled.

I dived back in. *Flap* ... nothing ... *Wings* BEAT ... something stirred. I concentrated, hunkering my mind down and felt the wind, an internal vortex, deep in its own mind, a muscle memory ... tendons flexed.

'That's it, he's got it!' Faucon shouted. Now was their moment.

... the tail feathers twitched and slowly the great vulture extended its wingtips. We jolted upwards and I would have fallen were it not for Sansonnet, who sensed what was happening and grabbed me. 'Jump!' she cried. Chassignol and all the rest must have already gone because then there was just mine, the bird's and Sansonnet's minds, still locked in. I knew I had to get out. I looked for an exit but felt my mind being torn away as Sansonnet wrenched herself free of the vulture and pulled me with her, half carrying me, her wings beating furiously to take the extra weight. The pain was excruciating this time. I had been in so deep that it felt like a huge thorn had been ripped from the back of my head, allowing my consciousness to pour out of the hole.

I must have blacked out because the next thing I knew was the feel of cold night air on my face. My own wings kicked in and I finally slowed. 'Gnagh ... phew,' I felt obliged to remark, heartily relieved to find myself hovering in the air, in good health with all the right number of arms, legs and, most importantly, my own brain. We turned to see the vulture flapping and trying to bank as it hit the ground hard but thankfully not hard enough other than to give it a few nasty bruises.

Then I remembered the flying ship that followed us and grabbed Sansonnet's arm. 'Let's go!' I shouted. Even today I have a clear vision of that terrible vessel sailing the troubled skies with as much serenity and menace as it had sailed the storm waters off the coast of England.

We landed on a thickly wooded outcrop, overlooking a small valley. Night made the scenery inky and indistinct, what little there was left of the Moon was shaded by thick branches and clouds that crabbed their way across the heavens. Exhausted, we wrapped our wings around each other and fell asleep. Finding the others could wait until the morning.

⟨⟩

That night I dreamt that an old man with a lined face, like a walnut, was telling me a story:

Reverie III
TALLWOOD

⤷ 'At the northern end of Tallwood there are some of the oldest and most extravagant trees in the entire forest. Their trunks are as wide as a cottage and each branch supports a blaze of bright leaves, so that the sunlight down below is green and rather mysterious.

Many years ago, long before the Wandering Kings had come and then settled in the Keep, a Nightingale lived in the uppermost canopy of the tallest of all the trees. She was a magnificent bird, far larger and more colourful than the Nightingales these days, and she sang exquisitely. Her voice was pure and it carried for miles through the forest, caressing the air and filling the lonely places. What is more, she sang all day.

The reason for this somewhat obsessive behaviour was that she was deeply in love. High up in the clear sky she saw a cloud every morning, drifting slowly by, like a floating lamb. This was the object of her love and whilst he idea of anybody falling for a cloud may seem silly to you, it had to be remembered that the Nightingale had a beautiful voice, and not necessarily a great intellect.

To her, the cloud was really an angel. The gentle wisps of whiteness at the edges were his wings and every morning, as she looked up, she saw new expressions of love for her on his face, as the currents coaxed the cloud into different shapes. And every day she flew through the forest, chasing her love through the skies and singing her heart out to him as the cloud drifted by, totally unaware of all the fuss it was causing.

⤷ Now, far below, under the gloomy canopy, a woodsman lived on his own. His was a lonely life of tree cutting, clearing and light household chores. He wasn't sure why he was there. Nobody ever gave him any money and he could not remember having applied for the job.

What he was certain of, though, was that he loved the Nightingale and she loved him. Her voice to his ears seemed to be the very expression of all the beauty that was so lacking in his life.

It made him want to laugh and dance to think that the forest was putting on this display for his benefit alone. 'I am the only living creature out here, apart from the wild piglets and my love, the Nightingale, could not possibly be singing for their benefit,' he reasoned.

His heart ached with joy and he wept hot tears of gratitude for the great gift he had been given.

This state of affairs went on for years. Every morning the Nightingale would wake and, shaking the morning dew that covered her feathers, uttered her first clear notes at the lilac skies.

As the sun rose, the cloud would appear and her song would reach new heights of joy. And far below, amongst the bushes, the woodman would blow his nose on an old sock and smile lovingly up at the trees.

)— Sadly, nothing ever stays the same forever. One day, the woodsman was drowned in the lake.

He had been clearing brush from the slippery bank, when one of the piglets he thought so little of broke from cover without warning and knocked him in the drink. The water was deep and very cold and the poor man could not swim.

The Nightingale died shortly after. Of old age.

Now, both died happy, having spent their lives dedicated to love, which is more than can be said for most of us. The piglets, with no one to hunt them, did very well and began to roam about in large numbers, oinking happily in the undergrowth. And the cloud serenely drifted across the landscape.'

His story finished, the old man got up, winked a rheumy eye at me and hobbled away.

It is very rare for a Vampire to be able to
fly until after his, or her thirtieth year.
Flight has as much to do with confidence
as wingspan. Many Eltern attribute
flightless Vampires to loss of magical
ability more than any other factors.

Grue, *Misc Notes.*

Chapter 12
rainbow Caves

I woke in the early hours, with an uncomfortable feeling that the latest dream was somehow about Sansonnet and me and my best friend, Chassignol.

Dew hung from the lower branches, which were richly draped in spiders' webs that stood out in silver and faint pink as the early morning rays of light penetrated the dense canopy of pine and mountain ash. It was certainly beautiful but I was grateful that spiders rarely come out at first light. The webs were pretty large and so, I assumed, were the vicious creatures that had made them the night before. I really can't stand spiders.

Sansonnet woke shortly after me. That morning we were somehow embarrassed in each other's company, so I did my best to stick to business. 'Are you ready?' I asked.

'Yes,' said Sansonnet, nodding at her feet. After a pause. 'They can't be far'

I'd already done some searching before she woke. 'I am picking something up. Down there.' I pointed further down the valley where some rocks were lying in a messy heap. Sansonnet followed the line of my arm.

'O K', she said. 'Best be off ... shall we?'

Half an hour later we had found them. By all accounts they'd had a better night than us. Sheltered by rocks, Chassignol had decided they could risk a fire and Peregrine had stunned a rabbit, so they'd even had a spot of supper. 'Any left?' I asked. My teeth always tingle when I am peckish.

'His fer-friend went that way,' said Milan.

'Down that hole,' said Faucon, pointing.

'No big deal,' I made an effort to look like I wasn't particularly bothered and ambled over to where Grue and Chassignol were talking.

'It has to be tonight,' Grue was saying.

'You're sure?' Chassignol looked paler even than Grue and

I wondered if he'd been injured in the crash.

'Of course I am,' stated Grue flatly and stalked off to stand under some trees and brood. Chassignol was fiddling with what looked like a sextant from the Sprite.

'That thing work?' I asked.

'Hopefully,' he said, barely looking up. Then, with a ghost of a smile, 'or we're in trouble.'

'Any idea where we are?'

'Pretty much,' Chassignol squinted at the horizon, toward the rising sun in the east. 'In fact, this whole outcrop and the valley below are near where we want to be.'

'Good,' I replied and then wondered why we weren't talking about what needed to be said. Then again, that was ever the case between us. We never even spoke of that terrible night when we were children and he seemed to want it that way. For someone usually so open, Chassignol certainly had a lot of secrets, these days. I decided to take the risk. 'That was the Thin Man I saw last night.' Chassignol jumped and nearly dropped the sextant. From the corner of my eye I saw Grue stiffen. He must have overheard, so I lowered my voice to a whisper. 'I know it was Him, it was the same ship I saw at Truant Island and then during the storm off the coast of England.'

'We ... you,' he corrected himself, smiling sadly in a slightly annoying way, 'cannot be sure of that. You've only seen a ship, not the person.'

'And my dreams ... ?'

'Are probably just dreams,' Chassignol finished my sentence.

'You know that's not true, where I'm concerned. You of all people, Chass.'

'What have you *actually* seen, Moüsch?"

I shrugged. By now we had moved closer to one another and when I looked into Chassignol's face I saw some of his old tenderness, his strength and his humour still there, at the fringes of his features. He wiped the back of his hand against his mouth and I couldn't help noticing that it was shaking more than it had been on the mule train. 'Can you,' he swallowed, '... for me anyway, at least try to do what I asked you before all this?'

I snorted, despite myself. I also felt confused at this sudden change in direction. Chassignol – the old Chassignol, anyway, was never this erratic. 'What, that time thing again? No, that's impossible. Chassignol, we've already been through this!'

'Some people would say that what you do is impossible,' he pointed out gravely.

'Yes but ... '

'If I asked you to, would you try?'

'No, it would be a waste of time.'

'But what if you tried with Sansonnet?'

'This isn't like Seeing, Chassignol, or even making things move. It's too complex. Magic uses the laws of nature, it doesn't break them, it simply amplifies them that's why it seems so amazing. This smashes all the laws of Nature and rubs its nose into the carpet. It's impossible.'

He glowered at me, like a sulky teenager. 'Impossible, you say.'

'Chassignol, you worry me lately.' But he had already gone. I looked after him and then felt a shadow move behind me. Sansonnet had crept up. I was regretting forcing the encounter with my friend, and perhaps unfairly I suddenly felt annoyed at her.

'So what were you two talking about?'

'It was private,' I all but snapped back.

Sansonnet ignored the tone and asked, gently, 'Is Chassignol alright?'

'He would be if people didn't expect him to be perfect all the time.'

Sansonnet went red. Tiny sparks danced in her eyes. 'If you're referring to the Standing Stones, I didn't ask him to save me, he could have saved Bud. It was ... I don't know, I've gone over it a thousand times in my mind since and reached the same conclusion every time, it was like he didn't save Bud on purpose. I was fine,' she tapped her leather breastplate hard, 'Bud was the one in trouble.'

But I was getting angry, too. 'There are lots of things you don't know about Chassignol.'

'And I suppose you do?' said Sansonnet caustically.

'Yes, as a matter of fact, I do.'

'Like what? How about you try me, Moüsch? You complain that Chassignol is secretive but I'm coming to the conclusion you're as bad as each other.'

That was it. I turned sharply and grasped Sansonnet by the shoulders, so that I could look her straight in the eye. 'OK, you asked for it. Years ago, when we were children, we were in the Rainbow Caves – exploring.'

Sansonnet, who had been struggling against my grip, went still. She glared at me. '*And?*'

'And there was an accident. I fell.' I let go; Sansonnet didn't move.

'How?'

'These,' and I pointed at my crooked legs. I actually felt self-regarding tears prick my eyes. I was so young. 'These stupid things let me down, as usual. But Chassignol didn't. We'd been there two or three days with Chassignol's father. Chassignol hated it: caverns, climbing and such like just aren't his thing. Anyway, for once I was excelling at something physical that he couldn't get the hang of. After a few days, he wanted to go back. But Chassignol's father was a kind man – he could see it was doing my confidence a lot of good, so he persuaded Chassignol to stay. For my sake! Anyway towards the end of the last day, there was an underground cliff, I was too busy showing off and I didn't see it. I fell.'

'How old were you?' Sansonnet was now looking concerned.

'Just Milk Imps. Our wings hadn't grown yet.'

'And you were in those caves? You must have been mad.'

'We were roped. Chassignol's father was leading and when I slipped he had his back to me, so I pulled him over the ledge too. Chassignol was quicker. He braced himself against a rock and was able to hold me and his father.'

'Couldn't his father just fly?'

'He was wearing a pack, so his wings were strapped. He

couldn't let go of the rope to untie his pack, so there we were, hanging over a rock into darkness. My sword dropped and I remember it spiralling away into the void. It fell for a very long time. And the rope was beginning to slip in Chassignol's hands. We were surely going to pull him over the edge too, but he held on, although he would have died with us.'

Sansonnet shuddered. 'How did you get out of it?'

'Chassignol's father cut his rope.'

'He killed himself!'

'No. He saved us. He may have thought that he could get his pack off in time, free his wings and fly up. But Chassignol and I both heard the thump of him landing on the rocks far, far below at the foot of the void and we both knew he was dead.'

'And Chassignol was able to pull you up?'

'Yes, that's why I owe him my life and also why I owe him my loyalty. Before his father sacrificed himself, he could have easily thrown down another rope and saved his own father.'

'But he would have had to let go of you.'

'Exactly, but he didn't. He made a difficult choice, just like he did with you and Bud. And just like Bud's death, he will have to live with the consequences of letting his father die for the rest of his life.'

Sansonnet held my hand. There were tears in her eyes. 'Moüsch, I'm sorry.'

I pulled away as gently as I could. 'Perhaps it's Chassignol we should both be apologising to,' I said quietly.

But in the end neither of us found the right moment. Had we done so, I often wonder whether things would have worked out differently.

'Vampires are like Humans in one major respect: Over the centuries they have both gradually turned their backs on magic (or what we call Lore), attempting instead to rely on a natural grace and cleverness for survival. This is a mistake.'

Count Dracul of Sigishoura. Vampire Eltern.

Chapter 13

bereck's muster

We spent the rest of the day mooching about in the forest, avoiding insects and each other. At about mid-afternoon, however, when the sun had started to dip, Sansonnet came to find me.

'Hi,' she said.

'Hello,' I replied, a little formally, though secretly glad we were still talking.

'Grue says he's ready and he needs some help.'

'Right, I'll go and get Chassignol.'

'No, he's asked for you.'

I was slightly surprised. 'OK, um, tell him I'll be there in five minutes. I have to do something first.'

I went some distance off and looked out at the view. I needed some time to think. The mountains to the west were high, almost impossibly so. We Vampires had been around for a long time but I found it hard to imagine the mesmerising force that created these peaks.

To the east, the mountains gave way gradually to a broad plateau, studded with strange volcanic protrusions – humpback hills, covered with emerald vegetation. Through the thin mist I could see a long river snaking its way around these hillocks.

Each river in this great land I had heard, was ruled by a Dragon. These Dragon Kings apparently lived in magnificent palaces under the water with great echoing marble halls – vast dwellings of even larger and more ancient sea creatures that once lived in the oceans. Their ceilings were held up by buttresses made from the ribs of the great fish that once swam the oceans in prehistory.

The largest river of all in China was called the Great Yellow River and its Dragon ruler was said to be so huge that a Vampire could not look upon more than one scale of its body at any one time. Just one glance from this great beast could burn a whole city to ash. If the Yellow River Dragon King left or died, then all of China would sink beneath the waves.

I suddenly felt very small and alone in this strange land that could harbour, let alone conceive of, such beasts.

$\gtrsim$

Grue, when I found him, was half way up a tree on the edge of a small glade. He was wearing a large hat that I'd never seen before. I'm not joking, it was covered with sparkly bits. 'Got a bunny in there?'

Grue glared at me. 'Take these', he said tersely, throwing down a leather bag full of what felt like a lot of small stones, 'and spread them in a circle around the clearing. They *must* be evenly spaced. Place the largest crystal in the exact centre of the circle, then find the body of a mouse or a small bird and bring me its heart.'

'Oh yuk, are you quite sure?'

'Just do it.'

Half an hour later I was back, carrying the still warm heart of a sparrow fledgling, which I'd found lying on the forest floor, its wing badly broken. It was half-starved and nearly dead but I still felt a little guilty about finishing it off with my sword. Unlike Humans, Vampires rarely kill for any reason other than self-defence. We don't even kill our food; as you know, we only suck it a bit. Grue was still up the tree, muttering to himself as he carved a series of complicated-looking runes and shapes into the bark with the tip of his sword. He kept glancing at the sky as if worried about the time. He looked up briefly at my approach, then continued what he was doing.

'Cut the heart into sixteen slices and bury it ten rapier lengths to the north, outside the circle of crystals', he said, his back to me. I made a rude sign behind his head. 'And grow up', he muttered. Feeling silly, I went about my business in silence for a few minutes, and he did his.

By and by I asked the question I had been dying to ask since Grue had brought up the subject of the Muster. 'Grue?'

'Yes, what is it now?'

'Have you really done this before?'

He paused what he was doing and sighed. 'Of course, otherwise how would I know whether I could do it or not?'

Fair enough, I thought. 'How come?'

Cue more sighing – it was like working with a steam iron. 'How come ... *what?*'

'How come you've carried out Bereck's Muster? It's not exactly something you learn from your mentor.'

'My father taught me.'

Grue's family were one of the oldest and richest Vampire families living in the Keep – respected, even feared. His ancestors had made their money mining diamonds thousands of miles south and rubies on the Russian Steppes. As said, rumours had flown about for a while, that on the quiet they had sided with Corbeau, but nothing was ever proven. Even so, no-one at the Keep knew much about them. You saw them about once in a while but they were always pretty aloof, so people kept out of their way. Most of the time they looked so miserable you were silently relieved not to have anything to do with them. I recalled that Grue's father was once one of the Elterns' closest advisors and I'd seen him walking with them many times. A tall, almost skeletal figure, unusually pale, even for a Vampire; the Eltern with their eccentric way of going through life actually seemed a little in awe of him. He was also known to dabble in Old Lore, so I supposed some of it must have rubbed off on Grue. As I looked at Grue, in his frankly daft hat, I reflected that it was odd that you can grow up with someone but not really know them.

'Good at that sort of thing, is he?' I said.

'Yes, he is,' Grue replied. 'He believes, as do I, that the old traditions must be kept up. The Lore is there for a reason.'

'What's that then?'

'To protect us from our enemies. It also forms part of our traditions, our culture and what makes us Vampires. The Old Lore is also a discipline, one in which most Vampires are sadly lacking.' He looked at me pointedly. For Grue this was a huge speech. 'Now I'd be grateful if you could get on with what you are doing. We haven't much time.'

The sliver of the New Moon rose steadily in the sky as the Sun began to disappear behind the outrageously imposing mountains, which formed the foothills of the Himalayas to the west. In its dying phase the sun shone with different colours for a time, turning the snow-capped peaks into a series of giant birthday cakes with multi-coloured icing. Darkness crept in from the east and frost quickly formed on the tops of the trees surrounding the clearing.

'It's a bit parky out here,' remarked Faucon, who always felt the cold.

'Can't you keep *quiet*,' hissed Grue.

Faucon shrugged. 'Temper.'

To tell the truth, we were all on edge. Grue because it might not work, presumably, and the rest of us because we were about to witness a rite that had not been performed successfully, with witnesses, for over a thousand years. Grue had spent the rest of the afternoon carving what seemed like an endless, mindless list of shapes, runes and half-formed ancient lettering onto four of the larger pines at each corner of the glade. I had to admit that it looked pretty impressive when he was done. The tender core of the small bird's heart lay buried in the centre, along with the largest crystal and I had spent a long time making sure the rest were as evenly spaced as Grue had insisted.

Thankfully, Grue had now removed his hat.

For a long time nothing happened and I found my mind wandering. Then, very faintly, I thought I heard music coming from some distance behind us. I may have imagined it, so I looked enquiringly at Peregrine who, despite being older than the rest of us, usually had the best hearing. He nodded at me and cocked his head in the direction the music seemed to be coming from. It stopped. Seconds later it started again, this time much closer but from another direction altogether. The music got louder, until we all heard it. *Panpipes*, I saw Sansonnet mouth at Milan. By now I could hear each lilting note, as it drifted through the trees towards us. Then, abruptly, it cut off. Nobody moved. Then something rustled and a Faun stepped into the moonlit glade.

Humans always imagine that most magical creatures are the same size as them. If this was the case, a lot more would have been discovered by now. Most supernatural entities are almost invisible to the naked eye, through a mixture of size, magic and camouflage. The Faun that now stood before us was about our size, that is to say not a lot bigger than your smallest finger.

The Faun seemed to be in a daze; his pipes now hung from the tips of his fingers and his head was lowered, as if in prayer.

Far larger than him (about twice the size) was the bloody great troll that came crashing through the bushes after him. His skin was a greyish-green colour, a tuft of dark brown hair stood straight up on his scalp and more hair, as thick as the bristles on a pig, carpeted his neck and heavily-muscled shoulders.

'Told you,' said Milan, 'now we're all ger-going to die.'

'I wouldn't be alarmed,' said Grue, visibly more relaxed than he had been half an hour beforehand, 'they can't see or hear us …, not until I complete the rite.' And indeed, for the moment both the Faun and the Troll stood there, gazing blankly into the distance, their eyes glazed and their mouths agape, as if they had been sleepwalking through the woods and had decided to stop for a rest. The Troll stank.

Half an hour passed and our two new friends were joined by a pair of underfed-looking wood Faies, an elderly dwarf carrying an axe that was far too large for him and a pack of Weres whose breath billowed in the frosty air as their menacing yellow eyes ranged to and fro, not seeing us but somehow sensing our presence and resenting it with their souls.

'Unbelievable, they can somehow feel that this is an enchantment,' remarked Sansonnet, 'and they're trying to see around it. My father told me he came across some of the older Weres during the War who seemed almost entirely resistant to magic.'

'What do we do now?' asked Faucon.

'We wait,' replied Grue. As he said that, Chassignol, who had remained silent until now, pointed towards a dense clump of trees and bushes about thirty paces away.

'Look,' he said. From the darkest part of the forest a few lights winked on. Then off. Then on again. They circled one another for a few minutes and then slowly came to a standstill, where they hovered in the air. It was almost as if despite the strong lure of the Muster, they were resisting it, or at least holding back until they were sure it was safe.

'What are they?' asked Sansonnet.

Chassignol frowned, as if dredging up a memory. 'Sprites, I think.' It wasn't long until they were off again, arranging themselves in a line. They stopped their hovering and shot up in the air, and like an arrow, they fell into the open circle of trees and hung there like decorative fairy lights, above everyone's heads.

'Oooh, gosh, I thought they were extinct,' said Sansonnet, not taking her eyes off them.

'Not around here it would seem,' said Grue looking as austere as ever but clearly tremendously pleased with himself.

Something moved like a wraith behind us.

We all went very still. Whatever, or whoever it was had managed to creep up on our exposed backs. All of us, to a Vampire, realised we'd made a big mistake not posting a lookout. We waited, the hair on the backs of our necks rising. The voice, when it came, was calm and full of good humour.

'Ah, Bereck's Muster. Very expertly performed, I must say. Can I be of assistance?' Very slowly we all turned, and saw another Vampire standing behind us. He was much the same in appearance as us, except for the kaleidoscope of colours that patterned the down on his body. He was very old but there was an energy about him I had never encountered before in a Vampire, except perhaps Raptor. His eyes twinkled, and when he smiled he revealed a set of canines that were far smaller than ours. He spread his small wings as he bowed low to us. As he did so, the pale moonlight lit the diaphanous webbing in planes of purple and gold. 'May I be of service?'

We had found the Dragon Clan.

'There are nearly always two reasons for doing something: A really good reason and the real reason.'

Militant. *Many Musings*. Chapter 46, verse 24.

the dragon clan

The sun streamed in through my bedroom window and flooded the space in the rafters with light. I felt clean white sheets beneath my fingertips and a soft pillow under my noddle. *I'm dead*, was my first thought. Vampires don't get this comfortable unless they're in a coffin or what passes for Vampire heaven. I was brought sharply back to reality by a nasty cold wave of air where my soft downy sheet had been moments before.

'Get up you fer-feckless Vampire!'

It was Milan and Faucon and they seemed to be in a good mood about something. Milan threw open a window. More cold air followed the sunlight into my bedroom. 'It's exactly the same as the Keep!' they both shouted, 'only a bit der–d–different,' Milan added, as an afterthought. Faucon nodded and I reflected that Milan never actually stuttered when they spoke together.

Stretching, I sat up in bed and stared out of the window. Below, a courtyard was positively teaming with activity. Brightly coloured Vampires bustled to and fro on individual errands or were just out for a morning stroll. Milan was right. At first glance, the layout of the Dragon Clan's Eyrie mirrored that, almost exactly, of the Keep. It was so similar that I felt an unexpected jolt of homesickness. Getting up, I pulled on a silk dressing gown that someone had helpfully left hanging by the bed and strolled over to the window for a closer look in daylight. Apart from the rainbow of reds and blues and greens marking the Vampires below, this could have been home. Even the stonework on the battlements, protecting the Eyrie from invasion, looked the same.

'Apparently,' said Faucon, reading my thoughts, 'when the Dragon Eyrie was built during the great migrations, they used the same plans, stonemasons and everything.' I scanned the horizon, noting that we seemed to be still quite close to where we camped two nights ago. Silver and white peaks decorated the horizon to the west and a thick forest of pine carpeted the valleys and hills all around us. The air was fresh and sharp with cold, in spite of the sun.

The night before seemed like a disjointed dream. After the Dragon himself had put in an appearance, we made introductions. He smiled kindly at Sansonnet, who blushed, and then he stared for a long time at me until I began to feel uncomfortable. To Chassignol he accorded the respect due a leader but I couldn't help noticing a reserve spring up immediately between them. It was Grue whom he singled out for the most praise. 'A very accomplished Muster, worthy of my finest practitioners of Lore. You must have had a very fine teacher.'

'I *did*,' said Grue, with more feeling than I'd ever heard from him before. 'My father.'

'You must converse with some of my practitioners, perhaps you have a lot to discuss.' He finished by inviting us all back to his Eyrie.

'What about this rabble?' Peregrine had asked, pointing at the crowd of magical creatures the Muster had now gathered. 'Can't have 'em hangin' around all night.'

'Piece of cake!' The Dragon waved his hand at the group who, one by one, seemed to wake and melt into the night. The ability to break a Muster with nothing more than a flick of his hand was clearly a big achievement. Grue stood there with a look on his face I'd never seen before. At first I thought he was seriously ill, then I realised he was just perplexed.

Now we'd found the Dragon Clan I felt better than I had since Bud was killed. 'Where's Chassignol?' I asked.

'We went to s-see him,' said Milan.

'But he was busy and asked not to be disturbed.' Faucon didn't seem bothered. He continued. 'We've been invited to a feast in our honour tonight but some bloke who works for the Dragon stuck his head round the door this morning and said we were free to spend the rest of the day wandering around, as long as we didn't nick anything.'

'He didn't really say that, did he?'

'Not really – the bit about pinching stuff, that was Grue. He's gone off with the Dragon's Chief Alchemist – says they've got a lot to talk about.' Faucon gave me an ironic look. 'It might be love.'

⁂

Half an hour later we all sat in the shade of some maple trees and ate a hearty breakfast. It was all odd but delicious, apart from the dried snake and Troll blood porridge. I was finishing off my third cup of something called *tea* when this minute fellow, with midnight-blue down covering his whole body, came trailing in. He carried something small on a cushion.

'What's that little chap got 'old of?' asked Peregrine through a mouthful of what looked and tasted like scrambled eggs.

'A key, I think.' Sansonnet flashed a bright smile. 'Can we help?'

'Shuur,' the man replied beaming, 'Keys to Eyrie. Fleedom of city.'

'Thank you,' said Sansonnet extending a hand to take them, 'What are they for?'

'Shuur,' the beam widened. 'Keys to Eyrie.'

Sansonnet smiled back. 'Thanks *again*, does this mean we can go anywhere?'

The smile faltered and then resumed with interest. If he smiled any more, I thought, the top of his head might fall off.

'Keys to Eyrie. Fleedom. Shuur,' he said again.

'Lets assoome he doesn't understand what we are sayin',' said Peregrine.

'Ker-keys or no ker-keys, I'm off to look at the market,' said Milan, wiping his mouth. 'I saw some incredible l-l-looking swords.'

'I'll come too cos,' said Faucon, kicking back his chair.

'Likewise, I'm sure,' commented Peregrine, grimacing as he finished his tea, which must have gone stone cold by now in the mountain air. This left Sansonnet and me. I hummed to myself and drummed my fingers on the table. Sansonnet held up the keys and gave them a shake, which made them catch the light and sparkle.

'*Fleedom of City?*' She grinned. 'Sounds too good to miss … let's go exploring, I say.'

'Where to?' I found myself grinning back.

'Well, did you happen to notice those steps over there?' She pointed to the corner of the courtyard where four Vampire Guards stood in front of some stone steps leading down into what looked like a cellar. Each guard wore a highly polished sword and a stern expression.

'Not until now,' I admitted. 'Looks interesting though.'

We got up and sauntered over, kicking stray stones about, whistling and doing our best to look aimless. As we got to the top of the flight of steps, we halted. The vaulted opening was dark almost from the third step down, which seemed unusual, given how bright it was in the courtyard. A dull, peculiarly foetid breeze came up through the archway and made my nose wrinkle. Sansonnet made as if to go down the stairs, a studied look of mild curiosity playing across her brow. As if pulled by an invisible string, all four guards sprang into action and blocked her path, swords drawn. We exchanged looks; then, dipping her hand into her bag, Sansonnet pulled out the keys. 'Keys to Eyrie,' she said, dangling them in one of the guard's faces.

I didn't think we'd get away with it, and for a moment or two they seemed loath to budge. Then, their expressions remaining impassive, they each took one step back and allowed us to pass. 'Hurry up,' hissed Sansonnet. 'In case they change their minds.'

Before too long the passageway became uncomfortably gloomy. The steps crept down into the darkness for what seemed like an eternity, then, just as I was beginning to think we'd die of old age before we reached the bottom, they levelled off and we found ourselves standing at the entrance of a long tunnel. A smattering of lamps, posted high on the walls, burned dimly, revealing an ancient archway in well-dressed stone. The two pillars, which supported the ceiling, were carved with a selection of hideous monsters and ghouls. Sansonnet and I stared at them for some time. 'They almost seem to be moving,' she remarked, and shivered. And perhaps it was just a trick of the light, but they really did seem almost to be in constant flux, snaking the length of the walls, as if to escape their surroundings and make their way up the stairs.

'Shall we?' I extended an arm down the tunnel where more torches made dim little orange orbs in the inky blackness. I half hoped she'd say no.

'Of course,' she replied and so off we went – more slowly now, the darker it became. Also, the further we went down the tunnel, the worse the smell seemed to get. The torches gradually became more spaced apart and the stone-clad walls gave way to bare rock. We were no longer in a Vampire-made tunnel but in what looked to be a natural cave, deep below the Eyrie. The floor continued its gradual downward slope and after about half an hour, I began to sense that we were approaching the end of our journey, and that it lay at the very root of the mountain. Abruptly the tunnel widened into what may have been a chamber, as the light from the last torch disappeared around a corner.

Initially there was no sound but the darkness itself became oppressive, as if the weight of something unseen was pressing down on the air around us. I suddenly felt very blind and very exposed, as the down on the back of my neck rose to currents of air from an indiscernible source.

Up until then I had assumed that we were in a fairly creepy place but that we were alone.

'W H O,' came a voice that managed to boom and drawl at the same time, 'A R E Y O U ?' Vampire night vision is excellent but I couldn't make a thing out in the chamber. Apart from being very loud, the voice was coming from far above my head, which led me to suspect that it came from something either very large or, if we were really lucky, a dwarf up a ladder.

'If you get eaten first, I'll tell the others you died bravely,' I whispered to Sansonnet who'd grabbed hold of my hand.

'WHAT?' boomed the disembodied voice far above us. 'Who's whispering? I can't abide whispering, it's so ...' the voice paused, as if searching for the right word, '*whispery*.'

There was silence.

'Is *whispery* even a word?' asked Sansonnet eventually.

Something moved, a drawn out sliding noise: if I wasn't mistaken, it was very much as if scales were moving across a stone floor. Bang goes the dwarf theory, I thought. Hot breath passed over my face and body, an inhalation and then more hot air, filling the room. I identified the smell as the same as the one we had picked up at the mouth of the tunnel, but less stale and therefore not so unpleasant. It put me in mind of saltpetre and tar. The voice came again – rich, the tone musing.

'Mmm ... Vampire, certainly. Well travelled ... not from these parts. Duchess and male, small-ish ... . Old Country, I would say. I smell fear, yes, but a goal ...' there was a long pause. 'What are you seeking?'

I don't know about Sansonnet, but I was impressed. I decided to throw caution to the winds. 'The Chalice, since you ask.'

'The Chalice! Oh, ho! And what makes you think you'll find it here, my fretful little creature, so full of doubt yet so strong in purpose.'

'*Is* it here?' I asked.

'No, it is not,' the voice was grave but it also sounded slightly defensive.

'Do you know where it is?'

'No more than you.'

'Who are you?'

'For most, I am Nemesis.'

'*What* are you, then?' I felt Sansonnet move forward a pace and I sensed her arm stretching out in the darkness, trying to touch what was in front of us and seeming to take up the whole cavernous space. I was impressed by her bravery. Yep, she'll definitely get eaten first, I thought.

'I am ... ' there was a pause and this time an enormous inhalation of breath. Something was about to happen, but whoever he was his intention had been so well hidden that I had no idea what it was until just before he did it. The inhalation stopped and was followed by a sudden exhalation of tremendous power. A vast pillar of flame rose up hundreds of feet to the roof of the cavern, licking the walls and scorching the granite until it glowed red, then white hot, lighting the chamber as brightly as day.

Before us stood the most magnificent creature I had ever seen. Dark green scales, each the size of a platter protected his massive flanks, and these gradually became smaller, lighter green, then bronze and finally red, like the leaves in autumn as they met along the line of his back. His claws were a flawless diamond and the scales around his shoulders petered out to be replaced by a dense plumage of gold and copper-coloured feathers. When he turned to look at us, his eyes were filled with all the wisdom and experience of the ages. 'I am ... well, I think you can see that for yourselves,' he said and smiled kindly at us, with teeth the size of scythes.

'Hello, Mr Dragon.'

'Pleased to meet you, Your Dragon-ness.'

The Dragon bowed his head. His great eyes twinkled. 'It is always a pleasure to meet new people, especially such distinguished guests of Qi LiFang, from the Old Country.'

'LiFang who?'

'You call him, *the Dragon*, I believe.'

'Er, yes, sorry about that,' I admitted, embarrassed, given the present company. I rummaged about in my head for something to say. 'Are you one of the great river dragons?'

'Oh, no! I'm a mere lizard compared with them, no older than their last moult.'

'Is this your mountain, then?' asked Sansonnet.

'Not really, but I am retired from dragoning about the place now, you might say ... so I reside here as Qi LiFang's guest and ...' he added, after a pause, 'his friend, I hope.'

'But don't you get bored down here all day?'

'No. I sleep, I ponder and I remember. I have a lifetime of memories to contemplate. I was born in the firestorms that forged the rocks and blew out the caverns the few remaining of my kind still call home. You might not know it yet but you and I are very similar in many ways.'

'After such an interesting past, being stuck down here does sound a teensy bit dull,' Sansonnet remarked.

The Dragon smiled ruefully. 'Oh, and I wait,' he added, as if just remembering.

'What for?'

'Well, you see, young lady, before a Dragon dies he has one last glorious flight, one last deed to perform. I am waiting for that.'

'But how will you know when it's time?'

The Dragon paused. 'You know, I'm not really at all sure … I suppose I'll … know. I mean I *could* go now, this afternoon perhaps – but it would seem a waste just to flap about for a bit, then perish. Yes. I think I'll wait for a special occasion.'

The rock above was cooling, going from a white glare at its hottest, to a dull red glow; bathing the chamber in darker colours, so that the Dragon began to take on a distinctly creepy and brooding appearance. Despite his kindly demeanour, there was a power about him that left us in no doubt that he could crush us and destroy the Eyrie and most probably the whole mountain without breaking sweat.

I bowed low. 'It has been nice meeting you, Mr … er …'

"– my name is 𝓧eurfgard 𝓓'eowuqcpiwqhui 𝓐't 𝓦quoqioovovdbidbugskanfxhajk'. He smiled again, through the gloom. 'But you can call me Xeurf … for short.'

'It has been a pleasure to meet you, Xeurf, my name is Sansonnet and this is my friend Moüsch,' said Sansonnet, bobbing off a curtsy of all things. 'I hope we meet again,' she added as we both turned to go back down the tunnel.

'I hope so too, my dear. Goodbye for now. Goodbye.'

A few minutes later we were back outside in the morning sunlight, breathing heavily and laughing, more with jangling nerves than anything else. Once we had got halfway down the tunnel, we had both broken into a flight that lasted until we got to the top of the steps. The guards pretended not to see us. We crossed the courtyard to where we could see the cousins arguing with somebody selling swords.

It was market day by all accounts. After giving the Milan and Faucon a thumbnail sketch of what had just happened to us, we decided not to take any more risks and spend the rest of the day shopping and keeping out of trouble. Apart from our swords and breastplates, most of our kit had been lost during the storm on board the *Sprite*, so we had a fair amount of stuff to stock up on. We still had some gold and jewels, mainly rubies, but most of the places just waved aside our attempts to pay, insisting that it was a gift, as honoured guests and Vampire cousins. Milan and Faucon had set their hearts on a beautiful pair of swords but it proved difficult to get the stall owner to agree to sell. He insisted they were family heirlooms and just there for show. In the end, Milan unstrapped his own sword and presented it to the trader.

The stall owner held the sheath gingerly at first, judging the weight with an expert eye. He then took a large magnifying glass from under the counter and studied the jewels, which decorated the hilt. Only then did he unsheathe the sword and test the blade by bending it from the tip and watching how the metal sprang back with a healthy *twonk!* sound. He then tested the sharpness on an old strip of leather. After a few more minutes' deliberation he turned to Milan with a broad smile. 'At your service!' he exclaimed, grinning, and presented Milan with his own curved sword.

Milan was delighted. He made a few practice swishes with it, then seemed to have an idea. He paused, rummaged around in his pockets and drew a silk handkerchief from it, which he tossed into the air and sliced neatly in two with a flick of his wrist as it wafted down.

'Ber-bloody hell,' he said studying the curve of the blade that made it so different from our own straight rapiers. He strapped his sword belt back on and wandered off with Faucon, presumably to find more things to chop up.

Peregrine, Sansonnet and I wandered through the market at our own pace, picking up new rucksacks, rope, hunting knives and other things that might come in handy. Even if we found the Chalice here, at the Eyrie, we would still have to make our way back through hostile country. Sansonnet found a new flint and strike that the stall keeper insisted would light a fire even in the pouring rain or a typhoon. Peregrine bought a set of throwing knives that had been made by a master metalsmith. They came in a leather satchel, which strapped tightly to his back, allowing him to draw them quickly and give his arms room to move. After a couple of throws at a large target behind the stall he turned in a blur, pulling a third blade from behind his back and threw it to where Faucon was standing fifty paces away. The piece of fruit he was tucking into flew out of his hand, skewered though the middle by Peregrine's spinning blade. Faucon was so surprised he bit his fingers.

Looking about at leisure, there was something about the colouring of these Vampires, which almost looked like fancy dress. The habit they had of going everywhere at a half-run seemed almost comic. They clearly found us equally amusing. Everywhere we went, there would be a small group of Imps, in reds, greens and golds; milk-fangs showing as they grinned at us like miniature clowns (albeit slightly grubby ones), laughing and clapping whenever we did anything unexpected. The small duchesses seemed to find Sansonnet especially fascinating. She responded to the attention with a kind smile, patiently letting them touch her hair or hold her hand as they showed her around the market.

At one stall Sansonnet stood in profile to me, next to a very elderly Nosferatu with extraordinarily long nails. All of her attention was taken with listening patiently to a long explanation about the uses of Troll blood for curing warts. As she nodded her head politely a stray hair or two escaped from the coils that were held in place by a braid of sapphires and cut diamonds. She pushed the hair back behind her ear and smiled. I found myself admiring her finely tapered fangs and the elegant fold of her wings that caught the light and reflected it back a hundred different shades of silver and electric blue. I thought about her holding my hand in the cave.

Our larger wings were a particular source of interest. I'd even caught the older Dragon Clan Nosferatu glancing at them curiously when they thought we wouldn't notice. No one was so forward as to ask for a demonstration of flying but Milan and Faucon gave them one anyway – swooping and diving around the central courtyard of the Eyrie, and generally making bleedin' idiots of themselves according to Peregrine. By the time they finished, we'd drawn a crowd of some hundred or so Dragon Clan. Then a squadron of guards appeared, barked a few orders and the crowd melted respectfully away.

After a bit of rummaging around in the market, I found what I was looking for. Vampires have an excellent sense of direction; nevertheless, I had always been fascinated by compasses. This one was a work of art. It was enclosed in a small case, made of rich, orangey gold. The case protected it from breaking if you decided to chuck it about and I guessed it must have been a travelling compass, built to withstand fire, water, and being lost for centuries. The compass face was creamy, made of pearl, and three of the points had been carefully inlaid with emeralds. North however, was decorated with a small stone I did not recognise. I insisted on giving the owner fifteen pecks of gold dust, as it was by far the most beautiful object in his collection.

Chassignol joined us for lunch and seemed to be in a better mood. Sansonnet even acknowledged his presence with a nod and I guessed that after our talk she seemed to be coming some way towards forgiving him for Bud's death. The food again was familiar, yet came with strangely spiced blood sauces from exotic creatures. After weeks on the road it was enough to have food served piping hot, without the addition of grit from the road or bits of leaves and sticks. I noticed that the Dragon Clan spent most of their time out of doors, in spite of the cold mountain air. It took some getting used to but it seemed to be healthier. Dragon

Clan Vampires took their colouring from their family line. Looking around the lunch table at our party, we somehow seemed rather drab. Peregrine told us that one of the Dragon Clan had confided in him that they thought we looked like penguins at a funeral.

Sitting next to Chassignol at the end of the bench, I told him about our eventful morning. He listened politely to the bit about finding the tunnel but then perked up no end when I told him about meeting Xeurf. 'Is he trapped down there?'

'No, he claims to be a friend of the Dragon. Did you know *his* real name was Qi LiFang? Perhaps we should start calling him that?'

Chassignol said nothing for a moment. Then, 'So he can get out whenever he wants?'

'I suppose so'. I shrugged. Chassignol looked worried by this, so I added, 'He seems OK though. Eccentric perhaps but then again, I've never met a Dragon before. For all we know, he could be the model of sanity compared to the rest'. I told him about the last flight of the Dragon but Chassignol seemed to have sunk back into his thoughts and nodded, not really listening.

Abruptly, he pushed his stool back and stood up. 'I have to go', he said. 'You chaps enjoy the rest of the afternoon'. And with that he walked away, back towards his rooms.

'I suppose everything is alright?' asked Grue, staring at me. He had just sat down to lunch and was looking quite perky for him. I noticed he had patches of blue powder in his hair, and filthy hands for one usually so fastidious.

'Fine', I said flatly and sat back down further away from him, next to a second helping of pudding.

As for the rest of the afternoon, we pretty much all did our own thing. The cousins went off for a sauna and I walked around the battlements for a while, lost in my thoughts, and then went to my chambers where I dozed in the late afternoon sun. I then had my first hot bath for about two months, reflecting that I would never get used to washing in lakes and rivers. I was finishing up when Sansonnet came in. She'd had her hair and make-up done by some of the local duchesses. 'Gosh, you look nice,' I said without thinking, then remembered that we were meant to be just friends.

Sansonnet said nothing. She walked up to me, smiling faintly; raising her hand, she brushed some stray hairs away from my forehead. 'There,' she said. 'Now you look nice too.'

We all met up downstairs at the entrance of a great hall where we were to have the feast. Looking around at our lot, we seemed transformed, barely recognisable from the grubby rabble which had come in from the woods the night before. It appeared that most of us had spent the afternoon looking in the mirror.

'Shall we go in, then?' said the Milan and Faucon, both hopping from one foot to the other, steam practically coming out of their ears.

'I think we 'ave to wait until we're called,' said Peregrine gruffly. He was wearing his best uniform, neatly pressed having spent several months at the bottom of his pack, and his hair was plastered down over his forehead and ears with something that must have been strong glue. We craned our necks to look inside the hall where hundreds, or possibly even thousands, of candles burned brightly. Sure enough after a few moments somebody up in the rafters blew on a great big horn and our friend from breakfast popped up.

'You come in now,' he said waving frantically.

As we all filed in, Chassignol fell into step with me. 'Do you still have that key from this morning?' he asked.

'*Shure, fleedom of city,*' I replied.

'I might need to *bollow* it later. Do some exploring of my own,' he said, with a slightly stiff smile.

'No problem, Qi LiFang probably meant for you to have it in the first place.' I unclipped the key from my sword belt. 'Here you go.'

'Thanks,' he said, slipping it into a pouch.

At that moment the chap with the foghorn gave another mighty blow and everyone started to clap. It took us a few moments to realise that they were actually applauding at us. We all stood there rather foolishly for a few moments, dazzled by the bright lights and the din, until Qi LiFang himself came forward and ushered us to our seats at the head table.

'Welcome,' he said kindly, a smile cracking his ancient, wrinkled face. 'Welcome, come ... *eat*, eat up!' So we sat down as the first in a succession of enormous platters was brought in. Each tray was designed not only to contain the choicest delicacies but each dish was shaped and styled into fantastic designs that resembled paintings more than actual food. I counted thirty such masterpieces in all brought into the feasting hall.

We ate fresh dragonfly eggs, grilled seahorse dripping in butter and roasted hummingbird heart, with rashers of tangy bacon wind-dried from a small, pig-like animal that apparently roamed the forests nearby. I counted at least twenty different types of black pudding, and miniature mountains of rice sat steaming on platters the length of each table. There were no Sanguines attending, I was disappointed to see, but there was a plentiful supply of blood drinks at the table – snow tiger, fresh water buffalo blood laced with cloud berry cognac – a new one for me – and Unicorn, very rare and perhaps the purest blood of all, from vintages over three hundred years old. Say what you like about the Dragon Clan, they did well for themselves.

After nearly two hours the empty platters were taken away and we pushed back our chairs, stomachs bulging. I loosened my sword belt a notch and noticed Peregrine surreptitiously doing the same. Chassignol, who had spent the meal sitting between a heavily made-up duchess Nosferatu covered in jewels, and Qi LiFang himself, came over. 'Qi LiFang has requested an audience with us after the meal.'

'Both of us?' I was surprised, but nodded. 'Do we go now?'

'Not yet, no. He's put on some entertainment in our honour. From what I can gather, I think we're in for a treat.'

'Goody, will there be clowns?'

But Chassignol had already turned away and gone back to his seat.

We did not have long to wait for the festivities to begin in earnest. First up were a troupe of Vampire acrobats, who tumbled and spun in increasingly complex patterns and shapes in the air. To spice things up they each carried a baton lit at both ends, so that when they twisted in the air the batons made flaming swirls that narrowly missed setting light to their partners' elaborate costumes or the rich tapestries which hung from the walls. Like a lot of these things it was pretty impressive to start with but a little dull after a while. After some enthusiastic applause from everyone, the acrobats melted away and a large bird was brought in on a big red cushion. At first I took this to be more food, then I realised the bird was actually alive, although it didn't look too perky from where I was sitting. Maybe we would all wait for it to die of old age and then we'd eat it.

I was half right, as things turned out.

The bird was placed reverently in the middle of the feasting hall, on a dais. There was some polite applause and the audience settled down to wait. To my untrained eye the bird looked like a cross between a large peacock and a pheasant. And, indeed, after a few moments it spread its tail feathers and we all gasped. The myriad of colours revealed in its plumage made even the opulent surroundings fade into the background.

The bird then raised its slender neck to the heavens and started to sing.

At first the tune was undemanding, a succession of notes held for a few seconds, like scales, and yet strangely moving for all its simplicity. More notes were added and the song changed into a complex lament that filled the great hall. Imperceptibly the song gripped us until all the bittersweet beauty of life seemed to be summed up in the melancholic airs and the audience wept as it reached its climax. With one final note that hung in the air for an age, the bird then unexpectedly burst into bright orange flames. Everyone around the room gasped in awe, as it disappeared from view in a ball of its own fire, its final heart-wrenching chord drifting off into the rafters high above our heads with a thick white column of smoke.

'Wod on Eard was dhat?' I asked Sansonnet, sounding emotional.

'That was a Phoenix.' She wiped away some tears with a small silk hanky. 'Before it dies, it sings a lament and is then consumed by its own fire. We're very lucky to see this.'

'Aren't they meant to be born again or something?'

'That's right. Look!' she said pointing at the dais. Sure enough, now the fire had died down, amongst the ashes there sat a large, ivory-coloured egg. The same people who had brought the bird in now filed back, and amidst more rapturous applause, left with the egg placed on a new golden cushion. Milan and Faucon, still crying like little girls, clapped the loudest.

After all this excitement there was a pause in the proceedings as everyone pulled themselves together, discussed what they had just seen with their neighbours and knocked back a stiff drink.

At the far end of the hall there was a large black curtain. The bloke in the attic with the big horn blew it again and the curtain was drawn back to reveal four fully-armed Vampire Warriors. Each carried one of their long curved swords and another smaller sword strapped to their back. Unlike us, they wore leather and not polished metal armour. I could see the sense in this: thick leather will withstand a sword cut and even a sharp thrust. You could probably march about all day in the armour they wore and fight for far longer than if you were wearing the heavy plate armour our warriors carried into battle. Their movements certainly seemed freer and somehow almost graceful. I noticed Grue, Chassignol and Peregrine – our best and most experienced warriors – taking a keen professional interest in the swordsmen as they marched to the centre of the room. There they split into two pairs, bowed to the top table, then to one another, and drew their swords.

At first their movements were deliberate and seemingly choreographed. In fact, they started to resemble dancers more than fighters. Then gradually their swords moved faster and their feet began to skip left and right as the fighters circled one another. Parry and riposte became more urgent as their blades moved faster and the cuts more probing of each fighter's defence. Within a minute or so, both bouts had developed into a concerted fight, with each combatant attempting to force his opponent onto the defensive. A Vampire from the Old Country fights one-handed, his rapier is light and more of a thrusting weapon. These swords, whilst also lighter than, say, the two-handed axe that some Vampire Knights use, still needed both hands. In doing so, the fighters had to use their small wings for balance. The thrum of their beating wingtips was drowned out by the clatter and scrape of metal blade on metal blade.

Suddenly one of the fighters, who had been looking increasingly desperate, tripped and fell. He crashed over one of the long tables, scattering cutlery, pudding and startled guests. His opponent, a much larger and more experienced-looking Vampire moved forward with amazing speed and grace for someone so heavily armoured and brought the flat of the blade down on the fallen Vampire's torso. There was a smattering of polite applause and both the winner and the loser stepped away with a low bow to the high table. Qi LiFang smiled and nodded at the victor, whose face remained utterly impassive beneath a slight sheen of sweat. 'That's the Dragon Clan's Champion,' whispered Sansonnet. 'He's also general to Qi LiFang's army.'

The two remaining fighters seemed to be very evenly matched. So much so, that after another five minutes fighting both of them slipped through their opponent's guard at exactly the same time, each scoring a direct hit on the other's armour. A small cross-looking Vampire ran to Qi LiFang's table and whispered in his ear. Qi LiFang nodded once and stood up. 'The contest is a draw,' he announced, looking perturbed. 'Both dead.' The two warriors, each looking rather ashamed, bowed sheepishly at the high table and left the hall to a smattering of half-hearted applause.

'Why's everyone looking like someone peed in the soup?' I asked Sansonnet, who seemed to be the expert on the Dragon Clan.

'No idea,' she whispered back as Qi LiFang stood.

'Honoured guests,' he bowed graciously at us, 'assembled Clan members, our remaining champion, General Zhang, has no opponent. This is very unlucky!' He shook his head in what could have been mock-sorrow. 'Who will fight this champion amongst Vampires?' General Zhang glared at the assembled company, flexing his muscles, giving the sword a practice swish or two. You could hear a pin drop.

"'Spose that I will,' said Peregrine, and stepped resolutely into the middle of the floor. Now Peregrine is pretty large but he stood at least a head smaller than General Zhang.

'Does anyone object?' Qi LiFang shouted across the assembled company, looking stern but quite pleased. Applause from the Clan members and our own small group signalled that, on the contrary, we were looking forward to a good fight. 'Then let the duel begin!'

A few moments later, the Vampire who had been defeated by the General came forward carrying his own armour, which he offered to Peregrine. Peregrine studied it for a few moments and then shook his head, refusing the gift. Zhang saw this and permitted himself what I guessed was a rare smile; he clearly thought he would make short work of a Vampire with no armour. The threat of getting seriously injured would make any normal Vampire overly cautious. However, I could see where Peregrine was coming from. The only way to defeat such a large and powerful opponent was to stay light on your feet. Even so, Zhang was no fool: he'd no doubt be expecting Peregrine to keep out of his way until a heavier sword and armour tired him out. I guessed that either he would try to force Peregrine into a corner and beat him to his knees by sheer strength very early on, or he would go for the sword. Sooner or later, a well-struck blow from his sword would shatter Peregrine's rapier and the fight would be over.

In the end he tried both tactics. Bows were taken, swords were drawn and within seconds of the combatants starting the General came at Peregrine with all the finesse of a rhino with a bee sting. It was clear that his intention was to beat Peregrine back, not by aiming blows at his body but by concentrating all his power into his blade and forcing Peregrine to parry, in the hope of breaking the latter's weaker sword. This would have been disastrous and Peregrine knew it, so he used his shoulders and forearms to soften each blow. Holding the blade more loosely than he normally would, he retreated against the onslaught in a tight circle, so as not to be trapped. The storm of monstrous cuts and thrusts from the General met with only just enough resistance to deflect but not stop his opponent's sword dead in the air. The General did not seem particularly worried: he seemed to have plenty of energy left and clearly assumed that it was only a matter of time before Peregrine made a mistake.

Now Peregrine was moving very quickly, but as someone who had known him for several decades I also knew he could move far faster. The General knew he could move fast but had no idea yet just how quickly, and Peregrine was holding back on this for when he most needed it. I suspected that if any chance at all did come against such an experienced and ruthless fighter as Zhang, then it would be momentary and it would only happen once.

By now, Zhang had realised that Peregrine was not fully committing his blade, so he changed tactics and started to go for his face and hands. This forced Peregrine into defending himself more doggedly and I could see tension build in his eyes. In refusing armour he had also taken a big risk. Although this was supposedly only a friendly fight, the swords they were using were real enough and accidents happen, especially if the bout is between two professionals who want to win at all costs. By now Peregrine was definitely on the back foot, retreating all the time and struggling to defend himself, yet he still did not move up a gear and use his full speed. Once or twice the General's sword passed within millimetres of his face, narrowly missing his eyes, and he had already taken a nasty gash on his forearm, which bled copiously onto the stone floor.

Things weren't looking good. I glanced across at the others. Chassignol stared impassively at the proceedings but Sansonnet had screwed up her napkin in worry and the cousins were shaking their heads. Even Grue winced when the General caught Peregrine once more on the forearm and made another deep cut, this time exposing bone. I knew Peregrine was tough but I really had no idea how much until now.

Then, by degrees, General Zhang began to tire.

It happened that one or two of his thrusts lacked the usual ferocity and speed and Peregrine was extremely quick to pick up on this. He blinked rapidly to clear the sweat from his eyes, and turned on his assailant.

Finally he was on the attack.

His sword arm a blur, he parried once, then feinted left, then right, in quick succession. The General looked startled at this new turn of speed and for the first time moved onto the back foot. This was probably Peregrine's only chance before Zhang got used to the new pace, so he lunged with all the speed and strength he could muster. The General parried the blade and we heard a crack as Peregrine's rapier snapped half way down. But his wings buzzed and he kept moving forward through Zhang's guard until the stump of his blade came to a stop barely an inch from the General's exposed eyeball.

Head tilted back to avoid the razor sharp remnant of Peregrine's weapon, the General's own blade fell to the ground. He'd broken his opponents blade but he was still beaten.

There was total silence for a few moments; and then slowly, one by one, the Clan began to clap, quietly at first and then more loudly as the hall erupted in applause and cheers. General Zhang looked annoyed at first and then nodded his head gravely, in recognition of Peregrine's victory. He bent down, picked up the broken half of Peregrine's blade and offered it to him. Both Vampires then bowed to each other and also to Qi LiFang, who was smiling and clapping.

'A great combat!' he shouted, 'You both fight with honour and great courage. No shame, only glory. Come, sit … refresh yourselves!'

'Blimey,' remarked Milan to no one in particular, 'I think I aged t-ten years during that.'

'An aspect of Humanness we Vampires really enjoy is eating with cutlery – chopsticks too. All the really trendy aristocratic families now have at least one course where the use of a knife, fork, and sometimes even a spoon is required. At first it did take some of the older Vampires some time to grasp that food eaten this way should, ideally, be dead first.'

Prince Uri von Pengar.
Observations on the lives and customs of the Keep.

Chapter 15
audience

As the staircase wound ever upwards I began to wish I hadn't stuffed my face with quite so much food.

Ahead of me Chassignol trudged on in silence, carrying a lantern on a stick, and Qi LiFang led the way, moving with surprising agility for someone so ancient and wrinkly. It was very dark, so I did my best to keep up with them as we climbed the highest tower of the Eyrie to where Qi LiFang had his private apartments, but in the end I gave up and hovered up even if it is commonly considered poor manners to fly indoors. The lantern that Chassignol carried threw our shadows across the wall, elongating our bodies and making our heads seem monstrous. We resembled the Human take on us.

Below, in the feasting hall, the other Vampires had begun to disperse. Most of our lot had gone to bed, except for Peregrine who had gone to the medical wing to have his arm seen to. The General had insisted on going with him to make sure the wound was stitched properly. It seemed that they were now the best of friends.

After a while, we came to a small door that swung open at our approach, as if pushed by unseen hands.

'So! Welcome to my private chambers,' Qi LiFang said brightly, motioning us inside. The lintel of the door was very low and even I had to stoop to pass through it. Expecting the size of the room to match the door, I was surprised to find that it opened out into a large space, lit all around by red and gold lanterns. Our host moved briskly across the room, motioning to a waiting servant to bring us some drinks, and then out onto a wide balcony that gave us a magnificent view of the mountains lit by the Moon and legions of bright stars pricking holes in the fabric of the night sky. Two enormous fires, held by iron baskets, burned red hot and heated the balcony at either end. 'Please be seated,' he said, motioning us towards two large leather cushions. The drinks, when they arrived, proved to be some concoction of strong syrupy liqueur that tasted vaguely of blueberries. The fumes went right up our noses.

When Chassignol had finished coughing, he bowed and with some ceremony drew the Weirish knife we had found on Truant Island from his robes. He presented it to our host. Qi LiFang took it with equal ceremony but I noticed a look of mild distaste cross his usually inscrutable features as he recognised the writing. 'Thank you,' he said eventually, handing the knife to a waiting servant who melted away with it. 'I have heard of the existence of this.'

Chassignol nodded briefly, then he lent forward and asked straight out. 'Sire, do you know where the Chalice is?' Well, that was to the point, I thought and turned to study Qi LiFang's reaction.

By way of answer the Eyrie prince smiled sadly and swirled the remainder of his drink in his glass. Looking up, directly into Chassignol's eyes, he started to speak.

'There was an English King, a Human – some say the last true English King. His name was Harold. For many Moon cycles, the Chalice had been held in his land, passed down from generation to generation, from one English king to another until It finally came to him. The Weres had given it to him under someone's orders – possibly the Vampire you know as Corbeau. If any species could exact the destruction he craved from the cup, it was the Humans. It was jealously guarded but at a great cost – for those Humans value the Chalice almost as much as we Vampires do. So many people had lost their lives looking for it and just as many had died protecting it from those who would steal this …' he paused waving his long fingers with their curiously sharpened nails impatiently, ' … this perilous *trinket* and use it for their own ends. Some English Kings used it wisely and the land seemed to prosper, others misused its power and then evil swept across England and its subjects. The last King was a practical man who did not hold with superstitions. He ignored the Chalice and perhaps he even treated its power carelessly, preferring to trust in the keenness of his sword and the fierceness of his warriors.

'But shortly after he came to power there was a great battle on a steep hill. He and his men held the high ground and for a while it looked as if they would vanquish their enemies. The Chalice, as ever, had other ideas and maybe you might say that it would have its revenge against someone who paid it such scant regard. A stray arrow pierced Harold through the eye and he fell to the ground, where he breathed his last, face down on the muddy grass surrounded by his despairing troops.

'The battle was quickly lost and the victorious army, led by a foreign prince called Guillaume le Batard, swept through England, killing more men and making slaves of the women and children. This conqueror commissioned his scribes to start a great book, which he called *Doomsday*. In it he would record everything that England had in its possession: its castles, its farms, the sheep in the fields, the fish in its rivers, and of course its treasures.

'One treasure, however, escaped these greedy scribes, these avaricious list-makers and this was the Chalice itself. The greatest treasure of all? I don't know.

'Shortly after the battle on the hill was lost, a Clan Vampire from your Keep, who had monitored the Chalice in Human care for many years and made sure these Humans did not indulge some of their worst excesses with it, took the Chalice back and brought it here, where it would be safe.'

'It's true then, what I read on the cross in Sarum – you have the Chalice!'

'Not anymore we don't!' We all turned.

Out of the shadows stepped a tall, strikingly beautiful duchess Vampire. Although she wore the black leather armour of the Dragon Clan, she was clearly one of us. Her wings fanned out in the moonlight and her step was perfectly balanced.

'You'll find it has been moved.'

'You're … ' Chassignol gawped, ' … from the Keep?' Attaboy with the obvious.

The duchess Vampire smiled. She held out an elegant hand. 'I am Lark. The Eltern sent me here ... and many other places, including England, then known as Angleland, oh ... *many* years ago.'

'What for?' I found it difficult to meet her gaze – whenever I meet someone this striking, I'm painfully aware of my bent, wasted legs and my squint. Her thoughts were ordered and calm. Beautiful on the inside, too.

'I was, *am* a sort of Ambassador – the Eltern seem to think a conflict between Vampires is coming and we – those of us who oppose Vampires like Corbeau anyway – must pull together. This Eyrie,' she waved an elegant hand to indicate the general sweep of the high walls, 'is where I have been for the last hundred years.' She smiled again, but this time more warmly. 'I've missed the Keep, though. How are things?'

'Same old same,' I said, but Chassignol wasn't going to be side-tracked.

'Do the Eltern not know all this? So why did they send us to Truant Island?' I started at this. From what I recalled, Truant Island had nothing to do with them – it had been Chassignol's idea.

However, the Vampire called Lark sighed. 'I've been asking myself what they know since you arrived. When my cousin Picus and I took the decision to take the Chalice from the Humans and have me bring it here, we kept its destination a secret ... however, I've long since learned not to underestimate what the Eltern know.'

'Please tell us where it is,' Chassignol looked almost desperate.

'No.'

And the words were said with a finality that made any argument seem hopeless.

'But why?' implored Chassignol, sounding petulant, almost childish.

Qi LiFang stepped in. 'I have had time to study this object. I have realised that the Chalice is not evil in itself but it has the power to cause great harm just through its being. Too many people have lost their lives trying to possess it. I swore that it would end here.'

'We're not Humans, and nor are we here to misuse its power. We're here to return it to where it rightfully belongs.' I saw sweat beading the top of Chassgnol's lip – a Milk Imp would have sensed his desperation.

'But you have a private purpose for it too,' said the old ruler astutely. I also did not like the feelings I was sensing from Chassignol. His urgent desire to get the Chalice seemed to be spilling over into something like violence. Perhaps Qi LiFang was right – It brought out the very worst in us.

Qi LiFang then turned and stared at me very hard for a few moments before changing the subject. 'You know the one they call *Raptor*.' Personally, I'm easily disconcerted, so I spilled my drink onto a very expensive looking rug.

'Er … maybe ... yes, actually.'

'This wasn't a question,' he said, eyes glancing down involuntarily at the large blue stain on what was probably his favourite carpet.

'Sorry,' I said.

The Dragon leader ignored me. 'He is your future, if you want to fight so bad.'

'And what about the Dragon Clan, are you willing to fight?' I asked. It was now my turn to get riled, partly because his tone was dismissive and partly because I still couldn't figure out how he knew about Raptor.

'What is this Corbeau to me?' he replied, his voice now containing an edge of steel. 'Why should I fear him? Why should I hate him? He leaves us alone, we should respond with same courtesy.'

'And for how long do you think he'll leave you alone?' I asked, glancing at Chassignol for support. But my best friend had moved over to the edge of the balcony, seemingly ignoring our exchange. 'He wants all the Vampire Nation under his control.'

'Then find Raptor and fight.'

'I have to find the Chalice first. We think that Corbeau has summoned the Thin Man. We might be able to defeat Corbeau with swords but I doubt they'll work on Him.'

'What makes you say this terrible thing?'

'He is following us,' I said simply and went on to explain what I had seen leaving Truant Island, during the storm and then finally on board the ancient bird. The Dragon's normally placid features showed concern at first and then raw anger.

'You have brought him here?' Until that moment I had not seen the risk but now I saw it all too clearly.

Chassignol, though, could keep quiet no longer. 'The Thin Man won't stop until he has the Chalice too, which is why you must tell us where it is!'

'No, you are irresponsible people!'

Sensing violence also, Lark stepped forward, but before Chassignol could do anything he might afterwards regret, there was a shout from far below and a horn sounded urgently somewhere close by. Whatever it signalled, this didn't sound good. We rushed to the edge of the balcony. Far below us Vampire foot soldiers were climbing the battlements armed with pikes and bows. More soldiers streamed across the courtyard to close the great gates and I could make out the distinctive form of General Zhang shouting orders to a squadron of elite Vampires strapping on their leather armour.

We looked out over the Eyrie wall, deep into the valley below, where a sea of lights was approaching to the steady beat of Troll drums. To the west I heard a lone Were howl and all across the valley a hundred more cries came in answer. Suddenly my head hurt, and I felt slightly sick. There was no doubt about it: the Thin Man was here and he'd brought an army with him.

'This is because of the Chalice and the madness it brings!' Qi LiFang looked angrily at us both. He raised a bony finger. 'You have brought this Thin Man, this … this *monster* to our sanctuary!'

Chassignol looked defeated but I felt a keen, righteous anger. 'Maybe today. But if he had not come now, he would have come in the end. He is seeking the same thing we are. And we can fight him here; the Eyrie is as good a place as any, probably better. We are at your service, what can we do?'

Qi LiFang still looked furious. His small wings opened and thrummed, seemingly preparing for flight. 'We can do nothing against such an army. It is too big. You can do only one thing.'

'What's that?' I asked.

'You can pray that the walls hold!' And with that he tipped himself over the balcony and half-glided, half-climbed down to his troops below.

'Meeting Lark was my first indication of
the larger nature of the Eltern's plans.'
                                    Moüsch.

Chapter 16
battle for the Eyrie

And hold the
walls did.

At first the army below us was small, it came in rags and
tatters up the valley and assembled at the foot of the Eyrie's huge
ramparts and buttresses. Most of the force was made up of our
recent foes – the Weres. They arrived in a pack of about one
hundred and fifty fully grown adults, though more were
appearing out of the forest as their calls to arms rippled through
the dark woods and lost ravines. The Weres' eyes flashed yellow
against the Moon and red against our firebrands as our flares
picked them out in the darkness. They had all taken their
fighting, wolverine form. A pack of Greebach Jackals also slunk
into view. These were far smaller than the Weres, the product of
a union between two ancient species of meat scavenger that died
out long ago – before the last ice sheets. Their howls sounded
like a torment – half physical pain, half misery.

Then a large regiment of Trolls came to a halt about fifty
rapier lengths from the main gate. Each carried a club the size of
a small tree, although a few carried rusty-looking swords and
axes. Far from being the lone, anti-social creatures that we
usually mistook them for, they were banded together in battle
groups of six or seven, each with its own drummer who kept the
pace while they marched. Half a dozen immediately started to
hack down a large tree to make a battering ram, until a single
arrow from the battlements arced out into the night sky and fell,
with piercing accuracy, into the middle of them. One Troll fell to
the ground, stone dead, the shaft of the arrow embedded in the
back of his neck. After that, the rest of them lost the urge to
make battering rams and retreated out of range.

Sansonnet and the others were running across the courtyard
and clambering up the battlements, so we flew down and joined

them. Lark followed but at the last moment she peeled off and flew very fast to where Zhang was.

At that moment a group of Dark Faies also decided to turn up. These are very different to the beings we had encountered back in England. They gave out a malicious presence, and their vanguard played a kind of fluting, ethereal music known for driving the opposition to such a pitch of despair that they would simply give up, lay down their weapons and wait to die.

The effect of the Faies' arrival was almost immediate. Abruptly the wood around us seemed to change in our hearts and minds, so that the branches and trunks appeared to us to stand out against the snow, like blackened stakes and hangmen's scaffolds. A low moan sounded from far off, and the music – a bitter lament – made us remember the loved ones we had lost. The moonshadows, thrown out across the frozen earth, re-arranged themselves into jagged letters that spelt out warnings and terrible omens.

But the Clan seemed to be made of sterner stuff. No sooner had the Faies' magic begun to creep across the battlements to chill our bones and force our souls to lose all hope, than a counter-spell issued from Qi LiFang himself. He stood, arms raised, in the centre of the compound, muttering incantations. Abruptly a sentiment of well being flooded over us, we lost our sense of despair and then anything seemed possible. The wood shrugged off its sinister aspect and the enemies at the gate seemed suddenly inconsequential and weak.

By now, there were perhaps one thousand beings out there. More individual creatures were joining the assembled ranks. These were the dregs of the forest and its forgotten places: strange, half-formed creatures that only somebody or something like the Thin Man could call upon using his own Muster. A poisonous swamp toad with the arms of a human child; drooling hags, their wild hair matted with the skulls of small animals and dried blood; and a Rock Giant. Even from a distance it was clear that, although fully grown, the Rock Giant still had the mind of a child, or worse. Naked, he walked in bow-legged circles, sometimes laughing insanely to himself, sometimes beating his head with his huge fists. His slack mouth dribbled continuously. These latest arrivals, the lost and broken creatures, made me feel pity more than anything else and a certain distaste that we might have to fight and kill them.

And, all the while, I felt the Thin Man's malevolent presence watching from close by.

The closer we got to the Chalice, the closer he seemed to get to us. As I surveyed the broken and seething mass of his malformed army below, I unexpectedly felt a strong sensation that he was very close by indeed. I scanned the wood, staring for a long while at a patch that seemed darker than the rest. He was in there.

But we had other things to worry about first. 'This doesn't look good,' I said to Peregrine, who was standing beside me, his arm neatly bandaged.

'I shouldn't worry,' he said. 'These walls could 'old back an army three times this size. This gaff's been around a fair old while – it would just be a pile of rubble by now if the Dragon Clan was a push over.'

The first to attack, presumably because they were still very upset about the arrow, were the Trolls. They decided to come forward in one block, making for the great oak gate. Even without a battering ram the sight of a few hundred irate Trolls lumbering towards your front door, shouting about all the horrible things they planned to do to you when they got in, is enough to spoil anyone's evening. By the time they reached the gates they were at full speed and they hit the solid wood portals in a great bristled mass of brown and green arms and legs. But the terrible impact made little or no impression on the gates, merely dislodging some dust from the rafters above the portcullis. I realised that there was probably more than just a simple matter of wood and iron holding the gates closed.

A few moments later a swarm of Dragon Clan Vampires

climbed over the walls and attacked the Trolls on their exposed flank. Despite their superior size and strength, the massed ranks of Trolls simply crumpled and started to flee back to the woods, leaving about a dozen dead and badly wounded scattered at the foot of the walls. For a moment I thought the Vampires would pursue the Trolls into the forest, where I noticed the Weres were gathering for a charge. Had they done so, they would have been caught and at grave risk of being torn to pieces by the pack. But they were well-trained enough to keep ranks. The General himself led the charge and I noticed he was frantically ordering them into a line. When I scanned the trees beyond, I saw why. A splinter force of Weres, unseen until now, had broken into a loping run and were making for the General's isolated band of warriors. He could have climbed to safety back over the wall, but instead decided to stand his ground. 'He's testing them,' said Grue. 'He wants to see what they're made of. I think we should go down and help.'

'I'll go along with that, sir,' said Peregrine, drawing his sword. 'Lets 'ave some fun!'

Rightyho, I thought as I flew down, at least Qi LiFang can't accuse us of doing nothing. We just had time to join the left flank of the General's small force, when the pack hit. There was a snarling and scraping of claws against shields, followed by a blur of blades from the front rank of Vampires. Their attack was ill-judged at best, as there is relatively little attacking which Weres can do against a well-trained Vampire behind a solid shield wall. The snarling was quickly replaced by squeals and yelps of pain and they turned and fled too. A couple of Vampires had been injured but victory was clearly ours, for now anyway, as a pile of dead Weres lay bleeding at our feet. The fight was so quick that I'd not had a chance to use my sword, but both Peregrine and Grue had dealt with a Were apiece. I looked around for Chassignol but didn't see him.

Sansonnet, who stood to my left, turned to me, wrinkling her nose.

'Can you smell burning?' she frowned. Now that she mentioned it ... I turned to look at the Eyrie behind me and noticed a plume of black smoke. Just then a shout came from the wall.

'The Faies are at the North Gate, and they've set fire to it!'

We all took to the skies and flew towards the smoke. Crossing the Eyrie to the North Gate was very quick, but by the time we got there a large crowd of Vampires under Lark's supervision had already gathered to make a bucket chain from the well to the source of the fire. The buckets of water were being poured over the wall onto the flames but their effect was merely to check the fire and not extinguish it. Dark Faies armed with long, dangerous-looking bows, shot projectiles up at us and a couple of the Vampires fell from the walls with arrow wounds into the fire below.

One of the arrows hit a young Strigoi warrior carrying a bucket. Although it pierced him through the chest, the arrow tip jutting out of his shoulder blade, he barely paused until he had tipped the contents of the bucket onto the fire. He then grasped the end of the arrow, gritted his teeth and pulled it through his body and out of his back. Blood welled from both wounds and then congealed almost immediately. I was amazed, Vampires from the Keep healed quickly but this was remarkable even by our standards.

The North Gate was near to a rocky outcrop, which on the one hand protected it, as it prevented too many attackers being able to advance upon it; but on the other hand, the rocks allowed the Faies to have some cover close to the walls. Higher up on the rock face, I noticed something that gave me an idea.

'Milan, Faucon!' I shouted through the noise and smoke.

'Wer ... what?'

'If I create a diversion do you think you can get up there and move that rock?' I pointed to the part of the cliff that had caught my eye.

'Sure,' they both nodded, 'no problem.'

I got ready to take off. 'Oi!' cried Sansonnet, trying in vain to grab my feet when she realised I was going over the wall and straight into the thick of the Dark Faies. 'Have you lost *all* your marbles!'

'Not at all, watch this,' I said, and I flew as fast as I could towards the surprised-looking Faies. Going low over their heads I drew my blade and flicked it left and right. I wasn't really aiming for them but I managed to knock off one or two hats. The Faies weren't expecting anything like an attack when there was a bloody great fire to deal with so, had no time to react. When I came back around again they had recovered their wits sufficiently to shoot a few arrows in my direction, but I was too high by now and contented myself with shouting names. My diversion had worked and I could see Milan and Faucon now safely in position, having flown up unseen to the rocks above the Faies' heads. 'Alright, give it a push!' I yelled as I landed back next to Sansonnet. 'Now!'

'You maniac,' said Sansonnet, 'and anyway,' she said, watching the Milan and Faucon, 'that's a tiny little boulder, I hope you're not planning on trying to squash all that lot with it. It won't work.'

'Not at all,' I said, feeling rather smug that she hadn't yet guessed what I was up to, 'it's what's under the rock that I'm interested in.'

By now the cousins had managed to shift the rock a few inches to the left. The trickle of water I'd seen seeping out from around the sides of the boulder they'd moved became a gush, then a torrent that poured down over the rocks, sweeping the Faies aside and some of them down over the cliffs. It continued its path, building more momentum and came to where I wanted it most, a bull's eye, right in the middle of the flames that raged below us.

There was a loud hiss and lots of steam.

'That,' admitted Sansonnet, as the smoke cleared to leave the gate heavily charred but intact, 'was actually pretty impressive for you.'

As the fire sizzled and spat and died, the sound of hundreds of running feet erupted from inside the walls of the Eyrie. I looked up, expecting to see crowds of Vampires standing jubilantly on the walls, as the surviving Faies retreated into the forest.

Instead I saw carnage.

I couldn't immediately work out how, but Trolls had somehow got into the compound whilst we dealt with the fire and now they marauded inside the Eyrie walls, smashing Vampires with their clubs, setting light to the thatch of the houses and kicking down doors where young Vampire children cowered. Weres poured into a breach in a hastily drawn up defensive line and I tried not to think about what might be happening inside some of the dwellings. I blinked again. How could they get in … ?

'Look!' Sansonnet pulled my arm. 'The main gates are wide open.' Sure enough, they were pulled back, with no sign of damage.

'The Faies may have used the fire at the North Gate as a diversion. They must have used magic to open these. Or the Thin Man …' I shivered despite the sweat pouring off me.

'Come on, let's go! Sansonnet cried. After the initial influx of Trolls and Weres, the Vampire troops had now rallied and, drawing our swords, we joined their ranks in a new line. After some hard fighting, I managed to kill one Were with a clean lunge, half in the air as I went through its eye socket with the tip of my sword. Dodging a swinging cudgel I back-swung and seriously injured a Troll, opening a huge gash in its stomach. The Troll staggered to one side and fell over, bleeding copiously through his huge hands, which clutched his gaping belly. All around Vampires fought on foot; Peregrine, Milan and Faucon coming in from the air in brief attacks that went to the heart of the enemy's ranks before wheeling away again. It looked like we were turning the tide. Standing shoulder to shoulder with Sansonnet and Lark, we were fighting for our lives now and the most dangerous thing on the planet is a desperate Vampire with a sword in his or her hand, no question. Slowly the Trolls and Weres began to retreat back out of the gates.

It was at that precise moment that disaster struck.

It started with a trumpet call. When I looked up I saw a sight to make me want to turn and run. We were finished.

A seething mass of Faies was now coming towards us. There

must have been over five hundred, well over double our force, and they carried long curved scimitars and round shields, embossed with intricate carvings showing terrible leering monsters. Each shield had a spike, which was a weapon in itself, and their formation spoke of good training. They must have been hiding in the forest all this time, waiting until now to show their full force. Despite the impregnable walls we had been out-played by the Thin Man. And behind them came the creeping and broken horrors we had seen earlier. I didn't fancy getting caught by one of the Hags, so I decided to kill as many Dark Faies as I could before getting hacked down myself. Thus, amongst the smoke and the debris of the battle, we formed a wall of Vampires to make our last stand.

'Well, it's been reasonably nice knowing some of you,' said Grue, between gritted teeth. He tightened his belt and gave the air a couple of exploratory swishes with his sword.

Just then, we heard a rumbling sound coming from deep beneath our feet. It felt as if the Eyrie itself was experiencing a sudden quake. I glanced around expecting to see rock fall caused by a large avalanche at the least, but saw nothing of the sort. By now the Faies had also stopped in their tracks and were looking around, as confused about the racket as we were, which convinced me that this new event just might be to our advantage. The rumbling sound increased, whereupon a jet of white-hot flame erupted from a tear in the ground that then split further apart into a gaping chasm. The first hundred or so Dark Faies immediately disappeared into it.

Xeurf the dragon, in all his magnificence, burst onto the scene like the personification of The Day of Judgement. Qi LiFang rode triumphantly on his back.

This was a side to him we had suspected but not seen – a purveyor of fire, protected by iron clad scales, and sinew like steel hawsers. He flicked his head from side to side, spitting flame into the heart of the enemy who turned to ash and crumbled. The survivors began to flee as Xeurf touched down in front of us.

Qi LiFang glided down from to us, holding something in his

hand. I expected him to still be angry with us and the destruction we had been responsible for bringing to his home. Instead he looked remarkably calm for someone who had very recently hopped off the back of a fire-breathing Dragon. He looked me in the eye briefly but intensely and then said simply. 'You were correct.'

'Sire,' I stammered, 'I am sorry … '

'What's done is done,' he said firmly, cutting me off. 'This Thin Man and the army his servant, Corbeau, is raising in the west must be stopped – at all costs. I was wrong! We are all in danger now and no one should hide behind their walls and pretend that the outside world does not exist. Too long has the Dragon Clan stayed apart from the Vampire Nation. If the Chalice can be found, then this may help.' He handed me the parchment he was holding.

'What is it?' I asked.

'It is a map,' he said. 'Long ago, when I decided the Chalice was a dangerous toy for fools, I sought to send it away. I made arrangements so that even I did not know its exact location. I thought to do so was to protect us and I had long resolved that to have it here was to invite danger into our homes. I was unwise: dangers should be faced, not run from.'

'But I understand,' Sansonnet stepped forward as the others stood intently by, listening as mayhem raged around us still. 'You only sought to do what is best.'

Qi LiFang bowed deeply to her. 'Thank you. The map will take you far away, to another continent across the sea, further west than you have ever been. A group of Vampire hermits left the Eyrie to live there peacefully in the rain forests, in contemplation as final guardians of the sacred treasure. I believe this map will help you locate them and possibly the Chalice, too.'

'How will we get there?' Grue asked.

'Xeurf has agreed to take you. He knows the way.'

'His last flight.' I said, managing to feel honoured and really guilty at the same time.

Qi LiFang nodded sadly. 'Yes. His last flight, a great sacrifice.'

He looked over our shoulders and frowned. 'But hurry, the Faies and the Trolls are regrouping. The battle is won but we have more work to do.' And sure enough I could see the Faies gather up the remainder of their forces just outside the gates for another attack. It was hopeless but the darkness in the corner of the wood remained and seemed to urge them on even if it meant certain death. 'There is one more thing,' he said, looking at me.

'What is it?' I asked.

'A long time ago, when the Chalice came to us, Lark came with this too.' He handed me a fragment of parchment upon which someone had scratched runes and signs I did not recognise. 'It came from the one they call Picus, but I think that it belongs to you?'

'Why?' I was completely nonplussed. A couple of Faie arrows fled out of the darkness and landed a few feet from us.

Lark came up. She had a nasty gash across her cheek but otherwise seemed unharmed. She glanced at the parchment, recognition showing on her face, then looked at us. 'Show it to the Eltern, when all this is over and you do not know where to turn. But only then!' she said emphatically. 'Now go! Hurry!'

I called over to the others.

Milan, Faucon, Sansonnet, Perigrine, Grue and I quickly climbed on Xeurf's back and he took off, his strong wings beating slowly, then faster as he tore back over the ranks of the Thin Man's scratch army that was trying to regroup. More white-hot flame erupted from his open jaws. This time they seemed to scatter for good, and I breathed a sigh of relief for The Dragon Clan who were now closing their gates again and putting out the fires.

But I hadn't seen Chassignol since the fighting began in earnest. Then I spotted him just outside the gates, standing alone. 'We need to pick up Chassignol!' I shouted at Xeurf who tipped his great head and dived to where my friend was standing.

'Take my hand!' I shouted to him as he turned, Xeuf hovering a few feet in the air above him, wings beeting the air, kicking up snow storms around my friend.

Chassignol looked up at me but then, quite deliberately, stepped away. There were tears in his eyes. 'No!' he shouted back. 'I can't ... I'm so very sorry Moüsch!' I noticed he held something. It was the keys to the Eyrie. My mind seemed to lurch sideways, remembering the conversation we had before going into the Feasting Hall.

'Chassignol, this is the most important thing I'll ever ask you – did you open the gate?' I half-expected, half-wanted him to laugh but I could tell from his eyes I wasn't wrong. I almost choked on the next word. 'Why?'

He looked like he was going to reply for a second or two, but then he turned and ran through the smoke and the flames, back towards the woods where I could make out the long silhouette of the figure waiting for him. The presence that had haunted me since our journey began.

＊

'At the start of the Quest, the Eltern deliberately kept their plans vague and what they knew hidden. In hindsight, this was because they knew there was a traitor in their midst but they did not know yet their identity. Later I discovered that Peregrine was the only truly trusted member of the Quest at the start, and the rest of us suspects. The plan was simple; whichever Vampire amongst us displayed a knowledge beyond what we ourselves discovered, would soon reveal themselves the defector who was in contact with the Thin Man himself or Corbeau. Chassignol's disappearance on Truant Island was suspicious and his mysterious possession of one half of the Were knife telling. His conduct before and after the death of Bud sealed it for the Eltern who had received a report Peregrine had sent in secret after the Standing Stones. Lark had been tasked to stop him at the Eyrie but unfortunately the Thin Man had attacked faster than anyone had imagined.'

Moüsch.

Chapter 17

last flight of the dragon

As Xeurf soared higher and the wind roared in our ears, I felt a
jolt, like a small charge going off in my head. With blinding
clarity I felt the Thin Man's white-hot fury and frustration as
we cleared the tops of the mountains, making good our escape.
Until now, I had sometimes suspected the dreams may have been
His doing; but at that moment I had a revelation. The dreams
had been my protection all along. For in my dreams I knew that
I could beat Him.

I felt Him now as plainly as if He was standing by me, fishing
about in my pockets for information. He was delving – and I
should know – sifting about in my thoughts to try to find out
where we were going. So these odd dreams had very possibly
been a refuge, a way of blocking out or even escaping his probing.
Ignoring the freezing cold, the rushing air and the terrible
knowledge of Chassignol's betrayal, I lay against the Dragon's
skin, and concentrating on the steady beat of his heart and
powerful wings, I willed myself into a sleep-like trance.

Reverie IV
CHASSIGNOL'S PACT
〜 *I was back at the Standing Stones. This time, my protection lay
in inhabiting the soul of a Wood Spirit who had lived there long
before the forest had been cleared and the first stones erected around
the four petrified maids. A chant rang in my head, and in the
distance a flute played. Pleasure stirred in the Wood Spirit's long
dead heart as the music became louder and the words of the chant
became clearer,*

I can see it, across the rushes every night,
I can feel it, the cold currents lit by the old moonlight,
And it makes me sad to see it flow,
Where my thoughts can only dare to go.

I can hear it, speaking softly to the trees,
I can see it, the branches softly sway to melodies.
And in winter she is silent as the snow,
So I wonder where her meanderings must go.

I can smell it, the sweetened air that lies upon the breeze.
I can sense it, the sharp salt air of far off seas.
And the winding water lilies flow –
Downstream, oh so wondrous slow.

*It was Midsummer Night and the Faies were out. I sank deeper.
The years rushed by and the forest and the Faies disappeared. A
small village grew up around the Stones and then that too dwindled;
its inhabitants growing old before my eyes and dying, leaving empty
huts that decayed into the soil and grew over with grass.*

*All this time the Moon waxed and waned and the Wood Spirit
stood by and simply watched.*

*I sank deeper still, until Xeurf's heartbeat became a distant
thump, the pendulum that marked the passing years and the Wood
Spirit longed for company. She waited.*

*Time slowed and the Moon rose slowly in the sky, until it hung
there, a fixed point of light surrounded by stars. This time there were
no Faies but the night was warm and Midsummer could not have
been far off. The Wood Spirit was poking around in some bracken,
close to a brook. She was thinking about the Faies and wondering
what had become of them. She had enjoyed their music, even if their
words had meant nothing to her but it was years since they had been
in these parts, not since the last of the forest had receded. Sometimes
she was sure she heard the piping sound of their flutes in the hills, far
off – but it may have simply been the wind blowing through the trees.*

Bud appeared.

He was on his own, wandering through the bushes, idly swishing at the grasses and humming to himself. The Wood Spirit felt glad; he seemed nice, so she decided to follow him. He continued up the hill until he approached the Standing Stones along the path of the stream by which the maids had sat all that time ago. Tall grass hid him from the three figures whose voices he heard long before he actually saw them. They were arguing.

'No!' cried a voice that Bud immediately recognised. It was Chassignol!

'I think you will find a grovelling "yes" is the appropriate answer in the circumstances,' another, powerful voice replied.

'Don't I have a choice?' Chassignol's tone was scared, almost whining, so unlike his usual self.

Bud drew closer to peer out of the long grass. He saw that the Vampire talking to Chassignol was older, and painfully handsome. The other figure was much taller, shrouded and unmoving, part of the scene but as remote and as silent as a spectre. The Wood Spirit sensed then that Bud felt more afraid than he had ever been in his life.

'How rare it is that any of us do have choices,' the Vampire smiled acidly.

'If I give my friends to you, then they will die!'

'That is for my master to decide,' the Vampire gestured at the shrouded, impassive figure.

'But at the Keep, when I told you the Eltern had ordered us to leave to look for the Chalice, you said that it was all He wanted.' Chassignol gestured at the mute silhouette.

'The Chalice MUST come to us through a betrayal; it will add greatly to its power. The Chalice has to have servants and your friend Moüsch is the servant my master has insisted upon. The rest of your friends will be sacrificed. In all probability. This is the truth, I have not had time for lies in over a century. That much you can expect from me.'

Chassignol hesitated, chewing his finger, staring fearfully about him.

'And I will have power over life and death?' he asked in due course.

'For a limited time,' the Vampire nodded.

'And I can bring my father back?'

'If that is the one you choose.'

Chassignol appeared to think again but Bud could tell he had already made up his mind. 'O K. As long as there are no more tricks or surprises.'

'You have my word.' At this the other Vampire gave a wide grin, as if some hugely funny joke had popped into his head. Bud and the Wood Spirit noticed that the teeth were flecked with blood and the gums blackened – the sure marks of a Vampire that fed off his own kind.

Bud, who could stand it no longer, gasped and took a step back in fear. Chassignol look looked up, suddenly alert. He stared at the tall grass for some time, his expression at first fearful, then slowly, by degrees, comprehending, then finally hard and unforgiving. Bud was sure he had been seen.

The malevolent and silent figure behind Chassignol gave a leaden sigh, like the lid of a coffin sliding shut, and melted away. But before he did so he looked to where the Wood Spirit was hovering. Used to being invisible for millennia, she was surprised when He extended a long scabrous finger and touched her lightly on the forehead. She screamed silently and what was left of her soul was ripped from the world in that instant.

When I woke, I lay staring at the sky for a long time. We were high up now, at such altitude that there was no wind at all and the air was very thin. Too thin for any creatures but Dragons, Vampires and, in all possibility, the Thin Man, who would soon be following us. This time he had another ally.

Chassignol, traitor! Sneak thief, lickspittle … Human Judas!

Chassignol who, I realised now with a drowning feeling of disgust, had let Bud die because he had discovered before all of us the deal he'd struck with Corbeau and the silent figure I was sure was the Thin Man.

Chassignol, my friend who was trying to bring his father back to life. The father I had pretty much killed.

Chassignol was born honourable and good. It was I that had created Chassignol the traitor.

The sky to the east was growing lighter as the sun rose, throwing rays of light across the surface of an ocean far below us, looking dimpled in the pale dawn light, like the surface of an orange. At the start of the night our destination had lain thousands of leagues to the west, but we seemed to be approaching a landmass that meant we had crossed almost half the planet overnight.

Magic must have been at play here, I thought. I had read somewhere that some highly developed creatures, like Dragons, had long ago learnt the ability to travel at great speeds whilst barely seeming to move; this is what we must have been experiencing first hand now.

We were so high up that I could even see the curvature of the Earth's surface. I felt no elation at the view, rather a vague feeling of dread as I turned my attention to where we were heading, and saw that it was still night. A band of blackness stretched across the horizon like the frowning maw of some great monster, towards which we flew.

'Turn around,' I said suddenly. 'Turn around!' This time it was a shout.

The others, who must have all been asleep or dozing fitfully looked up in surprise. Xeurf, though, carried on, oblivious – his wings beating the frozen air like giant sails. I punched the huge, granite-hard scales that covered his back and got no response. I shouted as loud as I could. 'Turn back, head north, the Quest is over, we want to return to the Keep. We want to go home.'

'Do we?' asked Grue, looking at me coldly. 'Did Chassignol the Defector advise that?'

'Yes, why didn't Chassignol come, what happened?' said Milan, glancing at Grue and I.

But I ignored both of them. 'Can't you see, we're after something and we don't even know what it's for or how to use it? Qi LiFang, studied it for years and came to the conclusion it was a load of junk that people fought over and killed each other for. No one's ever said how it might help us against the Thin Man – or even Corbeau, whilst we're on the subject. Raptor has the right idea and he's barely even a Strigoi. We have to go back to the Keep, raise an army and kick his arse!' Everyone stared at me. 'Corbeau's ... not Raptor's, obviously', I added.

'I say we vote on it.' Peregrine was business-like as ever. 'All those in favour of going back to Blighty, raise your 'ands.' Mine shot up. Hesitantly, the cousins raised theirs. 'And all those in favour of sloggin' it out like real 'eroes?' Three hands went up. At least Sansonnet had the decency to look guilty. 'It's a tie. We're carryin' on', said Peregrine firmly.

'What? *Who*? You just made that rule up?' I blustered. 'Anyway, you don't even bloody well know where you're going, *I've* got the map. Where we're heading, it's probably Hell on Earth.'

'Well it can't be any worse than being stuck on that ship being sick, or spending the night getting shot at by Faies', Sansonnet pointed out, not unreasonably.

'It could be a lot worse, we could all end up getting killed, like poor Bud, or we could betray our friends like Chassignol.'

'What are you talking about Moüsch?' Only Grue really had an inkling of what was going on and the rest still had not grasped what had happened before we left the Eyrie: so I told them what I had seen in my dream.

Everyone went quiet for a few moments, and then everyone started shouting at once.

'QUIET!' We all turned around. I don't think I'd ever heard Grue raise his voice, or at least not for a couple of decades; we all shut up immediately, out of shock, more than anything. 'Chassignol was right about one thing – The Age of Aquarius is upon us. We have everything to fight for. But ... ,' he paused and looked around, ' ... the Eltern always suspected Chassignol, but having him at the heart of the Quest was the best way to find out how much he knew and how far he had strayed,' Grue said, 'and that's why they requested Peregrine.' He stared at me. 'They needed someone on the Quest whom they knew was not loyal to him.'

'If you are saying what I think you are … ' I started but Sansonnet put a hand on my arm, silencing me.

'So how did they know he was dodgy?' Faucon, who had never taken anything at more than face value in his life, was still looking confused.

'They wouldn't reveal their sources,' Grue said, unperturbed. 'They weren't even sure where his loyalties lay, but it seems Corbeau may have approached Chassignol shortly before the Eltern asked him to lead the Quest. After that they spoke to Peregrine and he said he'd go along to keep an eye on him. When he disappeared on Truant Island, I had my suspicions, which I relayed to Peregrine who was the only one of us I could see any reason why the Eltern had chosen to go on this wild goose chase. The day after Truant Island, Peregrine told me in confidence why he was with us but, as ever, I suspect this is only part of the story as far as the Keep is concerned. Is there anything you'd like to tell us Moüsch?'

'The Black Ship,' I said, my heart sinking even further. 'I saw a black ship slipping anchor, as we were leaving Truant Island. It was the same one that followed us during the storm off the coast of England and the one I saw riding the clouds when our lift decided to crash. I kept quiet at the time because I also suspected someone on the Quest wasn't on our side. You remember that bull?' I looked at Grue who nodded. 'He warned me, that's why I left. The Hag found us too easily. Then, when the ship kept cropping up, I assumed that someone was giving our where-abouts away.' I looked at Grue. 'I thought it was you at first,' I said, 'I'm sorry.'

By way of an answer Grue inclined his head very slightly. Grue and I would probably never get on but I knew, then and there, he was honest. He stared down his long nose at each one of us in turn. 'No one is going anywhere,' he said evenly. 'No one is giving up.' He sighed. 'Yes, we've lost Bud, and it would seem that Chassignol has turned traitor to follow a promise that the Thin Man will never keep. I've studied the old Lore and I am certain that the Chalice has great power. Certainly the greatest power of any of the ancient treasures that belong to the Vampire Nation. If it didn't, then why would the Thin Man be chasing it so hard to steal it from us, or perhaps steal it *back*? He knows its value, and, in our hearts, so do we. We must carry on and hope that when we find it, we will know how to use it, or at the very least that us having it will prevent Him from using it for his own ends.'

After that little speech, I'd had time to calm down, and I felt a little ashamed at my outburst. But Grue had once again surprised us all. 'All those who say we go on?' asked Peregrine. All hands, except mine, went up.

'Moüsch?' said Sansonnet gently.

'*What*? Chassignol was my friend, you expect me just to forget that?'

'Chassignol made his choice, now you have to make yours.'

I paused, Grue was right, she was right, which meant I was probably wrong. Slowly, reluctantly, I raised my hand, as I did so, I caught Grue's eye. Instead of the look of triumph I expected, he simply nodded again, almost ruefully. I nodded back as something approaching an understanding had just passed between us.

Emotionally and physically exhausted, I fell asleep again. This time my dreams were mercifully free of prophecy and fable. When I woke it was fully daylight. Xeurf still flew steadily along, though much lower now. Craning over his neck I could see dense jungle spread out before us like a giant salad. Tall trees, topped with vibrant green foliage and festooned with creepers, stretched far away into the distance. Here and there the carpet of greenery broke to allow the passage of a river or the sharp drop of a cliff face. Underneath the trees was a thick down of moss, giant shrubs and assorted plant life.

'Oh ger-goody, more jungle,' said Milan, as he woke and stretched, no doubt thinking about what had happened on Truant Island. By now we'd learnt to keep our Memory Exception Crystals with us at all times, so we were unlikely to be bothered by insects, but I still didn't fancy the idea of spending the next few days or weeks hacking about in the vegetation below.

I looked at Qi LiFang's map. The final destination seemed to be high up, on a curiously square mountain with a flat expanse at the top, rising above the jungle. The map showed sheer cliffs on all four edges of the plateau and what looked like the remains of a city built by Man. In the centre of the plateau was another protrusion. The map wasn't clear but it looked to me like the crater of a huge volcano. Vampires will naturally settle in the highest vantage point in any area, so it seemed likely that they would choose to settle here.

I assumed Xeurf somehow also knew where we were heading, as he didn't seem to want directions. I also knew that were getting closer as his wing beat was slowing, and his colossal head was beginning to hang. His last flight. Without him we would not have been able to defeat the small army of Trolls and Dark Faies. He saved the Eyrie and by flying us here through the night had almost certainly bought us days, possibly even a week or two of extra time to try to find the Chalice. And distance was what I badly needed right now. Our magic trace from Xeurf would be obvious and the Thin Man's vessel seemed to cope with any medium. As long as he was able to track me, the Thin Man would come eventually, I was sure of that. And, when he did, Chassignol would be with him. Although I dreaded it, I was sure of that, too.

As if echoing my fears Xeurf gave a sudden great shudder and his head drooped lower still. By now he had been flying solidly for fourteen hours or more and had crossed over half the planet. It was an immense journey, even for a Dragon, and I realised that he must have been exhausted. We lost more height until the tops of the trees were less than a hundred feet or so below. A blue and yellow parrot took off in alarm as Xeurf cast his huge shadow across the landscape and monkeys chattered in that mad way of theirs, shooting along branches with their babies clinging to their fur, to hide in the thick foliage as Xeurf sank lower still.

Then Milan gave a hoarse shout. 'Look!'

I followed his line of sight and noticed, on the far horizon to the south, the sharp rock face rising up, high above the jungle canopy. Without a doubt, we were far too low now – we should have been aiming for the top of the plateau, as far as possible up the slopes of the volcano that sat at its centre. Xeurf must have seen it too, because he roused himself to one final effort. But as we came closer, I began to worry that we wouldn't make it even to the foot of the cliff, falling short by several miles.

'We need to lighten the load!' Grue commented.

'What?'

'He's right,' I said, 'we can get rid of all the tents and bedding for starters. This is the jungle, there should be plenty of animals we can feed off, so the food's out too. Milan, Faucon, I'm afraid that Dragon Clan armour will have to go, too.' They hesitated for a moment, then, reaching un-spoken agreement, tossed it all overboard.

Soon our swords and a few other essentials were all that remained. Xeurf had gained a bit of height but not nearly enough.

'Why don't we just fly?' said Sansonnet. 'It's not like we've any stuff to carry now.'

'Good idea,' said Peregrine.

'No way,' I said, 'we're not deserting Xeurf.'

Peregrine looked like he was about to argue but just then there was a loud crack of thunder and a white flash of lightning forked across the sky. Large droplets, the size of my head, began to fall, he looked up '…it looks like rain.'

That decided it: our dragonfly wings would be battered to pieces in a downpour like that. We just had to wait and hope that Xeurf would make it.

In the end, he nearly did.

By degrees his wing beats became less powerful and his huge

heart slowed to a single dull thump every ten or fifteen seconds. We were only a few hundred yards from the plateau but the ancient Dragon's belly was scraping the tops of the trees now and it was clear we were going to crash at the base of the cliff instead of on top of it. The landing, when it came, was surprisingly gentle – with one last great effort, Xeurf arched his back, and using his massive wings as an air brake halted in mid-flight, coming down with the gentlest of bumps.

We all climbed down in the torrential downpour as Xeurf's head sank to the forest floor and he closed his eyes with a sigh that was nearly a groan. Sansonnet went up and gently stroked his cheek with the palm of her hand. 'Can we help?' she asked.

For a moment I thought he was already dead, then he opened an eye and whispered.

'Some water would be rather nice.'

Sansonnet quickly gathered up some of the rain into the natural bowl of a cup-shaped leaf and brought it to his lips.

The Dragon took a few sips and rested his head on the ground again. 'I came here many years before, you know,' he said, his lungs heaving like giant bellows. 'There is no one here now,' he continued distractedly, smelling the air. 'Or … perhaps … ' he struggled for air again, '…far below, who knows.'

Sansonnet offered him more water.

'Thank you. You are kind.'

'Can we get you anything else?' she asked.

But there was no answer. As we watched, the scales along his body began to turn white as they calcified. Minutes later they began to crack and then crumble as they disintegrated into ash and his bones reduced to fine powder. Soon, all that was left of Xeurf was a pile of dust that would presently wash away in the rain. Like our tears.

As we moved towards the base of the cliff to find shelter, we were so absorbed in our grief that we did not see the egg lying in the tall pampas grass where the dead Dragon's body had been.

'Jungles — bloody 'orrible places, and we always end up in one, sooner or later, every time we step out of the door for a little adventure.'

Peregrine.

Chapter 18

the labyrinth

We all stood and stared in silence down the mouth of what was quite obviously a tunnel leading upwards.

'It's qer-quite obviously a tunnel,' Milan pointed out. 'Going upwards, for some reason.'

Outside, the rain streamed down in a way that I'd never seen rain stream: Individual droplets of water had rapidly merged into individual rivulets so that between the creepers that hung in fronds to the ground, it looked exactly like thousands of hoses pointed directly at the jungle floor, each pumping out tepid water at full blast. A constant draught of damp musty air blew from within, suggesting a large dark spaces at our backs.

'There will be Chitinarthropodea in there, I shouldn't wonder,' remarked Grue, casually peering up the hole.

'What's that then?' asked Faucon.

'Giant centipedes. The largest found anywhere in the world.'

'They sound s-s-so cute,' said Milan.

'What do they do?' asked Faucon conversationally.

'Well, on a good day, they usually try to bite your head off with their front mandibles to suck out your insides.'

'Yes, absolutely charming,' agreed Sansonnet.

'Quite so, and if that fails or if they fancy coming back to eat you later, they'll simply paralyse you with venom.' There was a pause whilst each of us weighed up the options. According to the map, it looked like we had to get to the top of the plateau and then into the volcano. And sometime soon, before the Thin Man caught up with us.

It was Peregrine who summed up what we were all thinking. 'I 'ate getting wet,' he said, and gestured towards the tunnel entrance, 'let's see if we can't find a way up through here.'

When I was a very young Vampire, Chassignol's dad would say to us. 'Boys, if you keep quiet and eat your soup before it congeals, I'll tell you a story.' Our favourite one went something like this:

Moüsch the Bat (no relation) lived in an enormous cave, somewhere in a far away place, with a lot of other bats who looked a lot like him. They spent most of their time flapping about the caverns, screeching and hanging upside down. Sometimes, just for a change, they would walk around on the cave floor, or stand upright for long periods of time. This was called Yoga.

Now Moüsch was a Vampire Bat and this meant that, much like us, he lived mainly off the blood from other animals. Because there were so many other Vampire Bats living in the cave, competition to go get one's teeth into really nice juicy blood was fierce. Special bat patrols were set up to go out and find where all the animals were hiding at night, so that the bats could fly there en masse and get stuck into a field full of unsuspecting sheep or a very surprised herd of oxen.

Anyway, one night our friend Moüsch got fed up with waiting about for the Blood Patrol to come back and tell them in which nearby field their supper was standing, and instead flapped off on his own into the night looking for prey.

About an hour later he came back looking exhausted. To all the other Vampire Bats it was obvious that he'd just had a really good supper. Blood covered his mouth, matted his hair and there was even quite a lot on his feet. 'Where's the feast?' they asked, practically beside themselves with excitement.

'Not telling,' muttered Moüsch and he closed his eyes and pretended to go to sleep.

'Oh go on!' they chorused. 'We're absolutely starving!'

'I'm so hungry I could eat a light salad,' said his best friend Chassignol (no relation).

'I don't want to talk about it.'

'Oh pleeeeaaaasse!'

Moüsch knew it was no good. They wouldn't give him a moment's rest until he showed them where he'd been. 'OK, OK,' he said, unfolding his wings and looking a bit shifty. 'I'll take you there.'

The sight of ten thousand bats all leaving the cave to follow Moüsch was impressive as well as pretty scary but no one was about to miss out on the meal of a lifetime, so they all tagged along.

They flew down the valley, a great black cloud of leathery wings flapping and screeching. Simple Human folk thought that the end of the world was coming, closed their shutters tight and started to pray for the first time in years. A crowd of frogs hopped for the safety of a large log and a solitary wolf howled in anguish against the backdrop of the Moon. At the end of the valley, a steep cliff with a waterfall cascading down its smooth, black surface led up to a frozen plateau.

Ten thousand and one bats, sensing that the journey was nearly over cried out in glee, licking their sharp little teeth and thin black lips.

And indeed there, in the midst of the ice-bound plateau, stood a huge dark boulder. Moüsch raised a batty hand and everyone stopped. There was complete silence. Finally Moüsch turned to them, his mouth still bloody.'There,' he said grumpily, pointing at it, 'do you see that big rock?'

'Yes, yes, we do,' they all cried, their tummies rumbling.

'Well I didn't,' said Moüsch.

Ha ha.

~

Anyway, bats and other things that lurk about in dark places were definitely at the forefront of our minds as we moved through the cave, which tapered and then narrowed into what looked suspiciously like a Vampire-made tunnel. Grue led the way. I still didn't like him, but if it wasn't for his little speech earlier we'd be trying to explain to the Eltern right now why we had come back without the Chalice and why an eight-hundred-thousand-year-old Dragon's last flight had been wasted as a fire-breathing taxi home.

Almost immediately it became apparent that it was not only an old Vampire tunnel, but that something wasn't altogether quite right about it. It wasn't that it was creepy (although it was) and it wasn't only that we didn't have the faintest idea where we were going (although we didn't). No, the main reason why this particular tunnel was so unusual was that it changed direction every few steps. I wasn't sure if the others were aware of it except Sansonnet, who was looking as puzzled as I felt. It was like walking down the insides of a tremendous snake that coiled and uncoiled at will. A sudden horrible thought occurred to me and I gave one of the walls a quick jab with the point of my sword. Solid stone.

'What are you *doing?*' asked Sansonnet, giving me a look.

'Nothing.'

'Can you smell marshmallows?' she asked, looking embarrassed.

'No,' I replied. 'All I can smell is bat droppings but mainly Milan.'

'Thanks,' said a voice nearer the front.

'Don't mention it.' I took out my compass and held it up. Even in the dark I had no trouble making out that we were heading due east, the exact opposite direction to the bearing we started out on.

We carried on like this for about an hour until we all began to get quite tired and cold. We'd had nothing to eat since the feast and Grue had chucked out most of our food and water when Xeurf was dying. Every few minutes I looked at my compass and it showed a new bearing. We weren't exactly heading upwards anymore, by my reckoning, towards the plateau itself. Our plan to use what now seemed more like a labyrinth to get to the top of the mountain did not seem to be working.

The strange thing was, the walls were entirely smooth but the floor was pitted and uneven. It was only when I put my hand down to feel what we were walking on that I realised the unevenness came through wear. At one time hundreds of Vampire feet must have trod these paths every day. The thought was vaguely reassuring.

Then there was the sound of something angular scraping across wet rock and the clatter of thousands of tiny feet. *Chatter-di-chack, chatter-di-chack, tak tak tak*, went whatever it was.

'What was that?' Even to my ears I sounded hysterical.

'Dunno,' said Peregrine.

'Where?'

'Up ahead, over there.' Further down the tunnel I could make out an odd silvery glow. We made our way towards it, cautiously. All the time I tried to look to the future, to see if I could sense any danger. None was apparent, but it was hard because at the same time, I was still trying to work out what had made the *chatter-di-chack* noises. Those worried me.

That the labyrinth seemed Vampire-made was soon confirmed when we turned the corner. The source of the strange light was still not apparent but there was enough to see that the chamber was covered from ceiling to floor with line upon line of some ancient Vampiric script, the like of which I had never seen. The hieroglyphs and symbols were familiar but I had no idea what they were trying to say. Occasionally the author would take a break from his carving and draw a picture. There was no mistaking the meaning here: one showed a Vampire having his stomach eaten by a large rat, whilst another was having his eyes pecked out by some sort of parrot and a particularly gruesome illustration near the ceiling showed a whole bunch of Vampires being eaten in a humungous sandwich by a large Troll.

'Anyone got any idea what any of this stuff says?' Peregrine scratched the end of his nose and peered at the symbols.

'It's obviously a local form of our ancient script,' said Grue, 'and we certainly don't have time to decipher it.'

Sansonnet was not convinced. 'What if it's really important?'

'I doubt that, judging by the pictures. Whoever wrote this was probably a moron.'

'How can you be so sure?' Sansonnet's cheeks went pink.

Grue shook his head, but did at least make an effort to sound reasonable. 'We could be down here with no food and water for the next two weeks. If we spend all that time trying to work out this rubbish it's just going to be a lot of stuff about curses for coming here in the first place and *beware* and *you're all going to die horribly*, which might well be true but there's no point in upsetting ourselves.'

'You haven't even given it –'

'Guys,' Milan and Faucon had wandered off towards the odd light.

'– a chance, it might …'

'*Guys!*'

'What?' We were all enjoying the argument between Sansonnet and Grue.

'You might want to come and have a look at this.'

A few moments later we had discovered the source of the light and the strange smell of marshmallows. It was a room covered from floor to ceiling with thousands of what looked like miniature mushrooms. Each one gave off its own whitish glow, like a tiny lightbulb. The mushrooms themselves were a creamy colour, and each had a purplish head covered with tiny white spots. 'Don't eat any,' said Sansonnet to me.

'Do I look stupid?'

I was hungry though. However, my appetite slunk off into the shadows when I turned and saw what Milan and Faucon had also found lying in the chamber.

Most of the Human skeleton's clothes had rotted away, leaving large white bones jutting through the tattered fabric. A leather belt was all that remained of his trousers and his long white leg bones stretched out in front of him. A carpet of mushrooms had grown around his long bony toes that poked out from old leather boots. What was most alarming about this towering human skeleton was the fact that all his hair was still there. Long, greasy locks hung down beside his hollow cheeks – the dirty blond hair seemed to have carried on growing for some time after he had died. And he sat there wearing a hat with two cow horns stuck on the side, grinning at us as if death was the funniest thing imaginable.

In his hand he held a tattered bundle of parchments.

'The Saga of Olaf the Maddening,' it said on the cover in scratchy handwriting we all recognised.

≫

We all crowded around. I reflected that at the start of the Quest, confronted with the hairy corpse of what was to all intents a giant, all of us, with the possible exception of Peregrine, would have run a mile barefoot over sharp pebbles. Admittedly it was pretty gruesome, especially since I had also noticed bits of mummified skin still hanging from the bones in places, all leathery and yellow. We had all toughened up over the months.

'Well at least we can read this,' remarked Peregrine, 'it's the old Faie the Angles learned – unless Grue has any of 'is objections?' So we all heaved this way and that and eventually got the first page to open flat.

≫

↲December 4, 421 Year of Our Lord
VENTA
So here we are, ready to set sail at long last. The proud vessel we have purchased for the expedition is called The Sacred Endeavour, an apt name, if ever there was, for a stout and holy purpose – aye, there! Please forgive the lapse into seafaring speak. Still in port, but the rough language of the old Viking salts who work the docks is already rubbing off on yours truly, Olaf the Christian, formerly - to his heathen friends, to whom he rarely, if ever, speaks (may they burn in helle) - Olaf the Annoying.

So, the stores are loaded, the sails unfurled and I must admit to a growing impatience to be off, to leave these shores and carve out adventure on the high seas in our long ship whose pagan Dragon

I have insisted on replacing with a more fitting cross.

... later, around teatime...

Sitting here discussing the trip with my old friend and companion, Garp, over toasted oat cakes, when we hear a shout from the dockside and feel the Endeavour list starboard (at it again!). This is it – we're off!

)—December 5, 421 Year of Our Lord
ENGLISH CHANNEL, CHOPPY
Sea Sick.

)—December 5, 421 Year of Our Lord
CHANNEL CHOPPIER
Sea Sicker!

)— December 6, 421 Year of Our Lord
ATLANTIC CRASHING WAVES
Feel like dying. Prayed to the Holy Saints and even Thor, on the off-chance.

December 7, 421 Year of Our Lord
ATLANTIC
Took a short turn on deck. Sick again. Entreat Garp to chop my head off with that axe of his and put me out of my misery. Captain laughs nastily.

)—December 8, 421 Year of Our Lord
ATLANTIC
Gloomy, but feeling better. Took some turnip for lunch.

)—December 9, 421 Year of Our Lord
ATLANTIC
Brisk, chilly weather, but awoke to bright sunshine – a glorious day! The frost on the rigging soon melted. Garp and I are feeling most

refreshed after days as virtual prisoners in the bottom of the boat whilst the crew rowed and trod on our poor heads. Gulls' cries filled the morning air and I was pleased to note that the waters had turned from a dull greenish grey slab, to an azure blue thingy.

No one has ever crossed this great ocean before, but I feel sure with the blood of Vikings in our veins and the Lord of this new religion on our side, we will make our goal. The end of the world!

'Well, I for one hope that the hunting is good,' put in dear old Garp, in that dashing way of his, polishing his axe.

꜊December 10
MID-ATLANTIC
Waxed moustache ... and tied nice things in it.

'Shall we skip a bit?' Sansonnet suggested.

꜊December 25
PACIFIC
We celebrated Christian Day when their god, who we now know as the One True Deity, was born, by crossing the Equator and taking the Endeavour into the warmer climes of the Pacific Ocean.

Christmas meal was thanks to sharp-eyed Garp, who managed to bag an albatross. Some of the crew oddly upset by this, apparently it is a bad omen. Dark mutterings below.

Really, you would have thought Christians and free Norsemen to boot, would have put away these childish superstitions. It's nearly the 6th Century after all. The albatross, I confess, was not quite up to the usual Christmas fattened goose standard but was very tasty nonetheless and a welcome change from cook's seagull and mouse stew.

Went to bed slightly the worse for wear after a bottle of ale and 18 glasses of mead. Kissed Teddy and fell sound asleep.

꜊December 26
RAFT! PACIFIC
Was rudely awoken by the ship's priest and the Captain himself.

It seems the crew had actually decided to mutiny overnight over this wretched albatross business! We just made it off the Endeavour before they threw us overboard. Some of the chaps really were quite rough.

Still, I faced them down like a gentleman and they agreed to let us take our axes and a box of ship's biscuits, two barrels of water, 3 barrels of ship's ordinary mead (for medicinal purposes), a crate of ale, one slightly off cheese and a map.

)—December 27
RAFT, PACIFIC
Have christened the liferaft The Endeavour II. Captain Ogg seems rather downhearted and hardly stirred a limb all day except when he happened to notice Garp securing his axe to the stern of the craft with some twine and a very large cork.

'Where did you get that?' he enquired, somewhat sharply, pointing at the cork, which was the size of a dinner plate.

'Oh, I found it below decks, moments before we were thrown off,' said old Garp, matching the brusqueness of the Captain's tone with an admirable nonchalance. 'I thought it might come in handy for something or other. Had a hell of a job shifting it. I say, what's up old chap?'

Captain Ogg had gone quite red in the face and seemed to be having difficulty breathing. 'You idiot!' he finally managed to blurt out. 'That's the ship's plug. They'll all be drowned by now, we've got the only raft.'

)— December 28
ENDEAVOUR II. PACIFIC
Things a little fraught on board. Ate a biscuit. Captain and our so-called priest spent all day drinking rum at the aft of the boat, singing sad songs of lament to Thor.

)— December 29
ENDEAVOUR II. PACIFIC
We've run out of water so it's onto the ale. Cheese caused strange imaginings and dreams. Still, mustn't get too glum. My own spirits

good. Garp and the Captain continue to be cold with one another, I am sorry to say. Priest acting funny.

〜December 30
ENDEAVOUR II. PACIFIC
Thirsty

〜December 31
ENDEAVOUR II. PACIFIC
So thirsty.
    Had a dream last night that Teddy was stolen and a giant octopus was trying to eat my ears. Woke to find that the priest was gnawing the side of my head.

〜January 1.
Gregorian New Year's Day 422 AD Year of Our Lord
ENDEAVOUR II. PACIFIC
Land sighted. We're saved!

〜 January 2,
DRY LAND. INDIA?
Spirits much revived. We found a small stream flowing near the beach and fell upon it like savages. The taste of fresh water after two days was better than anything I remember. The coast here is littered with palm trees, bananas and gigantic pineapples.
Garp shot a parrot in the afternoon with his bow and we ate that.
    Speaking of savages, we've all mentioned a feeling of being watched from the thick jungle that runs down almost to the shoreline. Once or twice I've felt sure I heard drums, and the priest, a man of a delicate disposition, is certain that, 'we'll all be eaten in our beds tonight by the locals!'
    Have placed own axe under a palm leaf bed, just in case.

〜 January 3
DRY LAND. INDIA?
Awoke in the early hours to a strong wind coming in from the sea.

Within minutes the wind had reached such a pitch that we were forced to abandon the beach and take shelter in the bosom of the jungle.

Wind and rain, the like of which I have never seen – even in Readingum – lashed at the shore as if the very Devil himself was trying to beat the forest flat in a fury. Fell into a strange and fitful sleep, where a dwarf in a grass skirt was pursuing me with a glove puppet. Woke up and the priest had gone. Captain very upset, thinks the natives may have got him in the night. Garp remarked that it was more likely he finally lost his marbles and wandered into the sea.

It pains me to say that our Captain and Garp are no longer on speaking terms, communication being conducted solely through yours truly or via terse little notes scratched in the sand with a stick.

)—January 4,
DRY LAND. INDIA?
Mindful of more tropical storms, we spent the morning building a shelter in a clearing with the Captain. Garp went off and shot a monkey, five brown and white furry things that look like fat squirrels but apparently don't climb up trees, a couple more parrots and a green snake. We were tucking into this feast when the priest suddenly reappeared.

Gave us a shock. In fact, it took me a few moments to recognise him. Seems to have gone native – painted face, lots of feathers and an uncomfortable-looking pair of shorts resembling a large nappy made entirely out of straw.

Captain rushes forward with a joyful cry of, 'Snookie, you're alive by gad!' only to be muscled out of the way by about thirty or so titchy native fellows who appeared out of nowhere.

)—January 5,
PYGMY VILLAGE. WHO KNOWS WHERE …
Seems as if the priest's quite the dark horse (come to think of it, he's never mentioned his name). The natives all think he is a type of god and sit around all day fanning him with banana leaves whilst their

wives dice pineapple chunks and other delicate morsels for his fancy.
He kindly granted us an audience after making us all wait around
in the blazing sun for half the day. Turns out they think we're
his servants!

)—January 6
PYGMY VILLAGE. LOST.
Spent all day fanning that bloody priest and chopping pineapple
chunks under the direction of the pygmies.

)—January 7
PYGMY VILLAGE. UTTERLY.
More of the same.

)—January 8
PYGMY VILLAGE. WANT TO GO HOME.
...ditto

)—January 20
PYGMY VILLAGE.
Garp finally cracked this afternoon.
    Unable to stand it a moment longer, and I can hardly blame him,
he picked up his axe and hit the priest with the blunt end. Priest,
clutching his head and bleeding rather copiously runs off, shouting.
'Help, murder most horrid!' and other such nonsense. Not looking
where he was going the silly little man falls into a large cauldron of
boiling water that was busy bubbling away in the middle of the
village. Priest dies immediately. Even the Captain, who had begun
to take a different view altogether of his beloved Snookie over the few
days past, looks pleased.
    However, hitting gods – however annoying they might be – is
a grave offence it would seem to the natives, so Garp, me (clutching
Teddy) and the Captain beat a hasty retreat out of the village.

⌒January 21
MIDDLE OF THE JUNGLE SOMEWHERE. BEGINNING
TO THINK WE'RE IN WHOLE NEW CONTINENT
*Spent all night dodging angry pygmies in the forest; began to realise
what it must be like to be Welsh.*

⌒January 22
MIDDLE OF THE JUNGLE SOMEWHERE. STILL.
*Pygmies finally gave up their search for us half way through the
second day. But if we thought our troubles were over, then we were
sadly mistaken. Captain Ogg fell down a waterfall this afternoon
and was lost to us forever.*

*The tragedy took place towards dusk when we came upon a sudden
clearing in the forest and a cascade that issued forth from a sheer
granite cliff. Fortunately our Captain, who was leading our now sadly
depleted party, stopped just in time. Unfortunately, Garp, who was
busy scanning the trees for something to shoot at with his bow and
arrow, carried on going, only stopping after he had pushed the
surprised Captain over the edge.*

*'Yoouuu, moooroooon!' were the poor wretch's last words as he
tumbled into the void and onto the treacherous rocks below.*

*And now, to make matters worse, dear old Garp, childhood
companion, has succumbed to a nasty bite from a spider. Looks
bad – great shudders are wracking his body, foam seems to be
turning green around his lips. He may not last the night.*

*To think, Teddy and me will soon be the only ones left from the
brave band of adventurers who set out barely one month ago from
Merry Old Lloegr. The tragedy of it!*

⌒January 23
MIDDLE OF THE JUNGLE SOMEWHERE.
Garp died in the night. Am bereft.

⌒January 24
STONE TEMPLE. JUNGLE AND CREEPERS.
Teddy and I wandered aimlessly in the jungle these past few days,

mourning the demise of our companions, drinking what was left of our meagre rations of mead, tripping over tree roots, only to lie for hours tangled in bracken, insensible.

Awoke on the third day of this tropical wake, relatively sober again, in a muddy puddle. It had been raining in the night and I had a faint recollection of thunder and flashes of lightning throughout the dense forest. The day was fresher and shafts of sunlight stole through the canopy above. I had been badly stung the day before when I had drunkenly assaulted a wild bees' hive for its honey. However, my spirits were greatly revived when I found that I had been partly successful in my endeavours and a good sized lump of honey comb lay in my day bag where I keep my diary, Teddy and a half bottle of mead that I poured away immediately and replaced with rainwater collected from a nearby stream.

I ate the honey, drank some water and started to make my way through the creepers towards a large rocky outcrop I could see in the distance. From there, I was hoping to plot a course back to the coast where I would wait to be rescued someone or other.

About six hours later, I was standing at the foot of the outcrop, looking up at the sheer walls and wondering how I could attempt an assault on the summit without breaking my neck when I chanced upon a narrow cave that led up into a chamber lit entirely by strange crops of glowing mushrooms. The walls of the tunnel here are entirely smooth and everywhere are tiny carvings in a strange language, which leads me to suspect this is a temple, hewn out of the solid rock by a culture that is far superior to those pineapple - chomping savages on the beach.

I say 'is' because for the past few hours I have had the distinct impression that I am not alone. The walls of the tunnel seem to creak and groan, as if continually on the move and I seem to keep hearing strange whispers in the darker corners of the room that I find to be empty, when I go over to investigate.

I am also gnawed at by hunger, the like of which I have never known. It is as if I have never eaten a scrap. It was hours ago since I finished the last of the honeycomb and there are only a few crumbs in the bottom of my bags and the mummified remains of the parrot.

Those mushrooms are starting to look decidedly tasty.

)~January 25
STONE TEMPLE.
I am enlightened. The scales have fallen from my eyes,
for I am The Chosen.

I see now that it was always my destiny to come here alone, to travel the oceans, endure great hardships, to know hunger and to feel thirst. It was my providence and mine alone to eat of the mushrooms that caused mine eyes to see and my lips to speak the truth.

'Oh, 'ere we go,' said Peregrine.

That which causes me to see will close my eyes, ere long. The flesh of the fruit that grows so abundantly on the floor of this temple has quickened my heart just as it will soon cause it to stop for ever. This magical labyrinth that twists and turns like the mind of a lunatic holds more secrets than one man alone could fathom. The greatest of all its secrets lies at its very centre.

The Tree of Life.

I close mine eyes now and I can see it standing in majesty; ancient and gnarled – the First Tree. Long before the ancient rain forest around us spread out to cover the vast continent, this tree grew in what was then called Eden. When Adam was banished for eating its fruit to wander the young Earth with his Eve, a great wall of stone was thrown up around the Tree of Life to protect it and to protect others from it and a labyrinth grew, like the roots of an oak through the rock and under stone. All alone, it has remained in its tomb for millennia, waiting.

But nothing stays hidden for long. It was found by the first tribes of the Lost Cities. Not knowing exactly what it was they worshipped it for, they sensed its terrible power and they carved the runes in the tunnels that spoke of its legacy. Then a plague came and they died and other beings inhabited the Labyrinth, the night crawlers, the Nosferatu. They came on an ancient beast, which breathed fire and scorched the plague from the tunnels and chambers. They were

*ancient and wise and they too understood the First Tree and
respected it. So they dug a hole at the base of the tree and placed
their most precious possession inside. Some call it 'The Grail'.
They call it 'The Chalice'. And a well filled the hole with a deadly
water that none can drink except the true keeper of the Chalice
and there it stays hidden.*

My eyes grow heavy now.
I think ... I'll die ...

There was complete silence.

'That's it guys,' I finished reading and coughed to clear my
throat.

Grue looked thoughtful. 'Nosferatu,' he mused. 'That's us.'

'Must be talking about the Vampire Clan and it sounds like
Xeurf brought them here all that time ago.'

'He said 'e'd been to this dump before. ' Peregrine remarked.
'He might have told us about the Chalice.'

'He was dying and he probably didn't think it was any of his
business,' said Sansonnet somewhat defensively.

'What do you make of all that s-stuff about the Ter-Tree of
Life?' asked Milan, clearly trying to stop an argument developing.

'Sounds like 'e was high as a kite on poisonous mushrooms to
me,' said Peregrine who, I think I have mentioned before, has a
soldier's view on things. ''Orrible 'ippy.'

'Actually it sounds plausible enough,' said Grue quietly, looking
like he was thinking very hard about something.

I found myself nodding. 'Clearly the man was a bit of a fool
when he went in. Then all of a sudden he's an expert on the
Chalice, ancient tribes and Vampires. Must have been a vision.
I should know, I get them all the time. Ha ha,' I finished weakly.

'So w-what do we do now?' asked Milan.

'Let's sleep on it.'

That night we decided to stay awake in turns.

The next morning we awoke cold and stiff from sleeping on the hard, draughty floor of the tunnel. Grue gathered us all together.

'We need a plan,' he said a little stolidly. We all agreed but none of us had a clue what to say next. I'd tried looking into the future several times since we had entered the Labyrinth but it was murky to say the least. All I could see were confused and blurry visions what looked like lava – or just lots of strawberry jam – an indistinct cavern with vaulted ceilings, and darkness. I hadn't tried too hard because I was beginning to suspect that using my gift was alerting the Thin Man to where we were, like a beacon. Sansonnet looked tired, like she had been trying too.

When he was satisfied that we had nothing to add, Grue went on. 'I've been studying the map. The entire plateau is about a mile across at its narrowest point and almost two miles in length. The Labyrinth itself could be twice that size and probably is. Given that it keeps moving about like a fairground ride, we could die of old age down here before we find this Tree.'

But I wasn't really listening. I had heard a sound similar to the one I heard the day before when we discovered the chamber. It was very faint but unmistakable.

' … we need a shortcut or a way to navigate the Labyrinth and I think Moüsch, with your Gift, you might be able to help.'

I didn't answer at first. 'There it is again,' I said out of the blue.

'There's what?'

'Shh.' I was listening intently, head cocked to one side. 'Did you hear that?'

'Er, no, what?' Everyone looked suddenly uncomfortable.

'You 'aven't eaten one of them mushrooms 'ave you?' asked Peregrine.

I answered by staring at him with as much disdain as I could muster. Peregrine shuffled under my gaze. 'I only meant that this isn't one of your premonition fingy wotsits is it?'

'No,' I shook my head. 'I definitely heard something.'

'What?' Sansonnet came and stood beside me, sword drawn. I didn't know it at the time but this was going to save my life.

'A *scuttle*.'

'A Scuttle? Like that thing for a fire?'

'That's a *skittle*, this is a *scuttle*,' I confirmed, 'and a *clickety-clack*.'
On cue, it came again, closer this time.

'Like that?'

'Yup, that's it … '

There was a sudden burst of movement from outside the
chamber and then about a dozen giant centipedes were in the
room, climbing the chamber walls and streaking up the ceiling
in a twisting helix. For a moment it looked as if they were just
passing through, but this was a ruse to get height. They dropped
down on us. The Memory Exception Crystals did not appear to
work on them, and before I could react one had me clamped
around the throat. I felt the small bones in my neck creak, ready
to snap at any moment as the centipede's two glassy eyes stared
into mine with prehistoric indifference.

Peregrine whipped out his throwing knives and threw four in
quick succession into the writhing form of the largest centipede,
which found itself pinned neatly to the rock.

Thankfully, before my neck was cut clean in two by the
centipede's pincers and my head actually came off, Sansonnet's
sword flew up and cut the bug in half. The part of its body
attached to my neck stiffened as I felt two burning pinpricks
under each of my ears. Then the centipede's grip relaxed and its
corpse fell to the stone floor with a *splat*.

'I guess those must be the Chitinarthropodea. Are you
alright?' asked Sansonnet. She touched the two spots where
the centipede had punctured the skin with its venomous jaws.
They burned like two coals on the side of my neck but her touch
felt strangely light and wonderfully cool.

By way of an answer I tried to smile bravely at her but my lips
felt like they were melting down one side of my face. 'Doom,' was
all I said, as the poison took effect and I slid down the chamber
wall into my nightmares.

'My first experience at the Tree of Life taught me that there is little difference, for me at least, between the dream-state and reality. One complements the other.'

Moüsch. *Letters to Sansonnet.*

the tree of life

When I apparently awoke I was standing – quite alone – on the edge of a deserted shoreline. In the distance an enormous rock face rose up from crashing waves; clouds and a sea mist obscured the top of the cliffs, and so too the sun.

I was munching on an apple.

This is alright, I thought and then I noticed the tree roots, spreading out like immense brown tentacles all around me. I dipped a finger in the water and tasted it. It was brackish, not salty – a vast inland lake. I looked again at the cliffs ahead and realised that the rocky face was grained and pitted, deep grooves running up into folds, and through the mist, directly above my head, I could just discern what looked like the start of a lateral branch. I realised that the rock was ancient bark covering an immense trunk the size and breadth of a mountain.

The Tree of Life.

I looked again at the apple I was steadily chomping through, and suddenly remembering my history dropped it into the water. I blinked slowly, and when I opened my eyes I experienced a terrible clarity. I now saw myself as others saw me: a cripple, weak in mind and body in equal measure. I was mean-spirited and could only ever laugh at all I saw, even making fun of the misfortunes of my friends; all the friends I had let down at one time or another, or left … I gazed with disgust at my reflection in the lake.

And so I wandered in despair from that lonely shore, beyond the Tree of Life until I came to a great forest of brambles; a dense tangle of thorns the size of carving knives and plants that oozed a yellow poison, like pus. I hated myself so much by this stage that I pushed on through regardless, revelling in my own pain. After a few miles my skin was a series of huge welts where the stings had burned through my flesh and my wings had been torn to shreds on the briars, so I could no longer fly.

Behind me, each time I turned, I noticed a golden thread, sometimes quite thick, glowing like tinsel, sometimes thin and very faint.

I continued as the forest got thicker and the obstacles greater. Once I came to a clearing where I stumbled upon a giant spider whose only purpose in life was to harm me. She had waited over five hundred years for me to come into her nest, but by now she was too old and too decrepit to do anything but spit venom at me from the safety of her web, which hung like a sack from two stunted trees. I drew my sword and saw her shrink back away from the blade, great tears of terror springing from her eyes when she saw I meant to kill her. As I slit her putrid belly, hundreds of smaller spiders spilled out and made their way towards me, their jagged legs beating a dry tattoo on the dead leaves underfoot. I ran away from that place in revulsion and fear.

I heard the familiar cries of my dead brother, Moineau, and my sister, Alouette.

Their voices came from far off towards the darker part of the forest where I was certain that more nameless terrors awaited me. I had to save them! I plunged on through the undergrowth, now almost in a panic; stumbling over roots, falling into stinking ditches of water ringed with slime, and each time I thought I was getting nearer their cries seemed to come from further away, or inexplicably from a different direction. Soon my strength began to leave me as my twisted legs buckled every other step.

Night began to fall and I came upon a deserted house made of timber and mud. The chimneystack had partly toppled due to neglect and stood bent against the dark sky like a harsh question mark. Inside I heard my baby brother cry out again, in fear, but the door at the front was thick and bolted from the inside, so I crept around the back. A coal chute that led down to a cellar was open, and I crawled inside.

What was left of the daylight was immediately extinguished as I landed heavily on a stone floor. The temperature inside dropped to almost freezing and it took several long minutes before I was able to pluck up the courage to move in the pitch darkness. Slowly, with an enormous effort to master each new surge of panic that gripped me, I felt my way around the room until I came to a door. The handle was so cold that the metal stuck to my fingers and tore the skin from the flesh. As the door swung open a new blast of freezing air hit me in the face and burned my lungs. I knew what lay ahead would try to kill me if it could.

In the corridor I met a beautiful girl whose torso ended with the hind-quarters of a dog; she was reading a list of my sins and betrayals from a scroll in a high-pitched, yapping voice that echoed throughout the house. Some had already come to pass, others were misdemeanours and crimes I was destined to commit. This time my sister cried out my name three times, each more urgently than the last – so I pushed past the half maiden and made my way towards the stairs. But each time I tried to climb to the rooms above, the steps would lead me back down into the cellar or into a room that led back into the hallway. The third time this happened I noticed a fireplace on the ground floor, so I crawled inside, hoping for a way through when I got level with the first floor. The chimney flue was small and cramped and the soot got into my eyes and wounds, filling them with infection. Two mysterious wounds either side of my neck seemed to hurt the most.

As I crawled through the darkness, my fingernails bleeding and broken as they scrabbled for purchase against the ancient brickwork, I was assailed by visions of the past and future: I was holding the sword that had murdered my own sister: It was I who was now running through the Black Woods surrounding the Keep, a fugitive, sleeping in a ditch, my clothes stiff with frost and hunger and impotent rage gnawing at my belly: It was I to whom the Thin Man came in the cold night as my life was ebbing away and offered me warmth and comfort. The scene shifted and the Thin Man's claw-like grip grasped my shoulder, telling me I was to be his Lieutenant, his Trusted One to lead the battle against the Eltern and the Keep, to rediscover the Chalice for the glory of all Vampires and I was to be their leader, appreciated at last and revered; second to none but the Thin Man himself, for I was Corbeau. 'No!' I cried and was abruptly back in my own body, in the cold and the dark, 'No,' I said again and although I was exhausted, I continued my climb as another vision assailed me.

This time faces of the dead rose up in front of my eyes, their skin pale and greasy, contrasting in some terrible way with the soot that covered everything in my self-inflicted tomb. Silently they mouthed my name, their gaping mouths toothless and bloody. These were the Vampires who had died dishonourably, and upon their deaths their fangs had been removed as a mark of their shame. As they called out to me soundlessly they reached up, tugging at my arms and legs, welcoming me to their Clan of the damned and damnable. I kicked out and their flesh fell away from their bones, but still they clawed and racked at me. Then Chassignol appeared, slightly apart from the others. I went to take his arm but he melted away from me, back through the blackened brickwork.

Then I saw a chink of light coming through the bricks and put my eye to it. The room I looked into was dimly lit by a single tallow candle that flickered and spat in the corner. Apart from that there was no furniture except two cots at either corner from where I could hear my siblings' feeble moans. Someone in an old-fashioned nurse's uniform, holding a cruel-looking hook, had her back to me and was bending over one of the cots. I braced my back against the wall and pushed, but the bricks would not move. I focused my mind. The bricks began to shake and the mortar binding them together started to loosen. My sister gave a yelp of pain.

Something ignited in my head. Spontaneously, as the bricks blocking me from the room exploded into fragments, I felt another presence in my subconscious. It was Sansonnet! As she sang gently to me, I felt the throbbing of my injuries subside and my mind seemed to clear slowly at first and then another presence stole into my being. The vagabond, Picus. I felt some of his power in me.

The nurse bending over the cots turned, ever so slowly, as if she was expecting me. Her head was that of a Were, her muzzle caked with dry blood, her eyes yellow with madness. She was wrapped in a bonnet from a nursery tale I half-remembered from childhood. She pulled her arm back and threw the hook at me; my mind did a sort of flick and the hook immediately turned into a white butterfly that flitted way out of a shattered window to my left. The She-Were bared her teeth and jumped ferociously at my throat. Without pausing, on my way to the nearest bed, I drew my sword and took her arm off cleanly at the shoulder.

However, when I reached the cot I found only a rag doll in a filthy cotton dress. I went over and looked inside the other crib, which contained nothing but a straw boy in blue dungarees. Both mannequins lay lifeless, whatever magic having left their raggedy bodies presumably to retreat to another part of the house. At that moment I experienced all over again the pain of losing them and the knowledge that they were gone forever. The pain turned to white rage and I turned on the She-Were who lay bleeding on the dusty wooden floor.

She died with a sort of resignation. Before her life fled, she rasped, 'He is upstairs. He is waiting for you.'

When I was a small boy, Chassignol, Milan, Faucon and me, used to enjoy playing a game we'd invented called *Crypts and Kings*. The idea was simple: One of us would hide a carved wooden knight, we dubbed a *King*, that belonged to Chassignol's father, somewhere in the Keep's Crypt, and the others had to find it. The person who hid the *King* had to make the search as hard and as scary as possible. This was relatively easy in a place like the Crypt, which was a vaulted series of tunnels where our ancient forbears were buried.

Half the thrill, if you can call it that, was going down there on your own to hide the *King* somewhere unlikely. Once, Chassignol actually managed to prise the lid off one of the coffins and place the *King* in the mummified hands of the coffin's current occupant, an ancient and venerable old Nosferatu by the name of Zebedee. Such is the way with a lot of our sort that the Vampire inside the coffin was only slightly dead and was therefore able to be very annoyed at the disturbance by a small, rather grubby Imp. He rose up from the nearly undead and in a voice he had not used for centuries complained long and bitterly to the Eltern who immediately banned us from playing such games for the next few months, and instead made us get rid of all the bats and rats, clean all the cobwebs and sweep up the piles of dust from inside the Crypt. Without centuries of dust clogging the skylights, and cobwebs like sheets to get tangled up in, the Crypt was not such a scary place and the game instantly lost half its appeal.

I now felt the same way about the house and its supposed horrors. My real body, the one that was back in the cave with my companions, fought back. The poison in my veins was receding and in my dream-state Sansonnet's voice soothed my mind and gave me back the strength I thought had deserted me in the Forest of Thistle and Thorn. Each thing I looked at now changed in aspect for the better.

A vase full of dead plants, its water foetid and stinking, spontaneously blossomed into bright red tulips and cornflowers. The girl downstairs stopped her narration of wickedness and began to proclaim my many acts of kindness. The polluted clouds parted and a spectacular sunset gilded the horizon, throwing out tendrils of red, amber and gold across the late evening sky. Finally, the cries of my long dead brother and sister became their laughter in memory.

Feeling my strength and courage return with every step, I climbed the stairs to where I knew the Thin Man was waiting. Finally, for the first time since our quest began, I felt ready to face Him.

⤙⤙

I pushed open the trap door, and was surprised. The room, instead of being darkened and bleak, contained a reassuring fire and a neatly swept wooden floor. Curtains on the window were of faded sunflowers and a pair of leather chairs stood next to the crackling hearth, whose warmth was a welcome contrast to the freezing air in the rest of the Pepper Pot Cottage.

'Come in! Take a pew,' said a voice full of humour, all twinkly and avuncular. The Human-ish face that turned and peered at me from around the wing of the chair was the biggest surprise of all. Good cheer glowed from it like coals on a frosty night. Here was a purveyor of hot scones and frothy milk chocolate. He wore soft gloves. I smiled involuntarily and made my way to the empty chair. 'You've come so far and the way has been hard,' he tilted his head, 'so very hard. I really thought you wouldn't make it.'

'No thanks to you,' I said, keeping my features deadpan and then felt a strange sense of disquiet, as if I had been unforgivably rude. The Man shook his head.

'I regret that, I honestly do – it's all been so ... *unnecessary*. The Eltern you know – so set in their ways. Jolly decent and all that, I'm sure,' he beetled his eyebrows and frowned, 'but rather, er ... stubborn, that's it. Known them for years.'

'What are you talking about?'

'My dear chap,' he said passing me a glass full of an amber fluid that smelled vaguely of almonds and handing me a plate of what, for all the world, looked like toasted muffins. 'The plan was that we should have been working *together*, from the very start.'

'So you could nick the Chalice when we got it and then slaughter us all?'

'Why would I want to do that? We're the same, you and I. Why should I kill my own? Why do we always have to have the Good Guys and the Bad Guys? I really don't understand it and that's the truth of the matter. But the Eltern never liked anyone to be different. Have they ever really accepted you, would you ever have been trusted with the task Peregrine was given?'

Somewhere in the back of my mind, I felt a small bitter seed germinate. 'But … but why have you been trying to kill us all along?'

The Man threw up his arms. 'When did I ever do that?'

'That storm, when we all nearly drowned.'

'I *am* powerful, I admit, but not that powerful.'

'The bird?'

'Old age. I was trying to warn you.'

I shook my head. 'At the Eyrie, then?'

'Bereck's Muster's to blame, it's not even proper Lore! I'm afraid your dour companion, Grue was somewhat … overzealous. The Muster he created was never properly broken. They weren't trying to take over the Eyrie, they merely sensed that their master, Grue, was within the city walls and in trying to do his bidding attempted to force their way in. A grave misunderstanding all round, I fear. But so many battles usually are!'

I searched around in my memory of events, exasperated. 'Chassignol!'

The Man paused, sorrow filled his eyes and a tolling, not unlike church bells at dusk, sounded somewhere not far off.

'Yes, your friend. Your childhood companion. Nothing hurts me more than when a friendship is broken,' he paused to study my face with an intense stare that made me uncomfortable. 'He misses you, you know. He told me as much recently.'

'I miss him.' I blurted out.

'He wanted me to give you this.' The Man held out his hand. Wrapped around his thumb and little finger was a cheap brass chain; dangling from it was a white crystal, meticulously carved. I knew the chain was cheap, as it was I who had bought it with all the money I had when I was no more than a Milk Imp. I also recognised the crystal hanging from it because it was I that had mined the rare Moon Quartz and my hands that had carved and sanded it into the shape it was now. A teardrop.

It had been my present to Chassignol when his father died.

My eyes pricked at the thought he had carried it all this time. The Man watched me carefully.

Even to this day, I have to admit that he nearly had me with the Moon Quartz. My eyes strayed to the arms of the chair where something caught my eye. Eventually I found my voice.

'I might be able to believe you but can I ask you one more thing?'

'Ask me a thousand things – dear old thing, this is why we're here, to talk, to get to know one another, to learn, to trust and be friends again.'

'Okey dokey, can you take off your glove?'

The Man hesitated. Something else now flicked across his face, mild panic, I thought, then annoyance. As quickly as they came, he gathered his features once more into a look of harmless incredulity. 'Whatever for?'

'Just do it,' I said, my voice flat and hard this time.

'Come, come … take the gift, be happy. Your friend wants to see you.'

'Oh, I will … but first remove your glove.'

He looked at me then, in a way that suggested that he was seeing me only now, for the first time. Something changed between us. The pretence was gone. I suspected he didn't want to be friends anymore. Slowly, deliberately, he removed first one glove and then the other.

Darkness came flooding into the room, as dense as a swarm of flies on a corpse. My senses corkscrewed and the jovial figure before me was replaced with a new Being.

'Scum,' said a wholly different voice – one that recalled all my nightmares and balled them into a tight knot of terror that twisted my guts and made me feel like fainting. He turned to face me and yet I saw nothing – his face was now a blank; a dark hole where the mouth should have been and two eyes, burning like red pinpricks, were all I could make out. All other features, skin, jaw, hair and nose were just a smudge, or at least they were there but the moment you looked away they were gone. The creature before me was now forgettable and somehow utterly terrifying at the same time.

His body elongated like a mantis as he extended his arm, and a hand that was no hand, just a collection of dried sticks, beckoned me. 'Come, slave.'

'I am not your slave.'

In answer he only laughed with a dry rasping sound. 'I have been waiting for a long time and I am becoming impatient. Go back to the Tree and bring me the Chalice ... slave.'

Every fibre in my body told me I should obey Him, a lunatic voice seemed to scream in my head that his summons was law, higher than any other. I took a step forward, my knee bending as if I was about to bow before him. His body seemed to relax, for I was to do his bidding but, at the last moment, I straightened up to my full height, looked at him and smiled with as much compassion as I could muster.

His face seemed to crumble before me. I realised then that this creature before me was no longer the Thin Man at all. Like my brother and sister this was no more than a puppet, one of his many masks.

Somewhere, though, not far from the Labyrinth, the real Thin Man was watching. I was sure of this. Why does he not come himself, I thought, surely, sick with poison, he could destroy me easily? But something at that moment told me he could not. I felt his frustration as the Pepper Pot Cottage seemed to shrug off its sinister aspect all the more, to bloom with roses and fresh grass in the brilliant sunset. I also felt His hesitation.

Then the truth of it came to me – He feared us here.

This place, the Inner Chamber that housed the Tree of Life had been fashioned by Vampires. It was *our* place and He daren't go there in person. This was why He followed us still. He needed *us* to retrieve the Chalice. It belonged to *us*. When Chassignol thought he had found out where the Chalice had been hidden by Qi LiFang it was only then he tried to destroy us, that he was able to, with Chassignol to help Him. Chassignol had opened the gates and His army had swarmed in. Indeed, we would all have been dead now if it had not been for Xeurf.

My mind searched outside the Labyrinth for His spirit and hunted it down to a dark place, not far from the plateau. Sansonnet's Song rose to a crescendo in the waking corner of my mind and Picus' power gave one last surge.

I saw the blood coursing through His veins, the same blood as that of the Vampires. The Thin Man was once one of us, or we were once part of Him. The flowing blood became a steady roar in my ears, broadened and changed into rivers of lava, the very same I had seen in my dreams. I recognised this place, I had been here before and I knew where we were heading, but not how or why. I looked down at my hand and suddenly I was holding a silver shard. I turned it over and marvelled at its complete smoothness; no blemish nor crease marred its purity and when I held it up to the light its surface rippled with a score of colours I had never identified before. Instinctively I put it to my lips and it became a cup, filled with a cold liquid that moved like mercury. I drank deeply.

Instantly my movement through the lava flows increased, in my mind I was now going at impossible speeds, making turns in a heartbeat, navigating hidden dangers no ordinary being could divine, long before they even appeared. My Second Sight guiding me, the quicksilver in the Chalice giving me the speed.

Without warning, we came out of the lava flow and into a hollow cavern the size of a small world. The walls wrapped around me in the shallowest of curves that arched off into the distance and then came back round and met thousands of leagues away. The air was hot and the atmosphere stifling. Even though I was not really there in body, my lungs burned with each breath I took and my chest heaved with some unseen pressure. As my roving mind flew closer to its surface, I saw that the walls were made of a porous stone, like pumice and that hundreds, if not thousands of dwellings, roads, bridges and even canals had been carved from the soft rock.

This was the Thin Man's realm. But there was also something Vampiric about the towns and villages below. This vaulted space was once our home too. I knew then that this was where the first of our kind, the Wandering Kings had come from. *Slave*, is what he had called me.

Suddenly I saw:

Our forebears had been imprisoned here. They had somehow escaped and had taken the Chalice with them. I closed my eyes and fished back, far back into the Thin Man's mind at our past. Seeing where I was going he tried to block me, but Sansonnet's voice drowned out his and the mysterious Picus' magic prevailed. I plunged ahead.

〜

When I opened my eyes again, I knew all I needed to know.

An ancient scarecrow, stuffed with old hair and faded straw was all that remained of my opponent who had been seated in the chair. The Thin Man's shadowy presence had fled from wherever he had been watching my progress. He was no longer the hunter but, for now at least, the hunted. Somehow, thanks to Picus, I knew his thoughts, and if I cared to his whereabouts, just as he had known mine. I felt stronger than I ever had.

So I left that dark room. The golden thread that had been with me before was back again, streaming out before me, and so was Sansonnet's voice, which I followed out of the Pepper Pot Cottage and towards the Forest of Thistle and Thorn, where I found myself on a narrow path. And so I followed the song all night, crossing the forest, away from the cottage and towards a great granite wall that lay far off in the distance. By dawn I had reached the wall and found the other entrance to the Labyrinth, the one that led away from the great chamber and the Tree of Life, towards my friends. The golden thread had all but disappeared but the song guided me as I walked for another day. I felt no tiredness nor hunger because this was not my real self, just my mind wandering back, following the golden thread laid by Sansonnet's song, as my body rested, sleeping off the effects of the Chitinarthropodea's poison.

Sansonnet's voice kept up its unceasing lullaby as I meandered through the turns and finally found myself back in the chamber with the others. I saw myself lying there, pale but sleeping peacefully, and gratefully my roving mind slipped back into my body, like putting on a favourite set of clothes.

My eyes fluttered open as Sansonnet's song ended. After three days and nights she was drained and could sing no more but her job was done; she had given me strength when I had none of my own and had guided me home. Rising up from my bed, I caught her as she fell. Her lips parted.

'You are back,' was all she whispered.

'Yes I am.'

Our eyes locked and we moved closer to one another, almost touching ...

'Ahem!' Grue cleared his throat loudly.

'Corbeau sees the Chalice only as a weapon.
I do not agree. Like all things of great power
it is more complex than that. I believe that
it is our last hope when war is no longer
a viable solution.'

Raptor. A General's Life, by Princess Chrisnu.

the key in argent

We sat in the chamber around a fire that Peregrine had lit. Some of the fuel he was using looked suspiciously like old bones. The smoke stung our eyes but the warmth it brought was welcome, and it dispelled the strange light that the mushrooms gave off, which was getting a little eerie. Earlier, the cousins had gone out into the jungle and brought back some misshapen-looking fruit that tasted like a very sweet peach and left a red sticky residue around our mouths. And so now we all looked like clowns.

I had just finished explaining everything to them as briefly as possible: I told them how the Thin Man had finally penetrated my defences when I was weakened by the poison and how he had tried to use this to get me to unlock the Chalice where it lay at the foot of the Tree of Life and bring it back to Him. That was the easy bit – we knew he was after the Chalice from the start. We now also knew that he couldn't get it without my help whilst it sat at the foot of the Tree of Life. Somehow he was shut out from this place by some magic or life force that our predecessors, the Wandering Kings, had left behind when they escaped through here, out of their subterranean prison, through the volcano.

The hard bit was convincing them of what I had seen about our past. Vampires are generally prouder than any species on the planet and the idea that we had once been slaves to the Thin Man in the vast lava-ridden kingdom where my mind had travelled, was hard to swallow. I ploughed on, ignoring the indignant looks and shaking heads.

'I saw other things too, when I finally broke down His resistance and saw into his mind. I have a theory too about the Chalice and, er … me.'

'Continue,' said Grue.

'I think I was … well, my sort anyway … we *were* some kind of Navigators.' I told them about negotiating the thousands of lava flows that led away from the cavern and how the liquid in the Chalice allowed me to do this at such great speeds. 'It would explain my Second Sight, otherwise we'd crash.' I said.

Sansonnet shifted in her seat. 'It does seem a let-down though,' she said, 'the Chalice simply being an ancient way of getting about.'

'Oh, I think it's a lot more that that,' I said. 'I think that this is just *one* of the things it can do. It seems to be able to change form and to provide whatever is needed at the time. The Thin Man knows its full value and probably how to use it. If I can get close enough to Him again I can find that out. One thing I am sure of though is that when He lost it, He lost his control over us and we were able to escape out of slavery. If we have it again, He can't harm us. Hiding it was all very well but a mistake, we need to keep it close.'

'Sounds like if He gets it back we're in big trouble,' said Peregrine. Grue nodded. 'I'd say we'd better get our 'ands on it first, then, before he works out a way of getting to this Tree of Life on his own or with Chassignol. I don't know much about the Lore,' he said glancing respectfully at Grue, 'except that any magic, 'owever strong can eventually be broken. Got any bright ideas?'

I paused. 'Yes, I do actually.' I looked behind me. The golden-coloured thread, still hung there, as if waiting. When I woke up it was quite strong but now it seemed to be fading. We didn't have much time. 'I know the way down,' I said, 'but it'll take us two days at least to get there. We need water and provisions and we need to leave now. It won't be easy.'

'Well,' remarked Sansonnet, pointing at the skeleton, 'anything's better than spending any more time in here with *that*.'

'I d-don't know,' said Milan, looking rueful, 'I've got rather fond of him these past few days.'

In response, the odd Viking wore the grin he would wear for eternity...

✒

Later, as we walked down the first set of tunnels, I pondered how much more of a team we had become over the past few weeks. Milan and Faucon had always been a unit, and somehow this had begun to rub off on everyone. Peregrine and Grue seemed to be getting along too, unofficially the new elected leaders of the Quest.

The golden thread was faint but still visible enough in the half-light given off by the mushrooms. Apparently no one else, not even Sansonnet, could see it. She now walked by my side, occasionally our hands would brush and she would squeeze the ends of my fingers affectionately. Once or twice our gaze met and she smiled at me in a way that lifted my spirits and made me feel rather odd at the same time. I didn't bother mentioning the thread to anyone, they'd already had enough of what Peregrine would call *mumbo jumbo* to swallow from me and I didn't want to push my luck. For the time being, at least, Grue and the others seemed happy enough to accept my ancient role of Navigator and be guided by me. Perhaps that's why I didn't need strong legs or wings – my sight would have been enough to give me a place in the old order.

I knew how to get back to the great central chamber and to the ocean that surrounded the Tree of Life but quite what to do when we got there was beyond me. Mainly to take my mind off this problem, I studied the walls and ceiling as we trudged the tunnels. It was now obvious to everyone that Vampires had been here and that they'd settled these tunnels for a long time. The carving in places was Vampiric and here and there was script in a version of the old tongue that was fairly easy for us to decipher. None of it had much to say of interest – it was either just civic stuff, like *Don't eat the mushrooms, Drinking water,* or graffiti, *Vlad smells.* We came across hundreds of chambers leading off from the main tunnel we were in; some looked quite small, and others, judging by the size of the entrances, were as cavernous as a cathedral. There was some evidence of later Human occupation in these larger chambers: intricate carvings of real or imaginary monsters lined the walls; buttresses and radiating arches, that looked extremely worn, held up the walls and roof in places where it looked in danger of caving in.

Though we kept a careful eye out, the tunnels now seemed to be deserted and we all wondered what had happened to the members of the Dragon Clan that had left with Xeurf and the Chalice all those years ago.

We were in good spirits and it all felt like a day out, after the trials we had been through. At first we were excited by everything we saw of the ancient civilization down here; however, as the day wore on and we got more tired, we started to feel less touristy and ignore what was around us in order to concentrate on the long way ahead. I was just promising myself that I would fly as soon as we got out of the Labyrinth and into the Great Chamber, to give my feet a rest, when Grue and Peregrine stopped abruptly. This caused a bottleneck and we all tried to push past one another. It then took a few moments of bitter recriminations to untangle ourselves from each others' swords, arms, legs and wings. Picking myself up off the ground, I looked up to see Grue shudder. He pointed at something just out of my view.

'Is that Him?'

I pushed past to get a clearer view and there, standing before me, in a chamber about the height of a human house was a sight I had hoped to avoid for some time. Whoever had carved it had obviously spent a great deal of time getting Him just right. Down to the last detail.

The Thin Man's mannequin – the one he used to try to terrify me into giving him the Chalice, after the jolly mannequin failed – stared down at me, hollow mouthed and weasel eyed. The rest of the visage had that now familiar and terrible blankness that left you feeling all hope had gone forever. At his feet, Vampires and Humans alike lay dead of a terrible disfiguring disease that left their bodies twisted and their faces worn away. A crow's claw extended from the dirty shroud that covered his frame, and a long finger pointed directly at us.

'You had to deal with that?'

'It's not the Thin Man himself. I think he uses lots of disguises and this is one of them. Anyway,' I said, modestly, 'he's a bit shorter in real life.'

Peregrine looked at me with new respect. 'You poor sod.' He paused to stare up at the colossal statue. 'I fink that explains why all the Vampires and Humans scarpered.'

'I think they managed to seal him out of these tunnels somehow.' I explained again how he could not get into the Labyrinth. 'He's close though. Somewhere hidden in the jungle.'

'And you let us go out and pick fruit!'

'I don't think He's after *us* ... it's me he wants now,' I pointed out.

'He'll wait until we have the Chalice and He'll make his move then,' said Grue.

'More likely He'll get someone else to do it for him. That's His way.'

'You mean Chassignol?'

I didn't answer because I didn't want to think about it at that moment. 'The Thin Man's a coward,' was all I said. 'He won't risk himself if he can get others to fight for Him.' And I thought of Raptor and his struggle against Corbeau's army and the mysterious Picus, somewhere at the fringes. Sometimes I felt overwhelmed by it all.

Sensing the disquiet that lingered after we'd left the statue, Sansonnet tried to lighten my mood by telling me how the giant centipedes had been defeated once I had passed out from the bite. Grue, it seemed had been the hero of the day, killing five on his own and helping the cousins and Peregrine fight off the others. No one else had been hurt, except for Milan, who had fallen on a rock. He still had a nasty bruise the colour of a ripe plum on the back of his head.

'As you lay there dying, or so I thought, I didn't know what to do. You had gone so pale your skin was almost transparent and you were hardly breathing. Then you became very agitated, you called out two names, Moineau and Alouette. That was your brother and sister wasn't it?' I nodded. 'I thought you were remembering your childhood, so I started singing to you; all the songs we sang when we were children. It seemed to calm you and some colour came back into your cheeks. I sang them over and over again.'

'You saved me,' I said simply.

At that moment the thread seemed to falter. I panicked a bit but then realised it was because the quality of the light was changing, getting stronger. We were finally approaching the end of the Labyrinth. A few hundred yards later, Grue and Peregrine stepped out of the tunnel and into the Great Chamber. Quite where all this light was coming from I had no idea, when I had visited this place in my mind – we were miles below the surface of the jungle. However, now when I looked up I saw the truth of it.

At the edge of the chamber where we stood the walls rose up almost a mile in height, but then stopped abruptly, the edge overhung with greenery, huge creepers and tree roots that swept around in a gigantic circle. The cliffs did not only lead to the plateau, as Qi LiFang's map suggested, but also to the volcanic crater that we now stood in. The Labyrinth had originally been the route the lava took to get to the surface. The same route we Vampires had used to escape the Thin Man hundreds of thousands of years before, when this was all fresh. I wondered if the Eltern knew about the Tree. Probably.

Standing in the middle of the crater, just as I had remembered it, was the Tree itself, massive and ancient; its bark was the same colour as the rock. The water around its base sparkled in the late afternoon sunlight. Closer to us, the Forest of Thistle and Thorn lay spread out in a tangle of briars and close-knit stems. The golden thread led off into the distance, towards the path I had taken from the Pepper Pot Cottage.

I still had no idea what we were going to do but right now my heart leapt at seeing the sun and feeling wind on my face again.

I took wing with a shout and shot off towards our destination. The rest of us took to the air behind me. We flew hard, now stronger and fitter than we had ever been in our lives, revelling in the joy of being out of the dismal Labyrinth.

That night we camped on the quiet shores of the lake by the Tree of Life and gorged ourselves on the tiny silver fish that flitted in shoals in its shallows. Then we lay down and looked up at the night sky, as the stars revolved above us, unaware and remote.

⤳

The next day I was up at sunrise. The air was chilly as I went and stood by the water's edge. The jungle, far above us, was shrouded in a silky mist that tipped slowly over the crater's edge and poured in, putting me in mind of a cauldron in reverse.

Grue came to join me, wrapped in a woollen cloak, which he must have brought with him from the Eyrie. He was in a gruff mood and, like me, he obviously hadn't slept that well. 'This place is too full of magic,' he remarked, glaring up at the Tree as if it was to blame. 'Too many dreams.'

'It is,' I agreed. 'There are.'

'What do you propose to do now?' he said, looking at the still waters at our feet.

I stood for a moment in silence, thinking. 'The Thin Man is keeping his distance for now. The next part of this fight is going to be between Vampires.'

'Chassignol, then?'

'Yes, he is waiting for us. Close by. And it's through him we'll have to go to get the Chalice back safely to the Keep, or wherever the Eltern plan to put it. Don't forget, Corbeau is raising a slave army in England. Raptor will need our help soon enough too.' I paused and shivered. 'If he's still alive.'

'Can't we just use the Chalice, once we get it, to destroy Chassignol and then Corbeau and his army?'

I fought down a surge of irrational anger against Grue, and at the same time the urge to explain that I still felt Chassignol, our friend, was worth saving. And yet it was a fair question, if a little heavy-handed.

'The Thin Man would use it for violence,' I admitted, 'but he knows how to use it better than us and I suspect if we did use it to kill, and even if we were successful we would be using it for the wrong job. Looking at the Chalice's history, it has a nasty habit of eventually destroying those who misuse its power and then disappearing. For ages.'

Grue nodded slowly. We never would be friends – his love for Sansonnet and his hate of Chassignol would always stand between us – but he was never a fool.

'No,' I continued, 'we're going to have to face him and whatever army he has brought.'

Grue stared hard at me. I could tell what he was thinking without reading his thoughts. He was sizing me up, doubtless remembering how, as Strigoi, Chassignol and I had goaded him, teased him about his oddness but he also knew that it was time to put the past behind us if we stood any chance of surviving. 'There are only six of us left.'

'I know, but you'll think of something suitably sneaky, I'm sure.' I tried to sound brimming with a confidence I didn't feel. 'The main thing is how do we find the Chalice now in all this?' I gestured at the water.

'I was under the impression that one of us had to drink it,' Grue said.

'Again, it's not that simple, I suspect.'

'But that's what the prophecy said.'

'I've drunk the water already, or at least tasted it.' I said.

'Yes but that was in your dream, wasn't it?'

Sansonnet had just joined us. She had a blanket wrapped around her shoulders and she also looked pale and cold.

'I don't think that makes any difference,' I said. Look!' I hadn't the foggiest notion of how to move things forward at this stage and it was making me reckless. I scooped up the water with my hand and drank it before Sansonnet could stop me. I held the liquid in my mouth for a few seconds, cheeks bulging.

'Moüsch, spit that out at once!'

But I didn't, I swallowed it instead.

My face did not turn black, my limbs did not shrivel to dry stumps. Nor, to be fair, did any waves on the shore part to reveal a shining Chalice held in an open seashell, or carried by a squadron of angels. No visions. Nothing. Diddly. Zip.

'This isn't the Well that the Viking spoke about,' I said at last, suppressing a smile at the fact they had both stepped back a couple of paces, presumably in case I exploded.

'Where is it then?' Grue looked cross.

Until that moment I hadn't a clue what I was going to say next but then I had a revelation. I couldn't believe I hadn't thought of it before. My dream. 'Baule, of course!' I shouted and, without any reflection I dived into the water. I just had time to hear Grue ask whether I had gone bonkers before the freezing currents hit me, and I had to concentrate my racing mind on not exhaling. I felt a disturbance to my left and saw that Sansonnet and then Grue had joined me. Vampires can hold their breath much longer than Humans – up to ten minutes, which can be useful, but we hate swimming and we absolutely detest cold water. I forced my heartbeat to slow and signalled to Grue and Sansonnet that I was going to dive deeper.

At first I could see very little until my eyes had a chance to adjust to the dim light that filtered through the water to the bottom of the lake. Then I began to make out a smooth flat lake bed, largely made of sand. We continued a little further and came to what I had been half expecting since my revelation.

The place was littered with the bones from the distant battle I had seen in my first dream all that time ago. Rusting armour and weapons protruded from the silt, wrapped in tendrils of weed and encrusted with tiny white shells. As in my dream, some of the skeletons were tiny and others were monstrous, and everywhere you looked they stretched out across the lake bed for mile upon mile. There must have been tens of thousands. Sansonnet and Grue looked shocked and seemed to want to go back to the surface but I shook my head and motioned for them to go on. After about five minutes, however, I was running out of breath and thinking about turning back.

And then it was there.

The small, sharp-pointed hill I had seen in my vision all that time ago when I fell from the rigging in the *Sprite*, now stood silently before us under half a mile of water. My heart leapt. I knew where the Chalice was to be found: it was Baule's precious *key in argent* – my dreams had led me there and confirmed the spot. I kicked for the surface.

⁂

'So,' remarked Peregrine as we sat by the fire to dry off. 'Let me get this straight – you went for a refreshing mornin' swim and then you saw some dead blokes?'

'Quite so,' said Grue looking daggers at me.

'Now don't mind me asking or nuffink, but where does that get us exactly?'

'Nowhere at all,' said Grue evenly. Even Sansonnet looked like she probably agreed with Grue.

'I've already told you,' I shrugged. 'I know where it is.'

'Yes, so you say, it's down a well that's already under hundreds of feet of water, waiting for us, easy as pie.' Peregrine scratched his nose; rather sarcastically, I thought.

'That's right.'

'And you're going to swim down and fetch the Chalice, just like that?'

'Now you're getting it.'

'No, can't say I do really.'

'Trust me on this,' I said in a way I knew was probably infuriating, 'I know it's down there and I know exactly where it is.' I sighed. 'The only thing I'm not sure of is how to get it.'

Sansonnet looked up. 'What do you mean?'

'Well, Peregrine's right, it does seem a bit simple. But first of all, it's a long way down and secondly the well is underwater, so it seems to me like it's not going to be a straightforward thing.

Some sort of trick or magic perhaps. I really don't know, I was going to see what was going to happen when I got there.'

'Sounds perfect,' remarked Grue.

Faucon came to my defence. 'To be fair, that's how we've done everything so far isn't it? And we've not done too badly, have we?'

'Bud's dead.' Peregrine looked like he was spoiling for an argument.

'That's a cheap shot if ever there was one, ' Sansonnet cried, 'and it's hardly Moüsch's fault!'

'Look,' Peregrine stood up, 'I wasn't sayin' it was, I'm sayin' we have to be careful now – we've lost Bud and Chassignol, we nearly lost Moüsch back in the Labyrinth and I reckon we'll need him when we do get the Chalice if all this stuff about being a Navigator is true ... I mean *correct*,' he added quickly, avoiding my glare. 'I've made up my mind,' he carried on firmly, 'Moüsch, you show me where to go, and I'll put me trunks on an' get it.'

'No,' I said, 'absolutely not. It's my idea, I'm not having your death on my conscience, especially if you think all this is a bad idea in the first place.'

'You know what I'm like,' said Peregrine, 'I'm a fighter, an' I like things to be either squared away neatly or beaten to a pulp. All these visions and funny feelings, it's just not my thing and frankly it takes getting used to but, for what it's worth, I'm with you down 'ere. This Tree, the Labyrinth, your recovery when I thought you was dead – this is your world down here, so I'll accept anything you say.'

'Then I'm going alone.'

'Except that.'

☙

In the end it was decided that we would all go, and when we got to the well Peregrine and I would work as a team.

The first thing to do was make a serviceable raft. Swimming or flying out to where the submerged hill lay was all very well but we would need all the strength we had to make the dive, so we spent the rest of the day combing the beech for useful-looking driftwood. Then the cousins, who liked making things, set about showing us how to lash it together with rope we made from the fibres of the thickest briars we could find. It was hard work but I was glad to spend the day doing something simple that was also fairly menial. It took my mind off what lay ahead.

In the end we had a sturdy-looking craft of which even Grue looked immensely proud. 'So, what shall we call it, boys?' asked Sansonnet playfully. We all thought about it for a bit.

'I know,' said Faucon eventually.

'What?' Everyone was secretly pleased they didn't have the first suggestion, as it was bound to be laughed at by all the others.

'The *Bud* II.'

And, for once in our lives, we all just nodded.

The next day we launched at dawn. There was little ceremony, only *grim purpose*. With both the cousins rowing hard, it didn't take long before we were bobbing about above the spot where I guessed the pointed hill and its well lay submerged. Peregrine and I looked at each other for a few moments before nodding at the others and tipping ourselves over the side. The water, oddly, seemed a little warmer than it was by the shore but I still had to fight against a Vampire's natural dislike of getting wet. No such misgivings for Peregrine, whose broad shoulders disappeared quickly beneath the waves as he dived like an eel, descending to the depths below so quickly that I struggled to keep up. The hill came into view almost immediately and it wasn't long before we found the staircase in my dream that wound round the hill from the base to its tip. The stork and the little cloud, if they had ever existed, had gone, but we found the well with no difficulty and with that, the explanation for the water being so warm.

A steady column of steam rose up from the well's miniature fortifications. The source of the steam (and possibly the little cloud before water swallowed it all up) was a dark red lava the consistency of semi-congealed blood, that frothed and spluttered up to the surface of the well. Spilling slowly over the side, it quickly cooled in the water and turned to the grey pumice that had built up over the years, and which explained how the tottering hill that stood before us came about in the first place. I tapped Peregrine on the shoulder and motioned to him that I was going down to investigate.

The temperature was almost unbearable and clouds of super-heated water kept getting in my eyes, making them sting. A strange thought crept into my mind: the lava looked like jelly. No sooner had this occurred to me than it was clear to me that it was the most delicious jelly that had ever been put in front of me. Blood jelly. I had to taste it there and then. It must have shown on my face because the moment I decided to scoop up a generous mouthful of the gelatinous liquid, Peregrine shot forward to prevent me. But too late – before Peregrine could lay his hands on me, I stuck my head in and greedily sucked in the liquid fire.

A brilliant, burning agony consumed me and instantly I was transported back to visions of arteries coursing with livid blood that broadened into tunnels and caverns of boiling lava.

I looked up into the vast canopy above my head, as the Tree of Life bent and spoke to me:

゜

'*In England, barely twenty miles south of Tidythatch, there is an area of marshland where reeds grow in abundance.*' It intoned gravely, as I forgot about the burning in my throat and listened, mesmerised or somehow lulled.

ʝ~ '*At one end of the marsh there lies a small wood, Smallwood, where ancient oaks grow and provide shelter for these many clumps of reed that sprout up all over, like the hairs on an old man's chin.*
    Now there was once a venerable old Oak that grew in this lonely

*spot, next door to the tallest and most elegant reed in
the whole district.*

*The Reed was very vain and carped on endlessly about her
attributes to the long-suffering Oak. 'Oak, oaf! See what an elegant
stem I have, long and graceful, like the neck of a white swan.'*

*'Indeed, Reed,' replied the Oak invariably and fell to scanning
the watery horizon for nothing in particular.*

*'Oak, oaf! See my noble head, how it nods wisely to the wind.
It speaks to me and I understand. I am beautiful and wise.'*

'Indeed Reed,' the old gentleman would reply patiently.

*The Reed, living on a marsh, was naturally obsessed by the wind,
just as Eskimos can't stop talking about the snow.*

*One November the weather had been worse than usual. It was
shockingly cold and when the wind blew, the bleak inhabitants of the
marsh would shiver in unison. All except the frightful little Reed.
'Oak, oaf! See how I arch and pirouette in the gusts, like a dancer.
The wind is strong, but I am mightier. I bend but do not break,
nothing can hurt me. You, however, are as stiff as a board. If this
wind gets any stronger you will be uprooted I should say. Oak, are
you listening?'*

'Indeed Reed,' replied the Oak as he took the strain.

*The Wind was now whistling down the valley and through
Tidythatch where it blew tiles off the roofs and sent chickens
tumbling down the street like feathered acrobats. But it saved its
venom for the marsh: laying the grass flat, it shot in all its fury
towards the Reed and the poor Oak.*

*'Fa la ha ha, isn't this fun!' trilled the Reed up at the Oak, who
was creaking like an old door.*

*The Oak flexed its old back and replied with dignity, 'Indeed,
little Reed.'*

*We all have our off-days and the North Wind was in no mood to
be merciful that morning. An old man was blown out of his boat
whilst fishing and the Oak began to groan ominously.*

*'Ha ha, I told you so,' laughed the Reed, 'it's all very well to have
your head in the clouds, but your roots are in the ground and they
are none too deep. Look at me I am dancing. I am in my element,*

the Element is mine, the envy of all, I am invincible,
I am having the time. –'

Without further ado the Oak toppled over and squashed the
Reed flat.

'Indeed Reed,' he sighed as he looked out once more at this
untamed world and closed his eyes.

'That's all very well,' I said a little impatiently, 'but I've really got
no time to be listening to these stories. I am looking for the
Chalice, and then I have to get back to my friends.'

'Drink that,' was all the antediluvian Tree said.

When I looked down, I saw that I was holding a simple
earthenware cup filled with liquid. As I stared at it the substance
within changed from bright silver to the grey of a winter's sky.

'Drink it all up,' said the Tree of Life, 'and you'll wake.'

As I put the cup to my lips and drank, I felt the fire in my
mouth and throat recede.

Then my legs were being tugged roughly upwards and bright
sunlight shone in my eyes. Someone was thumping me hard in
the chest, and when I opened my mouth to complain about the
rough treatment a stream of burning liquid spewed out onto the
floor of the raft, which promptly caught fire. There was a sudden
flurry of activity as everyone else leapt about, all shouting at
once. It only stopped when Grue had the presence of mind to
throw some water onto the flames. He refilled the container and
threw some water on me for good measure.

'What was that for?' I spluttered.

'That's for making me miss my lie-in this morning, leading us
on a wild goose chase, for nearly getting yourself killed – yet
again – and in the event there was anymore of that liquid in your
mouth,' he added, not unreasonably.

'Fair enough,' I replied, 'but you're wrong about one thing.'

'Is that the case?' asked Grue, looking down at me with a sour
expression.

'I wouldn't say we've exactly wasted our morning.'

'No, I dare say you enjoyed gargling lava. If it wasn't for Peregrine pulling you out, you'd be dead by now.'

'The Tree of Life spoke to me.'

'What did it say?'

'*He*,' I corrected. 'He told me a story. And then I found the Chalice.'

That got everyone's attention.

'How? Where is it then?'

'Grue has it in his hand. He used it just now to drench me.'

Everyone looked at Grue who was indeed holding a silver bucket. As the fire had taken hold of *Bud II*, the Chalice had changed again into the thing we most needed – a good serviceable bucket – and somehow Grue had laid his hands on it almost immediately. Slowly, before our eyes, it changed back into the silver oval I had first seen, not really a cup at all, unless you needed it to be. Ripples of colour played across its surface. Happy hues of red, aqua marine and silver.

'It does that,' I said.

⋉

Hours later, we were sitting on the shore. Sansonnet had her arm around me and I was playing with the Chalice as we bathed our feet in the cold, clear water of the lake. Despite the fact that we were still in grave danger, with Sansonnet here and the Chalice found I felt happy. I turned it over in my hand, shook it and held it up to the light.

'Don't break it,' she said, drawing a half-Moon in the sand. The Chalice was warm but the colours had dulled and it seemed to have shrunk to a size whereby I could easily slip it into my pocket. Despite its size it was surprisingly heavy, but whichever way I held it the weight seemed to shift so that it felt reassuring and comfortable – like a talisman. 'And I still don't know why you can't just use it to help us,' Sansonnet said, though this time sounding less exasperated. We had both been trying to work out how to get out of the Labyrinth, past Chassignol and whatever army he had brought with him, and safely back to the Keep.

'Like I've said, I wouldn't know how.'

'But you're a Navigator, or a Se'er or whatever, it's in your blood. Literally.'

I sighed. 'Even if I did know, it still wouldn't work. The Chalice isn't meant to serve Vampires in that way. It's more likely the other way around. We serve it ... or something like that.' I knew it sounded lame but it was the best I could come up with. Like hundreds of people, Humans and Vampires alike, I was beginning to suspect that having the Chalice could create more problems than it solved.

She looked at me for a long while, her eyes solemn and, as usual, knowing. 'You're probably right,' she said, and sighed. 'Are you hungry?'

'I nearly died twice and it's not even mid-week. I could eat a horse.'

'If we were French Vampires, we probably would.'

Nevertheless, as I twisted to get up, I felt the Chalice in my hand change and I nearly dropped it there and then. It was suddenly freezing – the cold metal burnt my hand and seemed to stick to the skin. I started violently, shocked, and looked at it. The colours had turned to stormstorm cloud grey and at the edges it was almost black. When I looked at Sansonnet she had gone deathly pale.

'He's here,' she confirmed. 'I felt it too. Chassignol's just entered the Labyrinth.'

And I'd just lost my appetite.

꿔

Page 261

'Impossible only mer-means
that it's possible in a way you
h-haven't managed to work out yet'

Milan, overheard mer-muttering to Faucon.

Chapter 21

the first battle

Gruel looked gruesome.

The others just looked battered. It had been a long time since we had seen our homes and we were tired, dishevelled and most probably a bit whiffy. Looking around at our grubby band, I wasn't sure if that made us more or less scary as opponents. More so, provided you had a sensitive nose, I concluded after some consideration, although I strongly doubted that whoever was leading Chassignol through the Labyrinth right now would be too terrified by bad breath.

One thing that was true was that we were far tougher Vampires than we had been when we set out. Any fat had been lost, replaced with muscle and sinew. I felt I could fly all day now and fight most of the night, even my legs felt stronger. We were also more formidable as a team and not so easily daunted at the prospect of unfair odds in a straight fight to the death. But we would need every ounce of this new strength if we were to have any chance at all of surviving the day.

But after all we had been through it was unthinkable that we should lose the Chalice so soon after we had found it. I looked out at the Tree. Now that we knew more of the threat of Corbeau and the intentions of the Thin Man to make us his slaves again, losing was not an option.

'We will fight them on the beaches,' intoned Grue. 'If we go back into the Labyrinth we risk being trapped, split up or getting lost.' The cousins argued half-heartedly for carrying out a series of guerrilla warfare strikes in the Forest of Thistle and Thorn. But, when all was said and done, it seemed somehow appropriate that we should stand and fight in the open. There had been too many cloak-and-dagger antics already.

Outside, by the shores of the lake and under the vast boughs of the Tree of Life, it felt somehow safer. We were where we should be, at the start of life on this planet, at the mouth of the system of lava flows where our race had first escaped their underground caverns and caves. It seemed fitting to end it here, where it all started.

That night we heard the Troll drums, pounding a tattoo on thick animal hides stretched across the hollowed and dried carcasses of their enemies. By the sounds of it they were still in the Labyrinth but coming closer. They would be with us by early morning. Judging by the speed they were moving, someone – or, something – in Chassignol's new army knew the way. None of us could sleep easily through the racket but nor did we speak to one another, preferring to lie wrapped in blankets and our own thoughts. The temperature in the jungle dropped surprisingly sharply at night, so Milan and Faucon built up the fire before we slept to keep out the worst of the cold. I must have drifted between sleep and waking, for in the early hours I came to and noticed how the hot embers threw out a flickering red light onto the faces of my friends and the tangled forest at our backs. The hellish light reminded me of my poisoned dream-state and I wondered if that experience would always haunt me. Probably, I thought, but that's something to worry about if I survive tomorrow. I closed my eyes again.

This time I must have fallen into deeper slumber, because the next thing I knew it was dawn. A watery light bathed our camp and the Tree was all but invisible thanks to a thick morning mist that smelled of rain to come. Peregrine was up already, strapping on his sword and flexing his wings. The calm expression on his weather-beaten face and the fact it was daylight gave me more confidence than I had felt earlier, when it was still dark, and I almost found myself looking forward to the fight to come. The next thing I noticed was that the drums had finally stopped.

A small, blurred figure approached through the fog.

Something about it seemed odd, even at first glance. As it got closer I realised that it was, in fact, a Gnochme. I'd heard about them, but never seen one up close. About half a Vampire's height, they have a reputation for being miserable, and dangerous when provoked, but otherwise content to let you get on with your business if you return the favour. There's a lot of the Old Magic about Gnochmes, too, like Wights – though nobody can ever tell you what that might be, exactly. He stepped out of the gloom into the circle where we had slept and Peregrine, deciding he wasn't much of a threat, sauntered up to see what he wanted.

'My Lord Chassignol sends his greetings,' he said in a surprisingly squeaky voice, bowing even lower on stumpy legs. Peregrine had now been joined by Grue, and the two made an imposing duo. However, if our visitor was intimidated he did a good job of not showing it. Instead, he regarded them with calm grey eyes, set amongst a myriad of deep wrinkles. His skin was the off-yellow colour of old tallow candles and he looked as if he had been around for longer than the volcano we stood in. The clothes he wore had seen better days too and even his boots, though well made, were split and heavily caked in mud.

Gnochmes usually stuck together but I had a feeling that this one was on his own, an outcast. Just like everyone the Thin Man seemed to recruit.

'Tell Chassignol he can rot,' said Grue, tonelessly.

The Gnochme shrugged. 'You may tell him yourself, when you see him. His army is barely half a mile away now. He asked me to repeat his greetings if they were not well-received the first time.'

'You didn't come here just to tell us that, I'm sure.'

'No, I did not,' the Gnochme conceded. 'I have another message from my Master.'

'Go on.'

'He wishes for peace between Vampires. Surrender the Chalice to him and he will grant safe passage through the Labyrinth and back to your home, the Keep. Anything he discovers about its use will be shared with the Eltern, for the good of the Vampire Nation.' He stopped and turned to me. 'To his friend, Moüsch, My Lord extends his special greetings and wishes you to know that everything he has done has been for the good of all Vampires.'

'By plotting to get us all killed at the Eyrie?' I replied evenly.

The Gnochme shrugged again and, not finished with his message, ploughed on. 'His master, the Grand Lord Corbeau, also expresses regret over the death of your family. One of the first tasks of the Chalice will be to revive your dead parents and siblings.'

'You don't seriously expect me to fall for the same trick he conned Chassignol into following him with?'

'And what if we refuse 'is offer?' cut in Peregrine.

'Then you will be slaughtered before the end of this day.'

Peregrine stepped forward a pace to tower over the Gnochme. 'And what if we send back your ugly 'ead on a stick as a present?'

A gentle breeze had got up and played itself out as a series of ripples on the surface of the lake. There was silence for a few moments, then the Gnochme looked away, as if the matter was of very little consequence to him either way. 'Then I too will die.'

'And this does not bother you?' I asked, coming to stand by the other two.

'No.'

I delved his mind rapidly and felt nothing but deep resignation and despair in his heart. This creature had lost all the hope he had ever had, perhaps centuries ago.

'So I see,' I said. I turned to Peregrine. 'Let him go. Anyway, it's bad luck to kill the messenger.'

'OK, little man, go and tell Chassignol we'll fight him if we have to and that if it comes to that, then he'll die. I'll be glad to do the job meself.'

'I will tell him you declined to accept his very generous offer.'

Grue smiled nastily. 'No, you will tell him we will avenge his treachery, and if you know what's good for you I'd make myself scarce today. I need a new ornament for my pond at home. Having you stuffed should do the trick nicely.'

The Gnochme regarded us coolly for a few moments, bowed again and left. His retreating form was soon swallowed by the fog, which if anything had just got thicker. Grue watched him go with interest. 'That's not the last we'll see of him, I suspect,' he commented.

'I doubt they're going to make a move before this fog shifts,' I said.

'No,' agreed Peregrine, looking suddenly energised, 'and we may be able to use this to our advantage. They'll be expectin' us to wait for them to attack, so let's pay them a jolly old visit. It'll be a nice surprise. The art of a good defence is attack, I believe it is said. Grue, Moüsch, fancy a morning stroll whilst the others rustle up some breakfast?'

Finding where Chassignol had camped for the night was easier than expected. Our vertically-challenged friend had left damp footprints in the morning dew all along the path he took, and the fog gave us perfect cover to follow him. Anything more than ten feet away was all but invisible and further into the forest it was so thick that it dampened any sound we made as we crept along.

After about twenty minutes we saw a huge grey outline by the side of the path. Peregrine to my left motioned us to stop and he crept forward. A few moments later he came back.

'Trolls,' he breathed, and held up four fingers. He closed his eyes and made a gesture as if asleep.

Barely a minute later all four Trolls lay dead around the campfire. Grue and Peregrine had made short work of them. Chassignol was clearly feeling over-confident putting Trolls on guard duty: everyone knows that they nearly always fall asleep after a few minutes if they're sitting down, unless it's actually on a fire.

'What shall we do now?' I asked.

'We'll have to go back,' said Grue. Peregrine shook his head; he was all for going on to have a look at the camp. 'No,' said Grue, emphatically, 'we've been away too long and the others don't know where we are. What if they go looking for us and get captured? We need all the Vampires we've got. Also, this fog seems to be lifting. Much as I'd like to see the surprise on Chassignol's face when it clears and they find all their guards dead, it'll be best if we were out of the area.'

'OK,' Peregrine agreed reluctantly.

'It won't do their morale much good to know we came this close to them. I can't imagine they've many Trolls left either.'

Peregrine looked much happier at that thought.

꿈

By the time we got back to the camp the fog had lifted entirely, so that all that remained was a thin mist across the surface of the lake and the branches of the Tree looked a little hazy. Grue was right, the others had risen and were looking worried about us not being there. Milan and Faucon were delighted that the first blood of the day belonged to us and agreed that losing Trolls would damage the enemy's morale as well as making Chassignol wonder if we had an army ourselves. Sansonnet seemed to think the Gnochme important and pressed me for more details.

'He was just a messenger,' I shrugged.

She frowned. 'Are you sure?'

'Well, I agree, you never can tell with those guys, or any Wight, in my experience. I guess he is some sort of outcast. It makes you wonder what the rest of Chassignol's band will be like. There was something inherently creepy about the Gnochme, I admit, but I don't think he'd be much good with a sword in his hand.'

Sansonnet did not look convinced. 'That's what people said about you, and you proved us all wrong.'

We all decided to get ready immediately thinking that now the fog had lifted, Chassignol would be keen to get things started.

In the end, it was late afternoon before we heard a curious noise, like the sound of tiny feet moving through dead leaves. It came from the forest. Really quite a lot of tiny feet. Milan and Faucon had been stationed as lookouts towards the entrance of the Labyrinth, where they were most likely to approach from. Sansonnet and I covered the left and the right, in case they attempted to outflank us. With the lake at our backs it seemed unlikely they would approach by boat. As it happened, Chassignol showed us how confident he felt by using the same path through the Forest as we had.

By the time they began to form up, about two hundred yards from our camp, the reddened sun was sinking in the sky. As it bathed the lake in rich colours and made the forest seem as if it were on fire, we began to see the full extent and nature of Chassignol's force. Our hearts sank into our worn boots.

Even before it was fully arrayed I knew we had virtually no chance.

Jagged-legged, their huge, coarse-haired bodies swaying gently to an unseen rhythm. Before us stood Chassignol's own private army of spiders. Their bellies scraped the ground, making the curious rustling noise we had heard on their approach, and their jaws worked obsessively, foaming poison the colour of thick custard. Each stood the height of a fully-grown Vampire but must have weighed two or three times as much. This did not prevent them from moving quickly. Here and there small fights erupted within the ranks where one spider moved too close to another, and then their turn of speed was impressive, even by our standards, as they grappled and bit into one another in fury. None of the fights ended until one of the combatants lay belly up, curled and dead, whereupon the rest would hungrily devour the body, sucking the juices from it until nothing remained but a curled husk that blew away in the wind, like giant tumbleweed. Instinctively I knew that these were the offspring of the spider that had attacked me in my dream state: now fully grown in just a few days. This was how Chassignol must have navigated the Labyrinth at such speed.

In the midst of all this stood Chassignol, with his back to the sun, his features bathed in darkness, like a mask. At his right stood the squat form of our morning messenger. I noticed that he now carried a heavy-looking bow, and a sheaf of arrows strapped to his back.

Now that the full force seemed to be there, I saw I was right:

the Trolls we had killed had been the only ones in the company. This was small comfort as Chassignol raised an arm and the first wave of spiders scuttled forward.

We had no plan but to stand shoulder to shoulder between two large rocks that made a gully and prevented them from coming in at the side of us. There was little chance they would come around the back – spiders hate water, I thought with some relief – even more than Vampires. Just before the first of the arachnids reached us Grue turned to me and said. 'If they break our ranks, we're dead.' I nodded. 'If that happens, you have to fly with the Chalice and bury it back where you found it.'

I shook my head, my eyes fixed on the approaching hoard. 'I'd prefer to stay and fight.'

'It's not about you and what you prefer, it's about saving the Chalice and you're the only one who can put it back where you found it. If it's any consolation you can still feel as heroic as the rest of us. When Chassignol catches up with you, which he will do if we're all dead, then he'll kill you too.'

I nodded. 'OK.'

And then the nest was upon us.

Peregrine's and Grue's flashing blades met the spearhead of their attack, two large males, which died almost instantly, blinded then beheaded, their bodies forming a barrier as more clambered over the top of the twisted corpses to get at us. The first spider that came at me was relatively easy, a smaller beast which squeezed between the legs of the others, its jaw straining to find the soft flesh of my belly. As it was a good deal shorter than me I brought down my sword with both hands like a skewer into its back. Surging adrenalin, and the final release of my pent-up energy, sent my sword thrust clean through the thickest part of its body and staked it to the ground like a giant museum exhibit. It made a screeching noise half agony and half fury before dying, its legs drumming on the ground.

I raised my head to shout in victory but the cry died in my throat. At the crater's edge stood a now familiar shadow, looking down on the scene. He was here.

The Thin Man had come to witness Chassignol's final act of treachery and the moment at which the Chalice became His.

My victory shout became a roar of rage and I hobbled the next spider with a cut across the back of its front legs. I slashed the mandibles and eyes from the front of its face with my sword, which now dripped grey green blood onto the slickening sand. A second wave of spiders hit but we hardly noticed. The world, for all six of the remaining Vampires in our troop, had retreated to a single tunnel of vision a few feet wide that was ours and ours alone to defend. Each time an arachnid stepped into the zone it was cut down, to be replaced by yet another almost instantly, with eager, clutching jaws. I lost count of the number I killed. I felt no fear, no tiredness, only a degree of madness.

To my left I was dimly aware of Peregrine's sword moving faster than I could imagine until not even the bravest of spiders would approach him. With no one to fight he roared with frustration, slashing wildly from left to right as the spiders cringed from his blade and stumbled back over the corpses of their companions to escape him. For a moment, despite the hundreds of spiders that stood fresh for the fight behind the ranks we now fought, I dared hope that Peregrine might swing the fight in our favour and save the day. Chassignol must have thought so too, as he now flew through his own ranks, slashing spiders out of the way with his sword until he stood before Peregrine. Even in the midst of the fight I noticed how much he'd changed in the few short weeks since we'd seen him. His square-jawed features had become hollowed and gaunt and there was dirt on his fur that looked like dried blood. I doubted if he had slept properly or eaten much since that night at the Eyrie. Nonetheless, he was still an imposing figure.

Very slowly, keeping his eyes locked on Peregrine's, he raised his sword and cast it to the ground. Realising the nature of the challenge, Peregrine did the same and showed both sets of his long teeth. Canines bared, Chassignol lunged forward, his wings beating furiously, and the two met in mid-air.

Now, I am a storyteller. Storytelling is about a lot of things, but mainly it's about entertainment. On dark winters' nights when there's nothing much to do, around lonely campfires and in crowded feasting halls, I am called upon to ply my trade. And it goes without saying that I need to keep in mind all sorts of things – descriptions, humour, pathos and the drama of the story unfolding, lest I lose the listener's interest. I am even ashamed to say that I may sometimes stoop to a white lie or two, a change in the sequence of events to make things seem more interesting or I may simplify things, so that they seem more real, less muddled. However, I must, above all things, keep to the truth of the *actual* events. A storyteller of real people and real events, such as I, is also an historian.

I really would have preferred to tell you that the fight between Peregrine and Chassignol was an heroic struggle. That they both fought with valour and with strength of arms and character; that their every move was a blur of breathtaking skill and that through it all the two learnt a new respect for one another and even perhaps that some of the old Chassignol came back. If only for a moment. I should, above all, like to tell you something with a happy ending. Yet, I cannot.

One of the spiders that Peregrine had cut down was not yet dead, and as Peregrine passed overhead a claw-like leg shot out and caught his wing tip. It was not much, and it happened in an instant, and yet it was enough to tip him off balance, his head snapped back as he tried to stay upright, and his throat was exposed.

This was all Chassignol needed.

Before Peregrine could regain his defence, he was upon his old friend and companion, attacking in the way that all Vampires excel from birth, teeth clamped around his jugular, severing it cleanly. Falling to the ground, Peregrine made no sound; he simply closed his eyes.

I alone witnessed his death – the others fighting their own private battles for survival. Exhaustion and despair swept through my body and I almost fell to my knees. With Peregrine gone the spiders began to advance upon us again. I looked for Chassignol but he had disappeared. I lifted my sword arm, which now seemed heavy and lifeless, knowing we were doomed. 'Go!' shouted Grue to me 'we have to fall back!' but I shook my head. I had to find Chassignol. More than anything now, I wanted to kill him.

Then a shadow passed over us – in silence it glided overhead, yet something about it made us all stop and look up. The spiders noticed it too. The sound of wings beating the sky like enormous sails could be heard and the spiders, sensing a new danger, abruptly halted in their advance to finish us forever.

'Xeurf!' Sansonnet shouted.

'It can't possibly be,' said Faucon.

'You're right, it's not,' I said, feeling energy flood back into me, 'it's his offspring, though. It looks just like him – the scale pattern is the same.'

'He's right,' said Grue, as close to being excited as I have ever seen him. 'When a Dragon dies, like the Phoenix, it leaves an egg. The egg contains not just a baby dragon but all of its parent's memories, all their experience and all their wisdom. In a sense it is Xeurf, re-born.'

The Dragon turned and swooped down, wings beating the air as the slipstream around it screamed. A jet of fire shot from its open mouth. Instantly nearly fifty spiders shrivelled to nothing but charred and withered forms. The rest hesitated and then made for the safety of the Forest of Thistle and Thorn.

'We've w-won!' shouted Milan, although it almost sounded like a question. Only a few moments ago all had seemed lost and yet now, for the second time in a few weeks Xeurf, or at least Xeurf's offspring, had saved us.

Only not.

A noise like a thunderclap hit the air and the Dragon faltered. Another thunderclap sounded and this time his whole body shook as if an immense fist had slammed into it. He turned to his assailant. I looked past him to the lip of the crater and saw the Thin Man, his long arms raised. A stream of white-hot flame spurted from the Dragon only to be blocked by an invisible barrier surrounding his attacker. Another bolt came from the Thin Man, striking Xeurf head on, and even his colossal frame buckled under the weight of the onslaught. He roared in anger and charged, spewing fire in all directions. This time the force of the flame knocked the Thin Man backwards. Momentarily he disappeared over the edge, out of sight. However he soon re-appeared, hands raised, ready to release another bolt, just as Xeurf hit him head on. Both were suddenly engulfed in a ball of blue and crimson flame that scorched my eyeballs even from a distance. Xeurf let out a mighty roar that made waves on the surface of the lake and bent the branches of the Tree. Tumbling away at great speed, we could make out a smaller ball of flame.

'It's Him!' shouted Sansonnet, 'the Thin Man is on fire, He's running!'

But our elation was short-lived. Xeurf's crumpled body was falling towards us, wings hardly moving. Then, ever so slowly, one wing extended and then the other. The huge leathery membranes caught the breeze and he seemed to hang there suspended before dipping into a graceful swoop. But by now he was too low, too near the ground. A lone arrow soared up in the air and found its mark, burying itself in his exposed chest where the feathers and scales were thin and his great heart beat like a fearsome engine.

Xeurf was dead before he hit the shoreline, his fall sending out sand in all directions like waves. I turned to look and saw the Gnochme standing there, shortbow in hand, his features, as ever, unreadable.

I let out a yell of fury and flew to him, sword extended. He didn't move and would probably have died if it were not for another sword that parried mine. A heavy body-check sent me sprawling to the sand and I looked up in time to see Chassignol's sword come down attempting the *coup de grace* – to sever my head from the rest of my body. I twisted and he missed me by millimetres, the blade harmlessly chopping down on empty sand. As I moved I thrust up my own sword towards his belly but it was parried away easily, as were my next two attacks. By now

I was on my feet, determined to avenge Peregrine's and Xeurf's deaths. Chassignol regarded me coldly, through dead eyes, and at that moment I almost feared him. Then I remembered Bud, my lost family and Chassignol's. I flew at him, fighting as I had never done before, and he slowly began to give ground. A desperate lunge to the left gave me first blood. Chassignol looked down calmly at the trickle of blood running down his sword arm and pressed his counter-attack.

For the first time since the combat began I was on the back foot and began to falter. Sensing my advantage slipping away I flew over him, attempting to get to higher ground and back into a position of superiority. However Chassignol was ever the swordsman, not me. He pre-empted my move by microseconds, repositioned himself, and as I landed kicked me hard in the stomach and brought the flat of his blade down on my hand, causing me to bend double and drop my sword.

And so, for the second time in my life, there was nothing to do but wait to die.

But history has a habit of repeating itself, and at that moment something made him hesitate. He had betrayed us, given himself to the service of our sworn enemy, had murdered Bud and Peregrine but something deep within Chassignol made him flinch from this final barbarism. In an instant I saw in his eyes that he could not kill me, his childhood friend. The very Strigoi he had spent years, from the time he was a young boy, protecting.

In the very next moment, I saw something else in his eyes. It was surprise. Then pain.

Blood started to spread on his white down chest like a blossom, and Chassignol fell slowly, almost gracefully, at my feet, Sansonnet's sword still quivering between his shoulder blades.

꜒ᴖ

'Until the two species unite for
a common good, the wars between
Vampires and Faies will never stop.
The best common good, for all,
would be to sue for peace with the Weres.'

Hibou, Chassignol's father.

Chapter 22

bye and bye home

And so it was over.

With Chassignol gone, and the Thin Man gone for now, the spiders crept back into the Forest of Thistle and Thorn and stayed there. As night fell we saw in the moonlight the occasional pair of eyes glinting at us from the thorns, but we had lit a large fire and they held back in terror.

The Gnochme had disappeared into thin air, although, as Grue had remarked, it seemed somehow unlikely that this would be the last we saw of him.

I agreed. 'He's dark, It's impossible to read him. Each time I tried, something blocked me, as if someone is protecting him or his purpose.'

By the morning the corpses of the dead spiders had mysteriously disappeared. Sansonnet speculated that their companions had taken them for burial or, more probably, food, under cover of darkness. Xeurf's corpse had also undergone a change. Dry bones, already brittle as chalk, marked the spot where he had fallen and, to our joy, an egg. Milan and Faucon rowed out to the base of the Tree with the egg and left it there, so it could hatch in safety.

We buried Chassignol's body with very little ceremony at the foot of the cliff by the entrance to the Labyrinth. Despite Bud and Peregrine, I could not find it in my heart to hate him completely. He had had his reasons, however misguided, for his treachery. Instead I felt just guilt – he had spared me, after all, and I had been the cause of his father's death and so the cause of his act of treason. I supposed that for now, at least, I would have to live with the guilt, until I found a way to make up for it. His headstone merely read *Vampyre*. And I would be a liar if I said that I did not miss him. Even now.

The Chalice had reverted to a silver oval of neutral colour, which I decided was a good sign.

It took us two days to follow the path that led out of the Forest of Thistle and Thorn and negotiate the Labyrinth. The centipedes tried to attack once more but we carried firebrands now, which kept them at bay. It took another week to reach the coast where with the last of our gold we bought a ship, not much better than the *Sprite*, from some local fishing Wights.

Our voyage home was uneventful, even a little dull, although a storm off the coast of Africa made us all sick again and served to remind me why I preferred dry land.

When we finally did make it back, the Eltern looked at us like they couldn't remember what we'd gone for in the first place and then complained that whatever it was for, it had taken far too long.

'If we expected or even wanted a hero's welcome,' remarked Grue, 'we should have handed the Chalice over to Corbeau and his lot.'

I bent to one knee to hand over the Chalice, but Prince Kasu just waved me away with an impatient hand.

'Oh, you keep it,' he said, 'it's been perfectly safe up until now in your possession, I'm sure that you'll take jolly good care of it and all that sort of thing.'

Then they disappeared off into the garden for an afternoon game of hide-and-seek.

⁂

For now, for us, things returned to normal. *-Ish*.

Sansonnet and I were still close but something, perhaps Chassignol's death, seemed to stand between us. Perhaps she missed him too, or felt a little guilty, like I did, at times that we could have turned him from his final decision if we'd paid more attention.

Sometimes she was carefree and loving towards me, at other times almost cold and austere. I was in love with her, so it felt like a bad toothache when I allowed myself to think of this – so I simply tried not to. Grue hid himself away with his books and his spells and still managed to look sour whenever we happened to meet, which was not all that often. I never did show him the parchment Lark gave me at the Eyrie but I did keep it: Picus' message to Grue stayed safe and un-deciphered in my chambers for now.

It was the cousins who made the most of our adventures, setting up a business trading weapons and artefacts between the Keep and our cousins at the Eyrie. Travelling suited them. Milan now wore his unkempt hair very long, full of beaded pearls and rubies. He'd shown a surprising ability to pick up languages and now spoke fluent Trollish without a hint of a stutter. On the occasions when they were back, Sansonnet and I would roast them black pudding for dinner, open a flagon of liverblood wine and talk about old times.

If he was feeling up to it our old friend Peregrine would join us all for a nightcap. This was usually after he'd closed *The Silver Fang* for the evening. As I have said before, it's very hard to kill a Vampire, especially if he's as tough and stubborn as Peregrine. He was almost dead when we found him soon after the battle, drained of blood and exhausted. It was then I noticed that the Chalice had changed colour yet again – this time to a livid red. Before our eyes, it had become a stone goblet filled with blood – the sweetest Peregrine had ever tasted, he said.

Everyone agreed that Peregrine was well-suited to his new role of innkeeper – he insisted that his fighting days were over for good. Holding court behind the bar most evenings, he wore his battle scars with pride – his weathered face and knotted forearms a hatch-work of ancient sword cuts and Were bites.

One scar that he kept hidden under a thick leather choker was the wound on his neck from Chassignol. It had never fully healed.

At night I would often take a stroll on the balcony before bed and look at the stars. Sometimes I would reach into my pocket and pull out the Chalice.

I have to say, the Eltern's attitude was typical but still a complete mystery to me. They prided themselves on pretending not to care, then usually surprised everyone by acting with ruthless efficiency when required. I mentioned it to Peregrine, who had served as one of the Vampire Knight elite and therefore knew them better than most.

He shrugged and said. 'They'll be keepin' a close eye on it and on you, make no mistake about that lad. They probably reckon that no one will suspect that such a titchy squirt like you would be left to babysit such an important arty-whatumacallit. Not that I can work out what it's supposed to do. First place anyone will look for it will be the Keep and if that there antennae of yours is still working, you'll know if someone comes lookin' for it, long before anyone else twigs and you'll be leggin' it out the back door whilst 'ooever as come knockin' will be getting ripped to shreds by some of our lads in the Fast Tower. Typical Eltern, if you ask me – they can make the wrong decisions look right. An' that just shows you 'oos really in charge.'

Since we had been back it had stuck with the same oval in a reassuring shade of burnished silver it had been since the morning of the fight. If I held it up against the light I thought I could make out a tear-shaped drop of blood at its centre. I wondered whose it was. I still had no idea what the Chalice was for or what it could do but I somehow trusted that, one day, if I were patient, then it would let me know.

In my heart I knew that we had unfinished business with the Thin Man, and I often thought of Raptor and his fight with Corbeau. I wondered if he had managed to track down Picus and persuade him to help. In my heart I also knew that Raptor would call, by and by, when we were needed.

For now though, I was content to stay put and enjoy the calm before the storm.

Here ends the second book